PENGUIN CRIME FICTION

MR. CALDER AND MR. BEHRENS

Michael Gilbert was born in 1912 and educated at Blundell's School and London University. He served in North Africa and Italy during World War II, after which he joined a firm of solicitors, where he is now a partner. His first novel, *Close Quarters*, was published in 1947, and since then he has written many novels, short stories, plays, and radio and TV scripts. He is a founding member of the Crime Writers' Association. Penguin Books also publishes his *The Empty House*, *The Killing of Katie Steelstock*, *The Night of the Twelfth*, and *Smallbone Deceased*.

MICHAEL GILBERT

Mr. Calder and Mr. Behrens

PENGUIN BOOKS

Penguin Books Ltd, Harmondsworth,
Middlesex, England
Penguin Books, 625 Madison Avenue,
New York, New York 10022, U.S.A.
Penguin Books Australia Ltd, Ringwood,
Victoria, Australia
Penguin Books Canada Limited, 2801 John Street,
Markham, Ontario, Canada L3R 1B4
Penguin Books (N.Z.) Ltd, 182–190 Wairau Road,
Auckland 10, New Zealand

First published in Great Britain by
Hodder & Stoughton Ltd 1982
First published in the United States of America by
Harper & Row, Publishers, Inc., 1982
Published in Penguin Books in the United States of America
by arrangement with Harper & Row, Publishers, Inc.
Published in Penguin Books 1983

LIBRARY OF CONGRESS CATALOGING IN PUBLICATION DATA
Gilbert, Michael Francis, 1912–
Mr. Calder & Mr. Behrens.
1. Spy stories, English. I. Title. II. Title:
Mr. Calder and Mr. Behrens.
PR6013.I3335M7   1983b   823'.914   82-22365
ISBN 0 14 00.6637 3

Printed in the United States of America by
George Banta Co., Inc., Harrisonburg, Virginia
Set in Trump Medieval

The stories in this book were originally published in
Ellery Queen's Mystery Magazine.

Contents

Daniel John Calder

Born 1913, only son of Rev. Joseph Calder (Canon of Salisbury) and Sandra Kisfaludy (Hungarian).

Educated: Bishop Wordsworth's School, Salisbury and Università di Perugia.

Reuters Foreign Correspondent, Athens, 1932; Budapest, 1934; Baghdad, 1937; Bucharest, Head Office, 1938.

Recruited to MI6, 1935.

Languages: (A) Standard-Albanian and Hungarian
(B) Standard-Greek, Italian, Arabic, Russian

War service: Partly still classified. 1939–41 at Blenheim and Hatfield Special Interrogation Centres. Member of British Military Mission to Albania, 1944.

Joined JSSIC(E) June 1958.

Special interests: Small arms; cello; history of the Peninsular War.

Club: R.A.C.

Residence: The Cottage, Hyde Hill, near Lamperdown, Kent. Tel: (ex-directory)

Blood group: AB. Rh+

Samuel Behrens

Born 1910, second son and fourth child of Alfred Behrens and Marie Messenger, of Highgate, London.

Educated: Shrewsbury (Oldhams House) and London University, and Heidelberg University, Specialised European languages. Taught at Munich High School, 1929–32; Baden-Baden, 1932–33; Leipzig, 1933–35; Berlin, 1935–39.

Recruited to MI6, 1933.

Languages: (A) +Standard-German
(A) +Standard-French
(A) +Standard-Greek, Italian, Russian

War service: Still classified (it has been mentioned in *Reminiscences* of Franz Mulbach, Bonn, 1963, that S. B. was in Germany for two months prior to the first attempt on Hitler's life and supplied the sabotage device which failed to detonate in the Fuehrer's plane).

Joined JSSIC(E) 1956.

Special interests: Beekeeping, chess.

Club: Dons-in-London.

Residence: The Old Rectory, Lamperdown, Kent. Tel: Lamperdown 272

Blood group: O. Rh+

Rasselas

Persian deerhound; by Shah Jehan out of Galietta.

Height: 32 inches. *Weight:* 128 pounds.

Colour: Golden with darker patches. Eyes amber. Nose blue-black. Hair rough, with distinctive coxcomb between ears. Neck, long. Quarters exceptionally powerful. Legs, broad and flat.

Club: Kennel Club.

Blood group: (canine classification) A5

I

The Twilight of the Gods

The German artillery observation officer said, "I shall now proceed to range one gun on to the slit trench. If you will use your binoculars, gentlemen, you will observe it quite easily at the foot of the small knoll due east of where you are now standing."

The small group of privileged spectators raised field glasses in gloved hands and focussed them.

"The trench is exactly one and a half metres deep and one metre in width. It has been dug into chalk and flint. Owing to unavoidable discrepancies in the charges, it would not normally be possible to guarantee actually to hit the trench more than once in a hundred rounds."

"I wager," said General Runnecke, who commanded XIV Corps in the Banja Luka area of Yugoslavia and who was, therefore, nominally at least, the senior officer present, "that he did all his ranging before we arrived."

"In his place I should have done so," agreed the staff officer with the gunner tabs who was standing at his elbow.

"Fire!"

The report from the gun, sited some five thousand yards to their rear, arrived at the same time as the shell, which threw up a puff of white chalk and grey smoke just beyond the slit trench.

"Correct for line," said the observation officer smugly. "Plus for range. I will drop fifty metres and repeat." The second shell landed, if anything, slightly further forward.

"You will see what I meant when I spoke of the inaccuracy of a high explosive charge," said the observation officer. "The range that time was shorter but the shell went further. I shall fire again at the same elevation."

This one landed almost on the lip of the trench.

"Two plus, one minus," said the observation officer. "I think we can accept that as the range. We will now repeat, using the new experimental fuse."

There was a stir among the spectators. This time it was different. Instead of a dull report when the shell landed, there was the sharp, distinctive crack of shrapnel.

"Height of burst," said the observation officer, "approximately ten metres. That should be very satisfactory."

"Damned uncomfortable, if you ask me," said General Runnecke loudly, and the officers laughed. The only man who appeared entirely serious, his gaze concentrated on the slit trench, was the single civilian among the uniformed group. He was a thin, serious, brown-faced man in his early thirties, with a pair of steel-rimmed glasses on his beaky nose. Despite the January weather he was wearing only a thin raincoat.

He said, in good but clearly not native German, "By my estimation, seven and a half metres."

The observation officer ignored this and said, "I shall order the same gun now to fire six rounds. This will avoid the necessity of ranging the other guns of the troop, but will produce the cumulative effect of a salvo of six guns."

The six cracks followed each other at twenty second intervals. The height of burst was unmistakably consistent. As fast as one cloud of yellowish lyddite smoke shredded away in the breeze, another filled its place.

"Stand your troop down," said the General. "We will inspect the target. Come along with me, Dr. Brancos."

The whole group moved downhill towards the slit trench, the general with the civilian in the lead, followed by a stout, white-faced officer wearing the insignia of a *gruppenfuehrer* in the SS, the junior officers a decorous pace or two behind. At the edge of the trench they paused.

There were six men in it. They had been fastened there by a chain attached at both ends to posts hammered into the ground and passing through iron shackles round the ankle of each. Four of the men were clearly and horribly dead. Two of them were still moving. General Runnecke motioned to the junior officer behind him, who drew an automatic, stepped forward and shot them both carefully through the back of the neck.

"I think," said the General to Dr. Brancos, "that we may regard the experiment as eminently satisfactory."

Dr. Brancos, who appeared to be unmoved as any of his military colleagues by the sight in the trench, said, "I should like to examine, with your doctors, the precise nature of the wounds in the four who were killed. It was unfortunate that you felt obliged to shoot the other two. If they had lived, it would have been even more interesting to have examined *their* injuries."

"No doubt," said General Runnecke curtly.

In a report which he sent that evening to the War Ministry in Berlin he said, "In this experiment we were able to make use of six Yugoslav terrorists who had been captured in plain clothes behind our lines in possession of explosives, and who were to have been executed in any event. One equivalent salvo of the new fuse killed four men and fatally injured two. This represents the quite dramatic superiority of this wireless fuse over the standard powder fuse for shrapnel, which, as every artillery officer knows, can never be guaranteed to detonate within a hundred feet of the ground, and, indeed, in half the cases buries itself in the ground and fails to detonate at all. I would recommend that Dr. Brancos be put in touch forthwith with the Army Bureau of Weapon Research –"

As he wrote these words the General paused. He knew that the all powerful *Reichssicherheitshauptamt*, or RSHA, the co-ordinating body of the SS, had recently added to its already inflated authority a Section VII concerned with scientific exploitation, and he suspected that they would want to grab Dr. Brancos for themselves as an important pawn in their constant struggle with the Army for power and prestige. What he was wondering was whether he could arrange for his report to go to the War Ministry *without* being seen by the SS authorities.

He might have spared himself any worry. The SS *gruppenfuehrer* had already reported through his own signals troop to the RSHA who received the report a day before the War Ministry.

*

When Dr. Brancos arrived in Berlin, therefore, he was not met by an Army Officer but by a polite *obersturmfuehrer*, who introduced himself as Lieutenant Mailler, and whisked the doctor off to a flat at Lichterfelde outside Berlin. Here, in the days that followed, Mailler proved himself a patient and instructed listener. He had been trained in the Communications section of the SS and knew a good deal about wireless. He had to admit, however, that Dr. Brancos knew a great deal more than he did.

The doctor said, "I am, by profession, a mining engineer. Coming from a small country like Albania there were few facilities, and I was therefore educated and trained in Italy, at Perugia, and later in Milan. I speak better Italian than German, I fear."

Mailler said, with a smile, "You speak our language very well and clearly."

"I am obliged. It was in the uranium mines at Marcovograd that I developed the technique of the answering fuse. Like most inventions, the idea came to me by accident. In the mines we used a type of geiger counter. You know what I mean?"

"I have heard of them."

"They are, in essence, small receiving sets. They answer to the radio-active emissions of uranium. Once we had a very difficult explosive blast to detonate." Dr. Brancos held out two thin brown hands. "In the mass of uranium we bury an explosive charge. The uranium emits radio signals. Could we not, I said to myself, cause those signals to bounce back and detonate the charge at any required distance? All that would be necessary would be to calculate the wave-length precisely –" The doctor brought his two hands slowly together "– and – pouf! – we cause an explosion at exactly the point we require without wires or apparatus of any sort."

"And did it work?"

"In mining, no. It was impracticable. But the seed of the idea was there. A shrapnel shell with a small and simple wireless transmitter in the head. It approaches the earth. The transmission bounces back – at whatever height you wish – the shell explodes. No more powder rings, no more fuse setting, no more guesswork. A detonation at precisely the most effective height."

"Wonderful," said Mailler, and meant it.

"There were difficulties. My prototype fuses were much too sensitive. They could be set off by a cloud of rain. Even a flock of birds. But I developed a system of shutters –"

Dr. Brancos seized a writing pad and pencil and started to sketch as he talked.

At the end of two hours, his brain whirling with technicalities, Lieutenant Mailler made his excuses. He spoke on the telephone to the head of his section, *Standartenfuehrer* Bach. "The man is a genius," he said. "I'm sure of that. He lost me half a dozen times in the details, but the idea *must* be sound. It operates on the same principle as radar –"

"It is certainly effective," said Colonel Bach. "I have received the close-up photographs of the target trench. I am only glad I saw them after lunch and not before."

"He could be a great asset to our section –"

"*If* we get him," said Bach. "The Army want him for themselves. There is a fight going on now on a level too high for me to interfere. By the way, I assume you have checked the security clearance?"

"All the ordinary checks have been made," said Mailler. "His papers are in order. His luggage has been thoroughly examined and contains nothing out of the way. It would, of course, be more satisfactory if we could get a positive identification."

Bach thought about this and then said, "There is a man in the Balkan Department of Section VI. The name, I think, is Munthe. He comes from Albania or Monte Negro, or one of those god-damned holes, and he was a professor at Perugia. He should know Brancos, by name at least."

Professor Munthe, old, grey-haired and white bearded, examined the papers which Mailler laid on his desk, and shook his head slowly. He said, "This man is a fake. Possibly a spy. I was at Perugia during all the years he states that he was there. We had not more than a handful of Albanians. There was no Brancos among them."

"You are sure?" said Mailler anxiously. "It is most important. The reputations of some very senior officers are now involved."

"If you doubt me, confront me with him."

"I will be back in half an hour," said Mailler, and was better than his word.

When Dr. Brancos came into his office, Professor Munthe rose to his feet and stared at him fixedly. The doctor stared back, then a half smile crossed his face. "It is more than ten years," he said, "but you have not greatly changed, Herr Professor."

The old man blinked as if he was trying to recapture an elusive memory. When Brancos would have spoken again, he held up one finger in a gesture of the classroom and said, "*Not* Brancos, Boris. Stefan Boris."

"It is true," said Brancos. "I had family difficulties. I found it expedient to change my name."

"Now that you mention it, I remember being told of it. I met a mutual friend a year ago in Ravenna. Alessandro Piero –"

Lieutenant Mailler said hastily, "I can see you are old friends. You will have much to talk over. I will leave you."

He made his way straight to his own office on a lower floor of the building, extracted a flask of brandy from a drawer in his desk and treated himself to a stiff drink.

If Brancos had been a fraud and his invention a fake and a lot of important people had made fools of themselves, he had a shrewd idea that his own head would have been one of the first to roll.

As he was finishing the drink the telephone on his desk purred. The man at the other end was so senior that the lieutenant clicked his heels and stood rigidly to attention when answering it. His end of the conversation was confined to saying "Yes" half a dozen times, and finally "At once". And to Dr. Brancos, later that evening, he said, "The Fuehrer himself has made the decision. Your invention will go to the Eastern Front. You yourself are seconded to Army Group North with the temporary rank of major. You will be flown to Rzhev on the Volga tomorrow."

Dr. Brancos said, "Impossible. I shall have to spend tomorrow doing some shopping." He seemed unexcited by this dramatic turn of events.

"Shopping?"

"If I'm to be a major I shall need a uniform surely?"

"All that will be provided at Rzhev."

★

All that, and a great deal more, was provided in the months that followed. Army Group North had been commanded, during the hard fighting of the previous autumn and the stalemate of that spring, by General Helmuth Busche, whose star was now so firmly in the ascendant that he was spoken of as a possible supreme commander of the Eastern Front. He was a tall, fair-haired, red-faced Saxon, nearly six and a half feet in height, and Dr. Brancos observed him from afar and learned that he was a great man; recognised as a good soldier by the hardest school of professional military opinion in the world, but managing somehow to be liked as well as admired.

The doctor himself was placed under the command of Colonel Franz Mulbach, head of the Army Communications section, and was allotted as his workshop and quarters a hut in the forest of huts which had sprung up suddenly in and around the ruins of Rzhev.

This hut, in the months that followed, became the centre of much activity, involving technicians from both the Artillery and the Signals sections of the Army. From time to time Dr. Brancos would pay visits to forward observation posts to check the accuracy of his fuses, which were now going into mass production.

"If they are to achieve maximum effect," he said, "we must be careful not to demonstrate them too soon. When we fire them we will get them to explode at irregular heights so that they will appear to observers on the Russian side no different from the old, inefficient powder fuses. They will then take no special precautions."

Colonel Mulbach, a jovial barrel of a man, agreed with this. He had walked over, as he sometimes did, late at night, to sit beside the stove in Dr. Brancos' hut, smoke a cigar and talk about the war.

"As you will have seen," he said, "from your visits to the front – you must not, incidentally, expose yourself unnecessarily; to lose you now would be a fatal blow to the Reich – we are up against a hard line of interlocked defensive positions. The Russians have had all the winter to deepen and strengthen their trenches. When our offensive starts, the neutralisation of these trenches will be the most important feature."

"Has a date been fixed?"

"It will depend a little on the weather. This cursed Russian winter is slow to relax its grip, but the last week of April or the first week of May is spoken of, and it is then that we may expect a most important visitor."

"You mean –?"

"I mean our Fuehrer himself. He will come in person to confer with our commanders, to lay down the general lines of strategy and to wish us good fortune. I understand that he has expressed a personal interest in the work that you are doing here. It may even be possible to introduce you to him."

As Dr. Brancos moved his head, the red light from the stove shone on his glasses. He said, "It would be an indescribable honour."

It was a week after this conversation, in the early evening, that Colonel Mulbach arrived to find Dr. Brancos at work on his blueprints. The colonel had brought his car and was in full uniform. He said, "I am to take you to see General Busche. He wishes to speak to you."

"About what?" said Dr. Brancos. He seemed irritated by the interruption of his work.

"That we shall see," said the colonel.

During the drive into the centre of Rzhev he was more silent than usual. They dismounted at the side door of the big square seminary which formed the personal headquarters of the general, walked along an endless and echoing corridor without meeting a soul, climbed flights of stairs and traversed further passageways, their footsteps deadened now by strips of matting laid on the floor. At the end of this corridor they came to double doors which opened on to an ante-room.

Here there were two desks set at angles and positioned to guard an inner door. Cards on the desks identified the men behind them as Major Nachtigal and Captain Heimroth. The captain rose to his feet, shook hands with Colonel Mulbach, cast a critical look at Dr. Brancos' creased and ill-fitting uniform, went over to the inner door, knocked and went inside.

There was a murmur of conversation, the door reopened and

the captain reappeared and beckoned the visitors in. It was a comfortable room. A fire of logs was blazing in the open stove and in front of it, tall, erect and strikingly impressive in the undress uniform of the Prussian Guards Regiment, stood General Helmuth Busche.

The General waited until the door had clicked shut and then turned to Colonel Mulbach and said in German, "So! This is the little English spy who has been sent to help us kill the Fuehrer." And then, in laboured but understandable English, "How do you do, Mr. Bairentz?"

Back in the Brancos hut, with the door safely bolted, Colonel Mulbach said, "I hope you will forgive my reticence of the last few months. It was necessary to make certain checks first."

"I was beginning to wonder," said Mr. Behrens, "if I was on a wild-goose chase. All we knew in London was that a plot was being hatched by a group of officers on the Eastern Front to kill Hitler and end the war by negotiation, and that they needed technical assistance. We thought that if I played my cards right I should be sent here and that the plotters would make contact with me. That's really all I knew."

"I must confess," said the colonel, "that I am surprised you have penetrated as far as you have."

"Part of it was calculation, part luck. The calculation consisted in giving away the new VT fuse. We reckoned that your scientists would arrive at it sooner or later. What we were presenting them with was eighteen months of our own research."

"A tempting bait. And the luck?"

"We happened to have a contact in your RSHA with exactly the necessary knowledge to check my credentials. In fact, my story was carefully tailored to fit in with his. So it was pretty certain that a confrontation between us would eventually be arranged."

"Even so," said the colonel, "Lady Fortune must have smiled on you. You can have little idea of the thoroughness of our security machine. Everyone – certainly every official in the Reich from the village postmaster to Commanding General – has a dossier in that giant card-index of the section known as *Amt IV (a)* 6*(a)* – harmless-sounding initials for an unparalleled instrument of tyranny!

"The information typed on those cards has been collected or extorted by the Gestapo, and when you consider that normal interrogation may involve a thin steel spike being driven down the centre of your finger until it reaches the knuckle bone, you will appreciate that very few men or women are likely to withhold information."

"No," said Mr. Behrens. "I do see that."

"You will appreciate also the risks which are run by those who dream of conspiring against the head of such a state. Even when those dreams are no more than thoughts whispered to oneself. General Busche is a patriot. His record is clean. When Germany has lost the war, as she will in a year or two, he could look forward to the certainty of retirement – Army Group Commanders are very rarely casualties, even on the *OstFront* – and an honourable old age on his estates in Prussia. Instead, so as to have the chance of shortening the war by two years with a negotiated peace, he is prepared to face ignominy and death. On the last occasion that a conspirator was detected he was hanged, yes, but not on a rope. He was hanged by a steel butcher's hook. It took him three hours to die. Every minute of those hours was recorded so that the Fuehrer might entertain himself that evening. A first feature film, you might say."

"Loathsome," said Mr. Behrens.

The colonel seemed not to hear him. He said, almost to himself, "We are coming to *Götterdämmerung*. The Twilight of the Gods. The time when the men of power at last realise that they too must perish, and determine to go out in a holocaust of blood and cruelty and death. When an Emperor of the Chaldeans died, five hundred slaves were killed to keep him company. Many more than five hundred Germans will perish if the Russians' hammer from the east strikes home on the anvil of the American and British forces in the west."

"Curiously enough," said Mr. Behrens dryly, "we should ourselves have no actual objection to ending the war two years early. Had we ended our previous war in 1916, England would be a different country today."

"You are right," said the colonel. His big face, which had gone red, now cracked into a smile. "As always, the British are practical. No more heroics. Down to details. When the Fuehrer arrives, he will come in a Junkers 52 of his own flight. When he returns to his headquarters at Rastenburg, it is normal for any high priority despatches to go with him in a special satchel. This bag will contain, in a compartment, enough explosive to destroy the plane and a time fuse which must be set for one hour and must be completely reliable. Do you think you can make it for us?"

"That is what I am here for," said Mr. Behrens.

"Good. Apart from the General there are only three men fully in the conspiracy. Two of them you met this evening, Major Nachtigal and Captain Heimroth. They are reliable. They are related to the General by blood. The third is Luftwaffe Major Lecke. He was absent today checking the probable flight schedules. He, too, is trustworthy. Unfortunately none of these three men can actually place the message satchel on the Fuehrer's plane. It would not normally be part of their duties, and to make a single abnormal move would invite immediate attention from eyes that miss nothing. However, at least we have Major Mendel."

"And who is Major Mendel?"

"He is an SS major, my subordinate in the Signals, and has, for some months, been in treasonable communication, by wireless, with the Russians."

"He has *what*?"

"It is not uncommon. Nor is it too difficult. When the SS capture Russian agents they torture them to extract their codes and frequencies and then use them for themselves. Their excuse, of course, is that they are using these means to convey false information to the enemy. Once contact has been established, liaison can safely follow. A wireless message leaves no incriminating copy behind it."

"And what does Major Mendel hope to gain by his treason?"

"He is not doing it for himself but on behalf of SS General Pohl who commands all SS troops in this area. General Pohl likes to have his bread buttered on both sides. If we win, he will protect himself by having Major Mendel murdered. Probably me too, since I know of it. On the other hand, if we lose and are surrounded and ordered to fight to the last – an order our Fuehrer is very fond of giving – then he can use this established line of communication to take himself over to the Russians as a welcome guest."

"But –" said Mr. Behrens.

"You wonder how this assists us? That, too, is simple. Once Major Mendel knows that there is a chance of Hitler being killed, the SS being reduced to impotence and the regular army gaining control, he will be faced with the possibility, in this event, of my reporting him to General Busche, who would have him shot. Therefore, to save his hide he will do what I tell him. As an SS Signals Major he is exactly the person to carry a message satchel to the airfield and place it on the Fuehrer's plane."

"You call it *Götterdämmerung*," said Mr. Behrens crossly. "For my taste it's not grand opera at all. It's low and vicious farce. Does no-one in this army play straight by anybody else? Does no-one trust anyone?"

Colonel Mulbach said, with a smile, "I trust you. Surely that is enough."

"I'm sorry," said Mr. Behrens. "I didn't mean to lose my temper. It's only because I'm so damned scared."

The work itself was not hard to organise. Mr. Behrens was able to do most of it openly in his workshop. There were technical difficulties.

"Remember," Colonel Mulbach had said, "what you devise must be silent, and it must not be too heavy. The satchel will be carried to the plane by Major Mendel, but it will have to be handed over there to one of the crew, and he must not have his suspicions aroused."

Mr. Behrens abandoned any idea of using a clockwork fuse. Instead he arranged two wires of identical thickness running through glass tubes into which acid was injected when the fuse was set. When the wire was finally eaten through, it released a plunger, which detonated the main charge of polar ammonite. If one failed for any reason, the other would do the job.

The whole apparatus had then to be carefully fitted into the bottom of a satchel, which was smuggled in to him by the colonel, and covered by a close-fitting sheet of coloured wood. The activating switch was underneath the handle of the bag.

During all this time, Mr. Behrens, mindful of the eyes that missed nothing, continued his normal routine of visits to the front line. It was on his return from one of these that he noticed that something odd was happening. Colonel Mulbach's driver, Lorenz, said, "It is true. The soldiers are going out and the SS are coming in." Mulbach confirmed this late that evening.

He said, "All three of the regular battalions which have been doing camp and headquarters duties are being sent up into the line. They are being replaced by *Waffen SS*. It is represented as a normal redeployment for the coming offensive."

The two men looked at each other.

"It *could* be no more than that," said Mr. Behrens.

"Or it could be the normal precautions which are always taken when Hitler visits his loyal troops," said the colonel, "but if so, it is in this case being carried to an unprecedented extreme. By an order posted this morning, command of the whole headquarters area, including both airfields, has been transferred to SS General Pohl."

"You mean that Busche has been superseded?"

"Not superseded. He remains in command of the army group, but during the period of the Fuehrer's visit, the troops in this area are not his troops and are not under his command."

"When is Hitler arriving?"

"According to present information he lands at Airfield South on Sunday afternoon."

In fact, Hitler landed at Airfield North at midday on Monday. At six o'clock that evening a Berlin acquaintance reappeared. It was SS *Obersturmfuehrer* Mailler. He shook hands with Mr. Behrens and said, "I have orders to bring you to headquarters. A historic privilege awaits you."

In an ante-room in the headquarters building, Mr. Behrens was subjected to a polite but extremely thorough and professional search. A small pair of folding nail-scissors was removed from him, with apologies, and he was conducted to a further room. This was crowded with high-ranking officers of the Army and Air Force, most of whom he had never seen before. They were standing about in groups talking softly.

"You must be nervous," said Mailler.

"I'll try not to be," said Mr. Behrens.

Thirty minutes later a stout major opened the far door and beckoned to Mailler, who laid one hand on Mr. Behrens' arm and propelled him forward.

A man of middle height and thick build, wearing a grey uniform jacket and black riding breeches, was standing behind a table looking down at the maps on it. There were other men in the room too, but Mr. Behrens had eyes only for one. The flat-tipped nose and porcine nostrils with the spout of black hair below them; the grey face and pouches of grey skin below the eyes; the eyes black and very small, tiny windows into the furnace inside.

The revulsion was so strong in him that Mr. Behrens felt his mouth dry up. Hitler lifted his lips in a brief smile.

"He is speechless. No harm in that. In the Reich, deeds come before words."

He half turned, and one of the staff officers handed him an open box. Hitler took out the small gun-metal cross, leaned forward across the table and pinned it to Mr. Behrens' coat.

Mr. Behrens had the presence of mind to throw up his arm in a Nazi salute. The next moment he was outside in the ante-room and Mailler was shaking him by the hand.

"A remarkable privilege," he said, "that he should pin it on you with his own hand." The medal was slightly askew. "You must never move it."

"It shall stay just where it is," said Mr. Behrens fervently, "until I finally take this uniform off."

Later he was able to examine his award more closely. It was the *Dresdner Kreuz* with crossed palm-leaves. The inscription underneath said "For Arduous and Faithful Service in the Cause of Right and Progress."

The convoy drove slowly out towards Airfield North. The Fuehrer's car, flying his personal standard, lay second in line behind the leading vehicle, which was crammed with guards, and a protective screen of motor cyclists. Third in line came SS

General Pohl; behind him General Busche, with his personal staff officers, Major Nachtigal and Captain Heimroth; then a second car load of SS, and a sixth car carrying Colonel Mulbach, Major Mendel and Mr. Behrens. A seventh car, full of guards, brought up the rear.

Mr. Behrens was not happy. Mulbach was sitting in front beside the SS driver and Behrens could see nothing but the colonel's bull-neck and massive shoulders. Major Mendel was in the back, beside him. Mendel had not spoken a word since the drive started. He looked a most unreliable conspirator. He was white and sweating, breathing quickly and unable to control his hands. "Good God," thought Mr. Behrens. "Why did we have to choose a man like this? A child could see that he's up to no good. He'll fall flat on his face before he gets halfway to the aeroplane."

A thought struck him. Had Major Mendel, not trusting himself to do it unobtrusively on the airfield under the eyes of the guards, already set the fuse, and was he now afraid that some unexpected delay might keep them hanging about for an hour before take-off? It would certainly account for his nervousness.

Mr. Behrens bent his head to look at the satchel which stood on the floor between them. It was then that the full shock hit him. *It was not the satchel he had prepared.*

It was very like it but it was not the same. He had worked on it too long to be deceived. The stitching was different and the colour was a shade lighter.

As he thought wildly, turning over various permutations of treachery in his mind, the car swung to the right, over a dry ditch and on to the perimeter of the airfield.

The driver jammed on his brakes so hard that the car behind them nearly ran into them. He shouted something and pointed out of the car window, as a pandemonium of noise erupted.

Six Russian fighter planes, coming low out of the sun, dived at the convoy, their cannons blazing.

Mr. Behrens jerked the nearside door open and rolled into the ditch. The driver landed on top of him. Round the airstrip, after a moment of paralysed silence, the German anti-aircraft guns opened up, but they were firing into an empty sky. The six planes, hedgehopping, had swung right with the precision of well-trained chorus girls and disappeared in the direction of their own lines.

In thirty seconds it was all over. As the firing died away, Mr. Behrens cautiously raised his head.

Most of the occupants of the rear three cars had reached the ditch. The people in the front four cars, having nowhere to go, had either jumped out on the far side of the cars and lain flat, or had simply stayed put. Most of the actual casualties had occurred in the thick lines of black-shirted troops surrounding the perimeter, and field ambulances were already on the move.

Colonel Mulbach was standing beside their car. He pointed. Whatever Major Mendel's troubles had been, they were over. He was sprawled across the back seat. A bullet had gone through the back of his skull. The satchel was still on the floor of the car. The Major's blood was dripping on to it from a pool which had formed on the edge of the seat.

Mr. Behrens took the satchel, feeling as he did so for the catch under the handle. His guess had been wrong. His fingers found the catch, and it was not yet set.

Footsteps approached the car. Mr. Behrens looked up and saw an SS colonel, unknown to him, approaching. The colonel took a quick disinterested look at Major Mendel, took the satchel, swung on his heel and walked back towards the head of the convoy where interest seemed to be centring round the front two cars. Mr. Behrens followed cautiously.

Every instinct told him that something had gone badly wrong and that he ought to keep clear. It was professional pride alone which took him forward.

A dozen Russian bullets had whipped through the back of Hitler's car, apparently without hitting anyone. The car itself was empty. Of Hitler there was no sign at all.

In front of the car stood SS General Pohl, squat and self-possessed, backed by a semi-circle of staff officers and guards. General Busche had got out of his car and was approaching with Major Nachtigal on one side and Captain Heimroth on the other. Approaching was the wrong word. They were being driven forward by SS guards behind them.

The scene reminded Mr. Behrens of something, but for a

second he could not put a finger on it. Then everything clicked into place. What he was witnessing was a field court-martial.

General Pohl said, "As you observe, General Busche, the Fuehrer changed his plans at the last moment. He decided to leave from Airfield South, and should by now –" Pohl made play of consulting his watch "– be well on his way back to Rastenburg."

General Busche examined the bullet-riddled car and said, "It was fortunate for him that he changed his mind."

"Very fortunate, and a demonstration that Providence intends that he should live and fulfil his glorious destiny. Yes?"

"No doubt about it," said General Busche.

"He instructs me, however, to add," said General Pohl, and the sneer in his voice was no longer concealed, "that the bag of despatches which was to have been placed in the plane, is of such importance that he insists they be taken to Rastenburg at once."

"I see."

"And since there are a number of matters, General Busche, urgent and important matters, which he desires to discuss with you, he has decided that you should yourself fly back to Rastenburg with the despatches. Major Nachtigal and Captain Heimroth will accompany you. The plane will be flown by Luftwaffe Major Lecke. He is already at the controls."

Pohl indicated the Junkers 52 standing on the airstrip. He added, "You will be in no danger *from the Russians*, General. A fighter escort will accompany you for the first hour of your flight. After that you should be in need of no further assistance."

There was a long silence. Then General Pohl said, in tones of elaborate surprise, "You are not hesitating, General, to obey the direct orders of our Fuehrer?"

General Busche glanced for a moment at the group which surrounded him; at the massed ranks of the SS beyond, and up at the clear sky above him. Then he gestured to Heimroth and Nachtigal and they walked forward and climbed into the plane. The SS colonel followed him and handed in the blood-stained satchel. The door shut, the props turned, the Junkers 52 taxied down the runway and took off into the light breeze, turned slowly and headed west. From the nearby Luftwaffe airfield came the roar of fighters as they followed the Junkers 52 up into the air. The men on the ground watched as the planes flew steadily westward, diminished in size, became specks in the deep blue Russian sky, and disappeared at last.

Mr. Behrens remembered little of the drive back to headquarters, or of the rest of that day. No-one took any particular interest in him and he was not sure whether this was a good sign or a bad one. After dark that evening there was a quiet knock on his door. He opened it with one hand deep in his jacket pocket. Colonel Mulbach came in, walking softly like a doctor visiting a very sick man, and closed the door carefully behind him.

Mr. Behrens went to the cupboard and took out a bottle of schnapps and two glasses and brought them across to the stove. He said, "What went wrong? Or don't you know? And what is going to happen next? Or don't you know that either?"

"What went wrong," said Mulbach, "is that Major Mendel changed his mind. He decided that Hitler's daemon would preserve him, just as it has in the past, in many such attempts, and that the SS would prevail over the army. Having come to this conclusion he behaved perfectly logically. He went to General Pohl and exposed the whole plot to him."

"The whole of it? You and me as well?"

"Rest assured that he did not mention you or me. If he had done so we should not still have our teeth and fingernails." Mulbach poured the schnapps down his throat with a quick twist of his wrist and held the glass out to be refilled. "He told what he knew. No more. That General Busche and his three staff officers were planning to kill the Fuehrer with a bomb which he, Mendel, was to place on the plane. The satchel was to be given him by General Busche personally. He knew no more. Whereupon Pohl – he is an able man; now that Heydrich has gone he might aspire one day to Himmler's job – Pohl devised the pantomime you saw this morning. It would have been too great a shock to morale if a popular commander like Busche had been relieved of his command and placed under arrest on the very eve of the offensive. So he and his three fellow conspirators were offered an easy alternative to the Gestapo torture cells and death on the hooks. A clean and sudden death in the air."

"It wasn't the bomb I made," said Mr. Behrens. "I noticed that in the car."

"It was a replica. They would keep the original for examination."

"But since it wasn't mine they'd have no means of knowing when it was going to explode. It might have been half an hour. It might have been three hours."

"That was why they threw it out of the plane soon after they were airborne. They had no desire to sit about waiting for death. They then flew the plane straight into the ground."

Mr. Behrens poured himself out a second glass of schnapps, rotated it slowly in the crimson glow from the stove and said, "How on earth do you know all this? About Mendel, I mean, and the SS counterplan, and that sort of thing?"

"General Pohl told me. I am his confidant, naturally. I arrange his communications with the Russians. He does not know that I had any connection with the bomb plot. I think the only man who may dimly have suspected that particular tie-up was our late friend, Major Mendel."

"I suppose that was why you shot him?"

"You saw me?"

"I saw nothing. I was too busy rolling into the ditch like everyone else, but I noticed that the bullet had gone through the back of his neck and come out at the top of his head. It seemed an odd sort of trajectory for a bullet fired from an aircraft. Incidentally, you were very lucky that the raid gave you the opportunity to do it."

"I arranged it on the wireless last night."

"Good God!" Mr. Behrens swallowed his schnapps. "Wasn't that rather dangerous?"

"Not so dangerous as leaving Mendel alive."

"I suppose not. What happens now?"

"What will happen next is that the team of experts who are being specially flown here from Berlin will examine the real bomb. They will do their work with great thoroughness. Each piece of material used in it will be subjected to microscopic analysis. Sooner or later they will conclude, without doubt, that it must have been made in your workshop."

"And then?" said Mr. Behrens.

"You are a very brave man," said Colonel Mulbach, "but are you sure that under the *special* methods of interrogation which they will surely employ, you might not weaken and implicate *me*?"

"A remedy has been provided for that."

"A cyanide pill? But that is a defeatist solution."

"Can you think of any other?"

"Certainly. I have arranged to have you captured by the Russians. I think that will be the best way of ensuring your safety."

"But what about you?"

"Oh, I have been very discreet," said Colonel Mulbach. "You will have noticed that my visits to you have been made after dark. My driver, Lorenz, knows of them, of course. I think you had better take him with you."

"I think you'd better come too."

Colonel Mulbach considered the matter, then he said, "No. With Mendel gone and Pohl perforce on my side, I shall be safe enough. The game is not yet over. I'll stay and see it out."

"You're a braver man than I," said Mr. Behrens.

The commander of the tank squadron looked doubtful. He said, "That village is almost no-man's-land, Dr. Brancos. Could you not get observation from here?"

"Of a sort," said Mr. Behrens, "but not flank observation."

"Then I shall have to send a troop to protect you. And for that I should have to have instructions from higher up. In view of the coming offensive we have been particularly ordered not to take risks with our tanks."

"That I appreciate, but there is nothing to prevent me going forward on foot. My driver can carry the wire and telephone. Your signaller will pay out the reel carefully and stand by to take down my messages at this end. You will be in no danger."

"I was not thinking of the danger," said the officer stiffly, "but of my orders. However, if you insist on risking your own life, that is entirely a matter for you."

26

He watched Mr. Behrens and his driver crawl forward up a ditch, reappear briefly at the far end and finally disappear into the rubble of what had once been a Russian village.

The wire on the reel snaked out steadily. The signaller, who was watching it, said, "He is going very far forward. He is a brave man."

"He is a bloody fool," said the officer.

From the far side of the village came a shot, more shots, then the beat of heavy Russian machine gun.

The officer swore. "Now we shall have to try to rescue him," he said, "and we'll lose a couple of tanks in doing it."

In fact, he ran into a very carefully prepared ambush and lost six.

Two hours later Mr. Behrens was seated in the headquarters of the 143rd Russian Infantry Assault Brigade. His knowledge of Russian was sufficient to enable him to carry on a limited conversation with the youthful brigadier and his much older brigade intelligence officer who had turned out, disconcertingly, to be a woman.

"We have informed Moscow of your arrival," said the brigadier, "and they will be sending a plane for you tomorrow. Meanwhile, we have been told to make you as comfortable as possible. We are a little primitive here, I am afraid."

"It looks just like home to me," said Mr. Behrens.

The woman, who held the rank of major, said something and the brigadier smiled. He said, "Yes. Play it back to us on the loudspeaker." And to Mr. Behrens, "You will be interested in a message we monitored and recorded this morning. It appears to have originated from an aircraft radio."

The loudspeaker in the corner clicked and cleared its throat; and then, out of the ether, General Busche spoke.

"With only a few minutes to live," he said, "I should like to speak to anyone who can hear me. Our country is in great peril. Unless we can come to our senses, awake out of sleep and throw off the gang of criminals and perverts, headed by the maniac who calls himself our Fuehrer –"

Here the message got buried in an outburst of static. "They are trying to jam the wavelength," said the major.

Then, for a moment, the interference died down and Mr. Behrens heard General Busche say, "I, who am about to die, salute you, my country. You will survive this foul tyranny and you will rise again, purer, stronger and greater."

Dominating the sound track now was the aeroplane note of the engine as it went into a power dive, a high shuddering scream of ill-treated machinery, rising to a crescendo. Then, at the last moment, silence.

The major got up and switched off the loudspeaker. "You don't hear the actual crash," she said. "The transmitter must have disintegrated at the moment when the plane hit the hill side."

Mr. Behrens was not interested in these technicalities. He was thinking, "One warring god gone to Valhalla. How long before the others join him, and peace comes into this grey, embattled world?"

2

Emergency Exit

It was six o'clock, on as foul a morning as could be imagined.

In Warsaw it was raining, in the way it rained just before the rain turned to sleet and the sleet to the first snow of winter. The wind from the east lifted the rain and blew it, in a fine spray, down the Grodsky Boulevarde and into Katerina Square. In the far corner of the square the electric sign of the Hotel Polanska was fighting a losing battle with the early morning light.

A man, dressed in an overcoat which hung nearly to his heels and armed with a long broom, was sweeping down the pavement which fronted the three cafés on the south side of the square; he looked up from his task. Something was happening at the Hotel Polanska across the way.

The front door jerked open and two uniformed policemen came out. They were half carrying, half dragging a man who looked as if he had been pulled out of bed and had not been allowed to put on all his clothes. A police officer raised a gloved hand. A car slid up. The four of them bundled in. The car drove off.

A fresh gust of misty rain blew across the square. It was as though a motion-picture director had said "Dissolve" and the scene had been wiped out. The square was once more quiet and empty.

The sweeper rubbed a frayed cuff over his eyes, and bent to his work. He was paid by all three cafés, and if he swept for one better than the others there would be complaints.

When he had finished, he shouldered his broom and shambled off. His course took him past one of the kiosks which sold newspapers and cigarettes. He stopped to have a word with the bearded stall keeper who was taking down the shutters. The man listened, nodding occasionally. Later that morning he himself did some talking, into a telephone.

The news reached an office in Whitehall with the afternoon tea trays and was passed on to Mr. Fortescue, the Manager of the Westminster Branch of the London and Home Counties Bank, as he was getting ready to catch his train home that evening. The message said, "They've taken Rufus Oldroyd."

Mr. Fortescue considered the matter, standing in front of the fireplace, with its hideous chocolate-coloured porcelain mantel. From the expression on his face you might have judged that the account of one of his most trusted customers had gone suddenly into the red.

Nine o'clock, on an autumn morning straight from paradise. The sun, clear of the mist, was full and golden, but not yet giving out much heat. In the drawing room of Craysfoot House a log fire was crackling in the grate, and the smell of percolating coffee was scenting the air.

"Damn the girl," said Admiral Lefroy, "how many times have I told her that I like my eggs boiled for four minutes!"

"I've told her a dozen times," said his wife.

"By the feel of this one it's been boiled for fourteen minutes."

"Give it to Sultan."

"I'll do nothing of the sort. The quickest way to ruin a dog's manners is to feed him at table. You'll have him begging next. Balancing lumps of sugar on his nose."

"When you were in command of a ship, I'm sure you were horrid to all the little midshipmen."

"It isn't a captain's job to be horrid to midshipmen." The Admiral glared at the official letter he had just opened. "Damn!"

"What's up now?"

"Got to go to town. The First Sea Lord's called a conference. It's wonderful how busy they manage to keep us, considering we haven't got a Navy."

"I'll go with you. We can come back together on Friday afternoon."

"Who have we got this weekend?"

"Your friend, Captain Rowlandson."

"Good."

"And Mrs. Orbiston."

"Oh, God!"

"You'll have to be nice to her. She's on the committee of the Kennel Club. We can't have her blackballing Sultan when he comes up."

Hearing his name, the dog got up from the rug in front of the fire and walked across to Lady Lefroy. He was nine months old, a puppy no longer, but a young dog with plenty of growth to come in his long springy body and barrel chest. A Persian deerhound of royal parentage, he wore the tuft of hair on the top of his head like a coronet. His eyes, which had been light yellow at birth, were deepening now into amber. His nose was blue-black, his skin the colour of honey.

Lady Lefroy tickled the top of his head and said, "Sorry, no scraps for you." And to her husband, "I forgot. There's one more. Mr. Behrens."

"Who's he?"

"You ought to know. You invited him."

"Oh, the bee chap. Yes. I met him at my club. He's written a book about them. Knows a lot about mediaeval armour, too."

"He can go for nice long walks with Mrs. Orbiston and talk to her about hives and helmets."

Admiral Lefroy abandoned the egg in disgust, and started on the toast and marmalade. He said, "What are you planning to do up in town?"

"Shopping, and having my hair done."

"By – what's the fellow's name – Michael?"

"Who else? And what are you snorting about?"

"You know damned well what I'm snorting about."

"Now, Alaric . . . Michael is adorable. The things he says! Do you know what he told Lady Skeffington last week?"

"I'm not the least interested in what he told Lady Skeffington."

The beauty salon was in two sections. The front had plush settees, low tables covered with glossy magazines, a thick carpet, and indirect lighting. At the back was a row of cubicles, with plain white wooden doors. On each door was the word *Michael's* in letters of brass script, and under each word the stylised painting of a different flower.

From behind the cubicles the snipping of scissors, the sudden gushing of water as a spray was turned on, the humming of a hair dryer. From in front, the hum of conversation. Mrs. Hetherington, county to the oblong ends of her brown shoes, was saying to Lady Lefroy, "So *she* said, when they have the next Cabinet reshuffle, Tom's been promised the Navy. Michael said – with a perfectly straight face – 'What'll he do with it when he gets it? Play with it in his bath?'"

A Mrs. Toop, who was nobody in particular, and knew it, giggled sycophantically. Lady Lefroy, who had heard the story before, said, "Oh. What did she say?"

"Of course she pretended to be furious. I mean, Michael doesn't bother to be rude to you unless your husband's someone."

How Mrs. Toop wished that Michael would be rude to *her!*

"He goes too far sometimes," said Lady Lefroy. "Did you hear what he said to Lady Skeffington?"

"No. Tell, tell."

"Well, you know how she's always carrying on about her husband's polo. What the Duke said to him and what he said to the Duke –"

"Hold it," said Mrs. Hetherington regretfully.

The door with a chrysanthemum on it opened and Michael came out. He held the door open for Lady Skeffington, gave her a gentle pat on the back as she went past, and said, "There now, Lady S. You look a proper little tart. I 'ope your 'usband likes it."

"He'll hate it," said Lady Skeffington complacently.

"It'll keep his mind off things. You ought to see the cartoon in the *Mirror.*"

"I never read the *Mirror.*"

"You don't know what you're missing. They've got him to the life. Quintin as the lion, and 'im as the unicorn."

It was noticeable that Michael dealt with his aitches quite arbitrarily, sometimes dropping them, sometimes not. He helped Lady Skeffington into her coat, showed her out, and came back, casting an eye over the waiting victims.

"Come on Lady L.," he said, "I'll wash your hair for you."

Mrs. Hetherington said, "What about me? I was next."

"Bert can take care of you," said Michael. "He'll be through in Delphinium in 'alf a mo'."

"It's sheer favouritism."

"You know what Mr. Asquith said. 'Favouritism's the secret of efficiency.'"

"It wasn't Asquith," said Mrs. Hetherington coldly. "It was Lord Fisher."

"Marcia Lefroy," said Mr. Fortescue, "is not English at all, although to hear her speak you would never guess it. She's a French Lebanese girl, of good family." Mr. Fortescue paused, as though the next words he had to speak were precious, and needed to be weighed out very carefully. "She had been a trained Communist agent since she was sixteen."

The Under-Secretary of State stared at him in blank disbelief. He said, "Really, Fortescue. This sounds like something Security Executive has dreamed up. I've met Lady Lefroy a dozen times. She's an absolutely charming woman."

"She was trained to be charming. In fact, her earliest assignment was to charm Lefroy. He was only a captain then, in command of our Eastern Mediterranean cruiser detachment. Her instructions were to seduce him. However, it served the purpose of her employers equally well when he carried her off and married her."

"This is quite fantastic. Who started this – this canard?"

"It was started by a disgruntled housemaid. She told us that once, when clearing away the coffee cups, she distinctly heard Admiral Lefroy telling his wife something – she was vague what it was but she was sure it was secret."

The Under-Secretary laughed. "And you believed that sort of evidence?"

"On the contrary, we put her down as a bad and spiteful witness. The information was pigeon-holed. However, three months ago, when Heinrich Woolf defected to us – you remember –"

"Of course."

"One of the things he told us was that details of our agents in Eastern bloc countries were regularly reaching Moscow via Warsaw. They were known to be coming from the foreign-born wife of a senior naval officer with a post in Intelligence. The Lefroys filled the bill exactly. He's the naval representative on the Joint Staffs Intelligence Committee.

"We still didn't believe it, but we had Lady Lefroy watched. And noticed that she had her hair – washed and set, I believe, is the right expression – by a fashionable hairdresser who calls himself Michael, speaks with a strong Cockney accent, was born in Lithuania, and has an occasional and inconspicuous rendezvous on Parliament Hill Fields with a Major Shollitov, who drives the Polish ambassador's spare car."

The Under-Secretary said, "Good God!" and then, "I hope you realise that this is a case where we can't afford – can't possibly afford – to make any mistake."

"I can see that it would arouse considerable comment."

"Comment! God in heaven, man, it's dynamite. And if it went off the wrong way it could – well it could blow quite a lot of people out of office."

Mr. Fortescue said in his gentlest voice, "I had not really considered the political angles. My objective is to stop it. You heard they picked up Rufus Oldroyd –"

"Was that –?"

"I imagine so. Admiral Lefroy knew all about Oldroyd. A single incautious word to his wife. The mention of a name even –"

"Yes. I can see that."

"It must be stopped." Mr. Fortescue's eyes were as bleak and grey as the seas which washed his native Hebrides.

The Under-Secretary shifted uncomfortably in his padded chair. He was a Wykehamist with a first-class degree. The fact that he was a chess player had apparently suggested to his masters that he might have an aptitude for Intelligence matters. It had not proved a happy choice. He disliked Intelligence work, its operations, its operators, and all its implications. It was only the accident of the particular seat he occupied at the Foreign Office which had forced him to have anything to do with it.

He said, "Alaric Lefroy's a public hero. Has been ever since he got his VC on the Russian convoy. He's a friend of royalty. He could hardly be removed from the committee without public explanation. And suppose we were forced – by questions in the House – to *give* an explanation. Could we prove it?"

"At the moment, almost certainly not."

"Then couldn't we pull this fellow Michael in?"

"It would be ineffective. Marcia Lefroy is a professional. She'd lie low for a bit. Then she'd open up a new channel of communication – possibly one we didn't know about. Then we should be worse off."

"I suppose you're right," said the Under-Secretary unhappily. "What are we going to do about it?"

"I had worked out a tentative plan – I could explain the details if you wished –"

The Under-Secretary said hastily that he had no desire to hear the details. He felt confident that the matter could be left entirely in Mr. Fortescue's hands.

Michael was uneasy. The causes of his uneasiness were trivial, but they were cumulative. There had been the trouble with the lock on the front door of his flat. The locksmith who had removed and replaced it had found the tip of a key broken off in the mechanism.

Michael had mentioned the matter to the hall porter, and in doing so had discovered that the regular porter, with whom he was on very good terms, had been replaced by a large and surly-looking individual who had treated him in a very off-hand way. And the final straw – there had been trouble with his car.

It had been his custom to make his trips to North London in an inconspicuous little Austin runabout. This had gone in for repairs a week ago, and had been promised to him for today. When he went to get the car it was not ready. Mysterious additional faults had developed. There was nothing he could do but use his second car, the extremely conspicuous, primrose-yellow Daimler with the personal licence plate.

This he parked, as usual, in the backyard of the Spaniards, and made his way on foot down the complex of paths which led to the open spaces of Parliament Hill Fields. It was an ideal place for a rendezvous, with an almost panoramic view of London. Major Shollitov would come from the opposite direction, leaving his car in Swains Lane, and walking up to the meeting place.

And now, to add to, and cap, all the other doubts which had been nagging him, Major Shollitov was late. Michael, although a very minor player in the game, was sufficiently instructed to realise the significance of this. A rendezvous was always kept with scrupulous punctuality. If one party was late, it was a warning – a warning not to be disregarded. The other party took himself off, quickly and quietly.

Michael glanced at his watch. 2:59. From the seat on which he was sitting he could command all the paths leading up from the Vale. It was one of its advantages. Thirty seconds to go. Major Shollitov was not coming.

When a hand touched him on the shoulder Michael jumped.

The man must have come up across the grass behind him. He was thick-set, middle-aged, and nondescript. He said, "Got a match?"

Michael's heart resumed a more normal rhythm. He said, "Sure."

"Mind if I sit down? Lovely view, isn't it?"

Michael said, "Yes." He wondered how soon he could move. To get straight up and walk off would look rude, and to be rude would attract attention.

The stranger said, "I wonder if you know why they call this spot Parliament Hill Fields?"

"No, I don't."

"You remember that crowd who were planning to blow up Parliament? Fifth of November, sixteen hundred and five. They'd got it all laid out, and were intending to scuttle off up north to start the revolt. And just about here was where they pulled up their horses, to have a view of the fireworks display. Dramatic, wasn't it?"

"Oh, very," said Michael. Give it one more minute.

"Only, as *we* know, the fireworks didn't go off. And they left

36

poor old Guy Fawkes behind to carry the can. Interesting, don't you think?"

"Oh, very."

"I thought you'd be interested."

There was something about this last statement that Michael didn't like. He said sharply, "Why should it interest me, particularly?"

"Well," said the stranger, "after all it's much the sort of position you're in now, isn't it?"

The long silence that followed was broken by the distant voices of children playing, out of sight down the slope. At last Michael said, "What are you talking about?"

"Your old pal, Major Shollitov – the one you usually meet here. He's gone scuttling back to Warsaw, leaving you sitting here, like Guy Fawkes, waiting for the rack and thumbscrew."

"Who are you?"

"Never mind about me," said the stranger, with a sudden brutal authority. "Let's talk about you. You're the one who's on the spot. You're a messenger boy for the Commies, aren't you? How did they rope you in? Through your old mum and dad in Lithuania? Not that it matters. They've finished with you now. You're blown."

"You're mad."

"If you think I'm mad I'd advise you to shout for help. Go on. There's a park attendant. Give him a yell. Tell him you're being annoyed by a lunatic."

Michael watched the park attendant approach them. He watched him walk away.

The stranger inhaled the last drop of smoke from his cigarette, dropped it, and stamped on it. He said, "You've had an easy run, so far. Listening to high-class tittle-tattle from Lady This, whose husband's in the Cabinet, and Mrs. That whose brother's on the Staff, and passing it on for a few pounds a time. They don't pay much for third class work like that. Well, that's all over now. It's you who's going to do the paying and –" The stranger leaned forward until his face was a few inches from Michael's "– it's not going to be nice. They get rough, those Intelligence boys. They know what happens to *their* friends when they get caught, and they like a chance to pay a little of it back. The last one they brought in had both his legs broken. Jumping out of a car, *they* said –"

"He's yellow," said Mr. Calder to Mr. Fortescue. "Yellow as a daffodil. By the time I'd finished he was almost crying."

"I'm not surprised," said Mr. Fortescue. "Verbal bullies are often lacking in moral stamina. You were careful not to suggest any connection between him and Lady Lefroy?"

"Very careful. I kept it quite general. Listening to indiscreet gossip was how I put it."

"Excellent. We must hope that he'll act predictably."

It had not been an easy weekend, even for an experienced hostess like Marcia Lefroy. Captain Rowlandson and Mrs. Orbiston had not mixed well. The only real success had been Mr. Behrens, who had filled in awkward gaps in the conversation with stories about his bees.

The final straw for Lady Lefroy was when her husband telephoned that he had to stay in London. The First Lord had called a conference for early the next day.

Lady Lefroy pondered these things as she lay in bed. Usually she fell asleep immediately after turning off the bedside lamp. Tonight she had not done so. Like all trained and experienced agents she possessed delicate antennae on the alert for the unusual. It was most unusual for a conference to be called on a Saturday morning. If there had been a crisis of some sort, it would have been understandable. But the international scene was flat as a pancake. Why then –

The first handful of gravel against the window jerked her back to full wakefulness. As she got out of bed Sultan growled softly. "It's all right," she said. She struggled into her dressing gown without turning on the light.

She made her way downstairs into the drawing room and opened the long window giving on to the terrace. As a man slipped through she adjusted the curtains carefully and switched on a single wall light. When she saw who it was her anger exploded. "How *dare* you come here!"

"I wouldn't have come unless I had to," said Michael sulkily.

"Your instructions were clear. You were absolutely forbidden to write, telephone, or even to speak to me, except in your shop."

"But I've got to get out. They're on to me."

"How do you know that?"

"They told me."

"An unusual proceeding," said Lady Lefroy coldly.

"This man, he met me, at the rendezvous. Shollitov's been sent home. He knew all about us."

"Us?"

"Well, about me."

"Did he mention my name?"

"Not your name particularly. He accused me of picking up gossip at the salon and passing it on. He made threats. They were going to – do things to me."

"Have they done anything?"

"Not yet. But they will. I tried to get through – to the emergency number."

"Fool. Your line will be tapped."

"I couldn't, anyway. They said it had been disconnected."

"I see," said Lady Lefroy. It was a few moments before she spoke again.

"How did you come down?"

"By car. I'm sure I wasn't followed – I should have known at once. The roads were empty. I hid the car nearly a mile away and walked the rest of the way."

"You showed that much sense." There was no point in panicking him. He was frightened enough already. "What do you want?"

"Help. To get out."

"What makes you think I can help you?"

"You know the ropes. They told me that if I ever had to clear out I was to come to you."

"Then," said Lady Lefroy, "I must see what I can do." She walked across to her desk. As she did so, the door was pushed open. Her heart missed a beat, then steadied. It was Sultan.

"That's very naughty of you," she said. "I told you to stay put."

Sultan yawned. He wanted the man to go so that they could get back to bed.

Lady Lefroy unlocked the desk, and then a steel-lined drawer inside. From it she took a bulky packet which she weighed thoughtfully in her hand. She said, "You see this. It was left with me against such a contingency. But before I give it to you I must have your promise to use it exactly in the way I tell you."

"Of course. What is it?"

"It's called 'Emergency Exit'. Inside you'll find a passport. The photograph resembles you sufficiently. You'll have to make a few small changes. Arrange your hair differently. That should be easy enough for a man of your talents." A smile twitched the corner of Lady Lefroy's mouth. "And wear glasses. You'll find them in the packet too. There's a wad of French and German money, and instructions as to what you're to do when you get to Cologne. From there you'll be flying to Berlin. There's a second passport to use in Berlin, and a second set of instructions. After you open the packet – which you're not to do until you're back in London – all instructions are to be learned by heart and then destroyed. And the first passport is to be destroyed when you reach Cologne. Is that all clear?"

Michael let his breath out with a soft sigh. "All clear," he said. "And thank you."

"A final word. *These things aren't issued in duplicate.* So look after it carefully."

Michael made an unsuccessful attempt to stow the bulky oil-skin-covered packet in his coat pocket. Lady Lefroy took it from him. She said, "Open the front of your shirt. That's right. Stow it down there. Now button it up again. Right. Don't open the curtains until I've turned the light off."

She stood for a few moments after Michael had gone. She was taut as a violin string. The young dog, crouched at her feet, sensed it and growled, low in his throat. The sound broke the tension.

"All right," said Lady Lefroy. "Back to bed. Nothing more to worry about."

★

Among other irritating habits Mrs. Orbiston was accustomed to turning on her portable radio for the seven o'clock news, and retailing the choicer items to the company at breakfast. Lady Lefroy had not appeared, so her audience consisted of Captain Rowlandson, who was never fully awake until he had finished his after-breakfast pipe, and Mr. Behrens whose mind appeared to be elsewhere.

"Burglars," she announced. "Stole jewellery worth fifteen thousand pounds. At Greystone House. That's not far from here, is it?"

"I've no idea," said Captain Rowlandson.

"Well, I'm sure it is nearby. Because the people were called Baynes, and I've heard Marcia talk about them."

"Serve them right. When you go away you ought to put your jewellery in the bank."

"That's just it. That's what made it so terrible. The men went *into* their bedroom, *while* they were there, and helped themselves to the jewel box *off* the dressing table. It makes your flesh creep. I was just saying, Marcia –"

"If it's the Bayneses you're talking about," said Lady Lefroy, who had come into the room at that moment, "I've just heard. Mary Baynes was on the telephone."

"One good thing," said Captain Rowlandson, "they wouldn't get away with it here. Sultan would see them off."

"He's a very light sleeper," agreed Lady Lefroy. "All the same, I can't help thinking that it might be better if he *didn't* give the alarm."

"Oh – why?"

"I gather these burglars are pretty desperate characters. And all my stuff is well insured."

"That's pure defeatism, Marcia. Don't you agree, Behrens?"

Mr. Behrens said, "Defeatism might be preferable to being shot."

Mrs. Orbiston, seeing the conversation drifting away from her, pulled it back sharply. She said, "And that wasn't the *only* exciting thing that happened in this part of the country. Roysters Cross is quite close to here, too, isn't it?"

"About four miles away," said Lady Lefroy. "Why?"

"There was a terrible accident there last night. A man blew himself up."

"Blew himself up?"

"That's what the news commentator said."

"Curious way of committing suicide," said Captain Rowlandson.

"The possibility of accident has not been ruled out."

"You can't very well blow yourself up by accident," said Mr. Behrens. "That is, unless you're carrying some sort of bomb."

"Perhaps it was a tyre blow-out," said Lady Lefroy. "Would you mind passing the marmalade?"

"It didn't sound like a tyre blow-out. They said the man *and* the car were blown to bits."

"Amatol or dextrol," said Mr. Calder. "Or just possibly good old-fashioned nitroglycerine. Although that's got rather a detectable smell."

"What sort of fuse?" asked Mr. Fortescue.

"Something silent. Wire and acid?"

"Very likely," agreed Mr. Fortescue. "It's notoriously inaccurate. I've no doubt the thing was intended to go off a lot further away from Lady Lefroy's house. Or maybe he took longer to walk back to his car than she anticipated. How do you think she arranged it?"

"I imagine it was something she gave him to take back to London. A parcel of some sort."

"The whole thing," said Mr. Fortescue, "is most unfortunate. Michael was responding nicely to treatment. He would soon have been ready to cooperate."

"Evidently Marcia thought so, too."

"It demonstrates what we have always suspected – that she's a ruthless and unscrupulous woman."

"It demonstrates something else, too," said Mr. Calder. "If she tumbled to what we were doing – twisting Michael's tail so hard that he'd incriminate her – she must have suspected that we were onto her as well."

Mr. Fortescue said, "Hmm. Maybe."

"Not certain, I agree. But a workable assumption. And if it's true, it must mean that she's decided to stay put and brazen it out. Because if she had decided to quit she'd have kept Michael on ice for a day or two, while she made all *her* preparations."

"It's not a happy conclusion, Calder."

"It's a very unhappy conclusion. Now that she's been warned she'll sever all her contacts and lie low for a very long time. Possibly forever."

"It would, I suppose, be a half-way solution," said Mr. Fortescue. He didn't sound very happy about it. "All the same, I don't think it's a chance we can take. Do you?"

"No," said Mr. Calder. "I don't." He added, "I read in the papers that there'd been another burglary down in the Petersfield area. It's some sort of gang. The police say that they're armed, and dangerous. They've put out a warning to all householders in the neighbourhood."

Mr. Fortescue thought about this for a long time. Then he said, "Yes. I think that would be best. It'll mean keeping the Admiral up in London for another night. I'll get the Minister to reconvene the conference."

"How's he going to get away with that one? He can't keep senior admirals and generals in London on a Sunday. Not in peacetime."

"Then we'll have to declare war on someone," said Mr. Fortescue.

Marcia sat up in bed and said, "Stop it, Sultan. What's the matter with you?"

It had been a savage growl – no gentle rumbling warning, but a note of imminent danger.

The moon, cloud-racked, was throwing a grey light into the room. As her sight adjusted itself, Marcia could dimly see the figure at which Sultan was snarling.

She twisted one hand into his collar, and with the other she switched on the bed-table lamp. A man was standing beside the dressing table, examining an opened jewel case. He put the case down and said, "If you don't keep that dog under control I shall have to shoot him. It won't make a lot of noise, because this gun's silenced, but I'd hate to have to mess up a nice animal like that."

"If that jewel case interests you, you're welcome to it. It's got nothing but costume jewellery in it – stop it, Sultan – worth twenty-five pounds, if you're lucky."

"And insured for five hundred, I don't doubt," said the intruder. "I'm not really interested in jewellery. That's just an excuse for meeting you. I wanted to get your version of what happened to Michael last night."

"Michael? Michael who?"

"The Michael who's been doing your hair for the last eighteen months. You can't have forgotten about him already. They've only just finished scraping bits of him off the signpost at Roysters Cross. That must have been a powerful bit of stuff you put in the packet you gave him."

"I've no idea what you're talking about," said Lady Lefroy. Her voice gave nothing away. Only her eyes were thoughtful, and the knuckles of the hand which held Sultan's collar showed white.

The door opened quietly. Calder's colleague, Mr. Behrens, looked in.

"You've come just at the right moment," said the first intruder. "Have you got the tape?"

"I have it," said Mr. Behrens, "and a recorder. I had to wire three rooms to be sure of getting it."

Lady Lefroy's look had hardened. She moved her head slowly, trying to sum up both men, to weigh this new development. It was the reaction of a professional, faced by a threat from a new quarter.

"You know each other, I see."

"Indeed, yes," said Mr. Behrens. "Calder and I have known each other for twenty years. Or is it twenty-five? Time goes so quickly when you're interested in your work."

"So you're in this together."

"We often work as a team."

"You do the snooping and sneaking, and he does the rough stuff."

"Exactly," said Mr. Behrens. "We find it an excellent

arrangement." He was busy with the tape recorder. "Now perhaps we can convince you we're not bluffing. Where shall we start?"

There was a click, and they heard Lady Lefroy's voice say, "It's called 'Emergency Exit'. Inside you'll find a passport –" They listened in silence for a full minute. "Open the front of your shirt. That's right. Stow it down there –"

Mr. Behrens turned the machine off.

"A nice touch," he said. "It must have been resting on his stomach when it went off. No wonder there wasn't much of him left."

Lady Lefroy said, "That tape recording proves nothing. You say it's my voice. I say it's a clumsy fake. It doesn't even sound much like me."

"You mustn't forget that I saw Michael, both coming and going."

"Lies! Why do you bother me with such lies?" Again her eyes turned from one man to the other. She was trying to estimate which of them was the stronger character, which one she should attack, what weapons in her well-stocked armoury she should use. It was confusing to have to deal with two at once.

In the end she said, with a well-contrived yawn, "Do I understand that this is all leading up to something? That you have some proposal to put to me? If so, please put it, so that I can get back to sleep."

"Our proposal," said Mr. Calder, "is this. If you will make a written statement, naming your employers, and your contacts, giving full details which can be verified in forty-eight hours, we'll give you the same length of time to get out of the country."

"We feel certain," said Mr. Behrens, "that you have all *your* arrangements made."

"More efficient, if less drastic, than the ones you made for Michael."

All expression had gone out of Lady Lefroy's face. It was a mask – a meticulously constructed mask behind which a quick brain weighed the advantages and disadvantages of the proposal. When she smiled, Mr. Behrens knew that they had lost.

"You're bluffing," she said. "I call your bluff. Go away."

"A pity," said Mr. Behrens.

"Very disappointing," said Mr. Calder. "We shall have to use plan Number Two."

"You do understand," said Mr. Behrens earnestly, "that you've brought this on yourself. We have no alternative."

Lady Lefroy said nothing. There was something here she found disturbing.

Mr. Calder said, "It's this gang of burglars, you see. Armed burglars. They've been breaking into houses round here. Tonight they turned their attention to this house. You woke up and caught one of them rifling your jewel case."

"And what happened then?"

"Then," said Mr. Calder, "he shot you."

Three things happened together: a scream from Marcia Lefroy, cut short; the resonant twang of the silenced automatic pistol; and a snarl of fury as the dog went for Mr. Calder's throat.

Mr. Behrens moved almost as quickly as the dog. He caught up the two corners of the blanket on which the dog had been lying and enveloped him in it, a growling, writhing, murderous bundle. Mr. Calder dropped his gun, grabbed the other two corners of the blanket, knotted them together.

"It was unpardonable," said Mr. Fortescue.

"I know," said Mr. Calder. "But –"

"There are no 'buts' about it. It was an unnecessary complication, and a quite unjustifiable risk. Suppose he is recognised."

"All Persian deerhounds have a strong family resemblance. Once he's fully grown there'll be no risk at all. I'll rename him of course. I thought that Rasselas might be the appropriate name for an Eastern prince –"

"I can't approve."

"He's beautifully bred. And he's got all the courage in the world. You should have seen the way he came for me. Straight as an arrow. If Behrens hadn't got the blanket over him, he'd have had my throat for sure. What were we to do?"

"You should have immobilised him."

"You can't immobilise a partly grown deerhound."

"Then you should have shot him."

"Shoot a dog like that," said Mr. Calder. "You must be joking."

3

One-to-Ten

The notice, in firm black letters on a big white board, said, "War Department Property. Keep to made tracks. If you find anything leave it alone. It may explode." The last three words were in capital letters. Beside it a much smaller, older, faded green board said, "Hurley Bottom Farm – one mile."

Mr. Calder read out both notices to Rasselas, and added, "You'd better keep to heel and leave the rabbits alone." Rasselas grinned at him. He thought that Salisbury Plain was a promising sort of place.

Man and dog set off down the path. After half a mile it forked. There was nothing to indicate which fork to take. Mr. Calder decided that the right-hand one, which went uphill, looked more attractive.

It was a windless autumn day. As they reached the top of the rise they could see the Plain spread round them in a broad arc, wave behind wave, all soft greens and browns, running away to the horizon, meeting and melting into the grey of the sky. Two pigeons got up from a clump of trees and circled at a safe distance from the man and the dog. A big flock of fieldfares swung across the sky, thick as black smoke, forming and reforming and vanishing as mysteriously as they had come.

Mr. Calder unslung his field glasses and made a slow traverse of the area. Rasselas sat beside him, a tip of pink tongue hanging out of the side of his mouth.

When the voice spoke it was unexpectedly harsh, magnified by the loud-hailer. "You there, with the dog."

Mr. Calder turned slowly.

It was an Army truck, and a blond subaltern in battle dress

with the red and blue flashes of the Artillery, was standing beside the driver.

"If you go much farther you'll be in the target area."

Mr. Calder said, "Well, thanks very much for telling me." By this time he had got close enough to the truck to see the unit signs. "I'm too old to be shot at. Don't you think your people might have put up some sort of warning?"

"The red flags are all flying."

"I must have missed them. I was looking for Hurley Bottom Farm."

"You should have forked left a good quarter of a mile back. We ought to put up a notice there, I suppose. All the locals know it, of course. I take it you're a stranger?"

"That's right," said Mr. Calder. "I'm a stranger, and if it's crossed your mind that I might be a Chinese spy, I could refer you to Colonel Crofter at Porton. He'll give you some sort of a character, I dare say."

The boy smiled and said, "I didn't think you were a spy. But I thought you might be going to get your head blown off. It causes a lot of trouble when it happens. Courts of Enquiry and goodness knows what. That's a lovely dog. What sort is he?"

"He's a Persian deerhound. They used them to hunt wolves, actually."

"He looks as if he could deal with a wolf, too. Are you a friend of Mrs. King-Bassett? Or perhaps you were just going to ride?"

Mr. Calder looked blank.

"She owns Hurley Bottom Farm. The place you said you were going to. And runs a riding stable. A lot of our chaps go there."

"To ride?"

"That's right." The boy, who seemed to think he had said too much, added abruptly, "You'll find the turning's back there."

Mr. Calder thanked him and trudged off. As he did so, the battery, tucked into a valley to his right, opened up and a salvo of shells came whistling lazily over and landed with a familiar *crump-crump* in the dip to his left.

The path to Hurley Bottom took him away from the ranges and into farmland. The soil was Wiltshire chalk with a thin crust of loam. It would not be very productive, he imagined. At a point where the path ran between two thorn hedges he heard a sudden thundering of hooves behind him and, removing himself with undignified haste to one side, he tripped and landed on all fours.

"What the bloody hell do you think you're doing?" enquired a magnificent female figure, encased in riding breeches, riding boots, a canary yellow polo-necked sweater and a hard hat, and mounted on what appeared to Mr. Calder, from his worm's-eye view, to be about thirty foot superficial of chestnut horse.

He climbed to his feet, removed a handful of leafmould from his right ear and said, "This is a public footpath, isn't it?"

"It also happens to be a bridle path," said the lady.

Mr. Calder had had time to look at her now. He saw a brick-red but not unhandsome face. Sulky eyes, a gash of red mouth, and a firm chin.

"When you come round a corner as fast as that," he said, "you ought to sound your horn. I take it you're Mrs. King-Bassett?"

"Correct. And if you're looking for a ride, I'm afraid all my horses are booked just now."

"Oddly enough, I was simply going for a walk."

"Then let me give you a word of warning. Don't bring your dog too near the farm. I've got an Alsatian called Prince. He's a killer."

"We will both bear it in mind," said Mr. Calder. Rasselas grinned amiably.

The cathedral clock sent out its sixteen warning notes into the still, bonfire-scented air and then started to strike nine times.

The wireless set in Canon Trumpington's drawing room said, "This is the nine o'clock news. Here are the headlines. In Chinese Turkestan, an earthquake has destroyed sixteen villages. After a football match in Rio de Janeiro the crowd invaded the pitch and was dispersed by tear gas. A subsequent bayonet charge resulted in twenty-five casualties. There has been an unexpected rise of twenty-seven per cent in the price of copper. The death roll from the as-yet-unexplained outbreak of cholera at the Al-Maza Military Research Station near Cairo has now risen to seven, and includes a number of Egypt's leading scientific experts. Professor Fawazi, head of the establishment, who was seriously ill, is now off the danger list . . ."

"For heaven's sake," said Mrs. Trumpington. "Turn that machine off, Herbert."

Canon Trumpington stretched out a hand, and peace was restored to the pleasant room in the South Canonry. In the garden outside an owl was serenading the full moon.

"Is it my imagination, or does the news get worse and worse?"

"There wasn't much to cheer anyone up tonight, I agree. What do you say, Behrens? Is the world running down? Are we all on our way out, in a maelstrom of violence and silliness?"

Mr. Behrens said, "Is it the world that's getting old? Or is it us? The older we get, the more we value calm and peace, and a settled routine. Our nerves aren't as strong as they were. Things which look like a desperate threat to us – if we were forty years younger, they might look like an adventure."

"I may be old," said Mrs. Trumpington with spirit, "and I may be nervous, but I can't see how anyone, whatever their age or state of health, could regard a thousand people being wiped out in an earthquake as an adventure."

"Certainly not. But the first reaction of a young man might not be one of horror. It might be a desire to go out and help."

Mrs. Trumpington snorted. The canon said, "He's quite right, you know." He made a mental note for his next sermon.

"And what about those poor Egyptian scientists?"

"There," said Mr. Behrens, "I must confess that my own reaction was one of incredulity. Cholera nowadays is controllable by quite simple forms of immunisation. If the outbreak had been in some primitive community, where serum was unobtainable – but in a scientific institution . . ."

"It said an *unexplained* outbreak. Might it be a new and more virulent type?"

"It's possible. I remember when I was in Albania before the war a particularly unpleasant form of skin disease, akin to lupus . . ."

"If you go on like this," said Mrs. Trumpington, "I'm going to bed."

Mr. Behrens apologised, and said, "Tell us what you've got planned for tomorrow."

"We're going to take coffee at the Deanery. There's a bring-and-buy sale in the afternoon. I'll let you off that. And we're having tea with Marjorie and Albert Rivers. Although I don't expect he'll be there. They have that cottage just outside Harnham Gate. He's one of the top scientists, out at Porton. She's a bridge fanatic."

"Not a fanatic, my dear. An expert. That's something quite different."

"They're both very good, anyway. No-one round here will take them on any more."

"When people say that," said Mr. Behrens, "it usually means they think they're a bit sharp."

"No. Nothing like that. They're simply above our standard. They're both county players. Indeed I'm told that if Marjorie Rivers had the time to devote to it, she might be an international."

"A scientist and a bridge international," said Mr. Behrens. "They sound an interesting couple."

"If there's one thing I can't abide," said Mrs. Wort, "it's rabbits. Rabbits and rats. They're both vermin. And as for *eating* them . . ."

"I'm not very fond of them myself," admitted Mr. Calder. "It was Rasselas who insisted on catching them. I should bury them and forget about it."

The great dog was stretched out in front of the fire, his amber eyes half shut, the tip of his tail twitching.

"I declare," said Mrs. Wort, "I think he understands every word you say. And isn't he enjoying his holiday! The Plain was a grand place for dogs, before the Army messed it up. I remember the time, when I was a girl, there wasn't a soldier in sight. Just a few airmen, in what they called the Balloon School. Now you can't move for 'em."

"You can't indeed," said Mr. Calder. He was as relaxed as Rasselas, full-length in an armchair as old and faded and comfortable as everything in the farmhouse kitchen. "I ran into them

53

myself this afternnoon. And *I* nearly got run into by a high-spirited female on a horse."

"Swore at you, did she?"

"That's right."

"Then it'd be Missus King-Bassett. Keeps a riding stable out at Hurley Bottom, and a kennels, and runs the farm. You know what they all call her up at the camp, don't you? The merry widow."

"Then Mr. King-Bassett is dead?"

"*If* he ever existed."

"I see," said Mr. Calder. "*If* he ever existed. That sort of widow. How long's she been here?"

"She bought the place – oh – three, four years ago. When old man Rudd died. She's pulled it up, too. She's a good farmer, they say."

"It's a lonely sort of spot."

Mrs. Wort sniffed, and said, "*She's* not lonely. Not if half the stories you hear are true. There was a major from Larkhill, made a perfect fool of himself over her. Married too. Now he's been sent abroad. So it's off with the old and on with the new."

"And who's the new?"

"I wouldn't know, and I wouldn't care. There's a lot of men to choose from round here. Soldiers and airmen, and all the scientists at Porton. They say the scientists are the worst of the lot. Would you be wanting anything more?"

"Not a thing," said Mr. Calder sleepily. "As soon as I can bring myself to stir from this beautiful fire, I'll be toddling up to bed."

When Mrs. Wort had departed on her nightly round of locking up, he sat for a long time, staring into the red heart of the fire and wondering why an attractive and capable woman should want to hide herself away in the wilds of Salisbury Plain.

"I'm sorry Albert couldn't be here this afternoon," said Marjorie Rivers. "They're keeping him very busy out at Porton just now. Some new gas. He doesn't talk to me about his work. Most of it's secret, anyway."

She was a thick, competent-looking, grey-haired woman and

reminded Mr. Behrens of the matron at his old preparatory school.

"I was telling Mr. Behrens," said Canon Trumpington, "what a formidable record you and your husband had established at the bridge table."

"Are you a player, Mr. Behrens?"

"I'm a rabbit. What I really enjoy about the game is the curious psychological kinks it throws up. I played with a man once who would do *anything* to avoid bidding spades."

"That must have been rather limiting. Did you find out why?"

"I discovered, in the end, that he stuttered very badly on the letter *s*."

Marjorie Rivers gave a sudden guffaw and said, "You're making the whole thing up. Another cup of tea, Mrs. Trumpington? Mind you, I agree with you about psychology. Albert's a scientist, you know."

"And a very distinguished one," said the canon politely.

"Oh, I wasn't talking about his work. I meant at the bridge table. He counts points, adds them up, calculates the probability factor, applies the appropriate formula, presses a button, and expects the answer to come out. And so it might, if the players were automata. But they aren't. They're human beings. Now I play by instinct, and I reckon I get better results."

"I entirely agree," said Mr. Behrens. "I'd back instinct every time."

"Are you in Salisbury for long?"

"The Trumpingtons are kindly putting up with me for a few days."

"We have a little bridge club. Mondays, Wednesdays and Fridays, at half-past two. Would you care to come along tomorrow?"

"It's quite safe," said Mrs. Trumpington. "Most of us are beginners. I shall be there."

"I can't manage tomorrow, I'm afraid. I have to run up to London. But I might come along on Friday."

"We'll look forward to it," said Marjorie Rivers with what seemed to Mr. Behrens to be rather a grim smile. Or maybe it was his imagination.

He carried the question up to London with him on the following day and propounded it to Mr. Fortescue, the Manager of the Westminster Branch of the London and Home Counties Bank.

Mr. Fortescue said, "She is certainly a remarkable woman. A top-class bridge player, with the sort of mind which that implies. A competent linguist in half a dozen languages, and the holder of very left-wing views which, to do her justice, she makes no attempt to conceal. But whether she, or her husband, or both of them are traitors is the precise matter which you and Calder have to decide."

"There *is* a leak, then?"

"That is one fact which had been established beyond any reasonable doubt. And it was confirmed by this outbreak at Al-Maza."

"I never really believed in that cholera. What was it?"

"It was the delayed effects of a prototype form of dianthromine."

"Remember, please," said Mr. Behrens, "that you're talking to someone whose scientific education never got beyond making a smell with sulphuretted hydrogen."

"Dianthromine is a non-lethal gas. It is light, and odourless, and it freezes the nerve centres of the brain, causing sudden and complete unconsciousness, which lasts from four to six hours, and then wears off without any side-effects."

"That sounds a fairly humane sort of weapon."

"Yes. Unfortunately the prototype had a delayed side-effect which did not become apparent for some days, when the subject went mad and, in most cases, died."

"How many people did we kill at Porton?"

"We killed a number of rats and guinea-pigs. Then the defect was traced and eliminated."

"I see," said Mr. Behrens. "Yes. How very fortunate. It was the experimental type that our traitor transmitted to Egypt?"

"It would appear so."

"The traitor being Albert Rivers?"

"That's an assumption. He was one of four men with the necessary technical knowledge. And his security clearance is low. So low that I think it was a mistake to let him work at Porton at all. He's a compulsive drinker, and is known to be having affairs with at least two women in the neighbourhood. He's also living well above his means."

"If it's him, how does he get the stuff out?"

"That is the interesting point. He would appear to have devised an entirely novel method."

Mr. Behrens said, "Do you think it could be his wife? She goes abroad a fair amount to bridge congresses and things like that."

"It was one of the possibilities, but the Al-Maza incident proved it wrong. Porton knew about the side-effects of dianthromine at the beginning of August. We must assume that Rivers would have transmitted a warning as quickly as he could. Yet the fatalities in Egypt did not occur until the third week in August. By the end of the month they, too, had corrected the defect."

"So we're looking for a message which takes two or three weeks to get through. It sounds like a letter to a safe intermediary."

"His post has been very carefully checked."

"Radio?"

"Too fast. He'd have got the news out before the trouble occurred."

"Some form of publication – in code. A weekly or fortnightly periodical?"

"I think that sounds more like it," said Mr. Fortescue. "You'll have to find out what the method is. And you'll have to stop it. There are some things going on at Porton now which we would certainly *not* want the Egyptians to know about. Or anyone else, for that matter."

"I'll have a word with Harry Sands-Douglas. He knows as much about codes as anyone in England. I can probably catch him at the Dilly Club."

The University, Legal and Professional Classes Club is never referred to by that full and cumbersome title. Its members long ago rechristened it the Dons-in-London, abbreviated to the DIL, or the Dilly Club. It occupies two old houses in St. John's Wood on the north side of Lord's Cricket Ground. It has the best cellar and the worst food in London, and a unique collection of classical pornography, bequeathed to it by the Warden of one of the better-known Oxford colleges.

Mr. Behrens found the club very useful, since he could be sure of meeting there former colleagues from that group of temporary Intelligence operatives who had come, in 1939, from the older universities and the Bar, created one of the most unorthodox and effective Intelligence organisations in the world, and had returned in 1945 to their former professions, to the unconcealed relief of their more hidebound professional colleagues.

"The idea which occurred to me," said Mr. Behrens, "was that you might conceal a code in a bridge column."

Harry Sands-Douglas, huge, pink-faced, with a mop of fluffy white hair, considered the suggestion. He said, "Whereabouts in the column? In the hands themselves?"

"That's what I thought. Every self-respecting bridge column contains two or three sample hands."

Old Mr. Happold said, "Most ingenious, Behrens. What put you on to it?"

"Rivers and his wife are both bridge fiends. It's become the rage of Salisbury. So much so that the local paper now runs a bridge column. A *weekly* bridge column, you'll note. If, as I rather suspect, one of the Rivers is contributing it –"

Sands-Douglas had been making some calculations on the back of the menu. He said, "It'd be a devilish difficult code to break."

"I thought nowadays you simply used a computer."

"You talk about using a computer as if it was a tin opener," said Sands-Douglas. "It hadn't occurred to you, I suppose, that you'd have to programme it first. The fifty-two cards in a pack can be arranged – in how many ways, Happold?"

"One hundred and sixty-five billion billion – that is, approximately. We shall have to do something about this claret, we ought to have tackled it earlier."

"It's the 1943. The only war-time vintage they produced in the Médoc."

"I expect the vignerons had other things to think about in 1943," agreed Mr. Happold. "It's our fault. We should have drunk it at least ten years ago. What were we talking about?"

"Bridge," said Mr. Behrens. "The possible permutations and combinations of a pack of cards."

"A large computer probably *could* deal with that number. But there's a snag. I don't suppose your chap is sending code messages every week?"

"Almost certainly not. Half a dozen times a year, probably. He'd key the column in some way – put an agreed word or expression into the first paragraph so that they'd know a code was coming."

"Exactly. So if we took, say, fifty-two examples, and fed them into a computer with instructions to detect any repeated correlations between the cards in the hand and known alphabetical and numerical frequencies in the English language, and the mathematics of physics – which is roughly how it would have to be done, if you follow me . . ."

"I didn't understand a word of it," said Mr. Behrens. "But go on." He was sipping the claret. It was quite true; gradually, imperceptibly, over the years it had built up to maturity, had climbed from maturity to super-maturity, and was now descending into gentle ineffectiveness. "Like us," thought Mr. Behrens sadly.

"If only ten per cent of your examples were true," said Sands-Douglas, "and the others weren't examples at all, but only blinds, even a giant computer would turn white hot and start screaming."

"Is that true?" said Mr. Happold. "I've often wondered. If you abuse a computer, *does* it really start screaming?"

"Certainly. It's only human!"

"I'm sorry I can't be more definite," said Mr. Calder to Colonel Crofter. "And I do appreciate the awkward position it puts *you* in – as head of the department and Albert Rivers' boss."

"And it's really only suspicion."

"Most security work starts like that. Something out of the ordinary –"

"Rivers isn't ordinary. I grant you that. Very few of our scientists are. They've most of them got their little peculiarities. I suppose it's the price you have to pay for exceptional minds. All the same, *if* it's true, it's got to be stopped. The stuff we're working on now is a damned sight more dangerous than One-to-Ten."

"One-to-Ten?"

"That's our laboratory name for dianthromine. It's not instantaneous. If I gave you a whiff of it, and counted slowly, you'd go out as I reached ten. That's one of its attractions. Imagine a Commando raid on enemy headquarters. One of our chaps lets off the stuff in the guard room. Until they start dropping, they'd have no idea anything was wrong. And when they did catch on, it'd be too late to do anything whatsoever about it."

"Commandos! It's light enough to be humped around easily, then?"

"Oh, certainly." Colonel Crofter unlocked a steel cabinet in the corner and pulled out something that looked like a small fire extinguisher. "A man could carry two or three of these in a pack. And it's very simple to operate. Just point it and pull the trigger. Only don't because it's loaded."

"Fascinating," said Mr. Calder. "Useful bit of kit for a burglar, too." He handed it back with some reluctance. Colonel Crofter locked it away and said, "Just what are you planning to do next?"

"We're looking for the outlet. The line of communication. For a start, we'll have to investigate both his girl friends."

"Both? I only knew about one."

"He's running two at the moment. One's called Doris. She's the wife of an Air Force WO at Boscombe Down. The other's Mrs. King-Bassett."

"Yes," said Colonel Crofter. "The merry widow. Quite a character."

"You know her?"

"I know of her," said the colonel, with some reserve.

"She seems to have had a succession of boy friends in the stations round here. A Major Dunstable at Larkhill, a Captain Strong from the Defensive Weapons Establishment at Netheravon, a light-haired subaltern from the 23rd Field Regiment whom I spoke to the other day – I rather think – I'm not sure about him yet, so I won't mention his name. And Albert Rivers."

Colonel Crofter said, "H'm – ha. Yes," turned on his stupid soldier look for a moment, thought better of it and became his normal shrewd self.

He said, "Have you met Rivers?"

"Not yet. Deliberately."

"When you're ready to meet him I can organise it. We have a guest night every Friday. Nothing chi-chi. We're a civilian establishment. But we observe the decencies – black tie. Why don't you come along?"

"When I'm ready," said Mr. Calder, slowly, "I'd like to do just that."

After lunch at Mrs. Wort's, Mr. Calder grabbed a stick and set out once again for Hurley Bottom Farm, Rasselas cantering ahead of him, tail cocked. The weather was clearer, ominously so, with the wind swinging round to the north and great cloud galleons scudding across the sky.

As he approached the farm Rasselas spotted a chicken and gave a short, derisive bark. The chicken squawked. A deeper, baying note answered.

"That sounds like the opposition," said Mr. Calder. They rounded the corner and saw the farm-house and outbuildings. A big, rather top-heavy Alsatian gave tongue from behind the farm-house gate. Rasselas trotted up to the gate and sat down with head on one side. The Alsatian jumped up at the top bar of the gate, scrabbled at it, failed to clear it, and fell back.

Rasselas said "Fatty", in dog language. The Alsatian's barking became hysterical.

Sheila King-Bassett added her voice to the tumult. "Call that bloody dog off, or there'll be trouble."

"Good evening," said Mr. Calder.

"I said, call that dog off."

"And I said, Good evening."

Mrs. King-Bassett looked baffled.

"Don't worry. They're only exchanging compliments. Yours is saying, 'Come through that gate and I'll eat you.' Mine's saying, 'Be your age, sonny. Don't start something you can't finish.' They won't fight."

"You seem damned certain about it."

"Open the gate and see."

"All right. But don't blame me if . . . Well, I'm damned. That's the first time I've ever seen *that* happen."

The two dogs had approached each other until their noses were almost touching. Rasselas had said something, very low down in his throat, and the Alsatian had turned away, sat down, and started to scratch himself.

"It's probably the first time his bluff's been called," said Mr. Calder.

Mrs. King-Bassett transferred her attention abruptly from the dogs to Mr. Calder and said, "Come inside. I want to talk to you."

She led the way into the front room of the farm and said, "What's your tipple? And, incidentally, just what is your game?"

"Whisky," said Mr. Calder, "and croquet."

Mrs. King-Bassett gave vent to a sort of unwilling half-guffaw, somewhere deep down in her throat. It was not at all unlike the noise Rasselas had made. She said, "I've seen you walking round a good deal with that dog of yours. And using a pair of field glasses. What are you? Some sort of security guard?"

"Sort of."

"And who are you watching?"

"This may be a bit embarrassing," said Mr. Calder slowly. He took a pull at the whisky. It was good whisky. "The man I'm chiefly interested in is, I think, by way of being a friend of yours. Albert Rivers."

Mrs. King-Bassett spat with force and accuracy into a vase of ferns in the fireplace. "That's what I think of Albert Rivers," she said. "And if he was here, I'd spit in his face."

"What –?"

"He's a slimy, two-timing, parsimonious pansy and no friend of mine. If he comes near here again, Prince has orders to take the seat out of his trousers. And he will."

"But –"

"Look. I don't mind him inviting himself round here every other day. I didn't mind him drinking all my whisky. I could even put up with him talking a lot of scientific mish-mash. God, how he talked! Talk and drink was all he ever did. All right. But when it comes to trying to run *me* in double harness with a bloody airman's wife . . ."

"Not very tactful."

"And *if* you're now telling me that he's a Russian spy and you're planning to run him in, all I can say is, bloody good show. In fact, come to think of it, I might be able to help you. Some of that stuff he told me about his work – nerve gases and all that caper. I can't remember all the details, but I'm pretty sure it was against the Official Secrets Act. What are those bloody dogs up to now? Fighting again?"

"I'm afraid they're *both* chasing your chickens."

Mrs. Trumpington put her head round the door after breakfast next morning and told Mr. Behrens that his bank manager wanted him on the telephone.

"I expect it's your overdraft," she said. "Mine's quite out of hand these days."

Mr. Fortescue said, "There's some news from Porton which I thought you ought to have. It came to me from the Defence Ministry this morning. They've had a burglary. Someone broke into Colonel Crofter's office last night and stole a fully charged cylinder of dianthromine."

"Why on earth would anyone do that?"

"I've no idea," said Mr. Fortescue. He sounded tetchy. "You and Calder are the men on the spot. You'd be more likely to know than I would. I think it's time you two got together over this. You've been operating at different ends long enough. Get together."

"I'll arrange a rendezvous," said Mr. Behrens. "Before I ring off, could you pass on a message to Harry Sands-Douglas? The Dilly Club will be able to find him. Tell him that I think I've located the key to the bridge articles. The hot ones have all got a reference to 'science' or 'scientists' in the third sentence."

"I suppose he'll understand what you're talking about?"

"He'll understand," said Mr. Behrens, and rang off.

After that he did some complicated telephoning, had lunch at the Haunch of Venison, and wandered slowly back along the

High Street, under the crenellated gate and into the close. Ahead of him loomed the bulk of the cathedral, like a grey whale asleep in the sun. A pair of falcons, male and female, were flirting in the air-currents round the top of the spire. Mr. Behrens entered the precincts and made his way to the seat by the west front. Mr. Calder was already there, Rasselas flat on the turf beside him.

Mr. Behrens said, "The old man wanted me to find out how things were going at your end. He's had no report from you for forty-eight hours."

"I've been busy. Clearing the ground. I don't think either of Rivers' girl friends are involved. I'm on rather good terms now with Mrs. King-Bassett."

"How did you fix that?"

"I sent her an anonymous letter, giving her the ripest details of Albert's liaisons with the airman's wife at Boscombe Down. Then I called on her, with Rasselas. We all got on together famously."

"I don't think," said Mr. Behrens, "that he's using either woman as a courier. In fact, I'm pretty certain that we know how he *is* doing it."

"Through the bridge columns?"

"Yes. I had a telephone message after lunch. There's a positive correlation. They should have the code finally broken by this evening. I gather the old man is already thinking about how to use it. He had the idea of sending them out something pretty horrific to try out next."

"*If* the messages are going out through this bridge column, does it mean that his wife's in it too?"

Mr. Behrens paused for quite a time before answering this. He seemed to be wholly engrossed in watching the falcons. The male had spiralled up to a height above the female and now plummeted down in mock attack. The female side-stepped at the last moment; the male put on the brakes and volplaned down almost to the transept roof.

"No," said Mr. Behrens at last. "It doesn't. For two reasons. First, because it's Albert Rivers who writes the bridge columns. His wife has no hand in them. I've found that out. By itself, it's not conclusive. But it was a remark by her, about Albert being a scientist, which put me on to the key to the cipher. If she'd been guilty she'd never have done that."

"It seems to me," said Mr. Calder, "that *if* we pull in Albert Rivers, simply on the basis of the code messages, we may be in for rather a sticky run. Fancy trying to persuade an average jury that something a computer has worked out on the basis of a few bridge hands constitutes treason."

Mr. Behrens said, "I once knew a Baconian. He was convinced that all Shakespeare's plays were full of code messages. He demonstrated to me, very cleverly, that if you applied his formula to Hamlet's soliloquy, 'To be or not to be', you could produce the sentence, 'F.B. made me for Q.E.'; which meant, needless to say, 'Francis Bacon wrote the play for Queen Elizabeth'."

"Of course."

"Sands-Douglas applied the same formula to a later speech and produced the message, 'Arsenal for ye cuppe.'"

Mr. Calder laughed. Then stopped laughing and said, "I've got a feeling we may have to consider an alternative solution."

"Was that why you broke into Colonel Crofter's office and stole the dianthromine?"

"How do you know I stole it?"

"It had to be either you or Rivers. You were the only two disreputable characters in the neighbourhood. He had no need to steal it. He could have got some legitimately. So it must have been you."

"What a horrible mind you have got," said Mr. Calder.

Albert Rivers leaned back in his chair in the mess ante-room, lit a cigarette which he extracted from a packet, and put the packet back in his pocket. As an after-thought, he took it out again and offered it to the two men sitting with him. Both shook their heads.

"You're a civilian yourself, Corker," he said.

"It's Calder, actually."

"Calder. I beg yours. I never remember a name for five minutes. Never forget a formula, but never remember a name."

"Perhaps that's because formulas are often more important."

Rivers squinted at Mr. Calder as though he suspected the remark of some deep double meaning, then laughed and said, "You're damned right they are. What was I saying?"

"You were pointing out that I was a civilian. I imagine that goes for the majority of the people here, too." As Mr. Calder said this he looked round the room. Most of the diners had disappeared to their own quarters, but there was a hard core left. Four were playing bridge with silent concentration. Two younger men were drinking beer. A man with a beard was finishing a crossword puzzle and a large port.

"That's just my point. Why do we have to confuse scientific research and the para-paraphernalia of military life? All that nonsense after dinner. Mr. Vice, the Queen, and sitting round for half an hour in our best bibs and tuckers, drinking port, when we'd all rather be down at the local or enjoying a bit of slap and tickle in the car park."

"Really, Rivers," said Colonel Crofter. "I don't think –"

"That's all right, Colonel. You can't shock old Corker. I've seen him sneaking off down to Hurley Bottom Farm. Lechery Lodge, we call it round here. What did you think of the merry widow, Corker?"

Mr. Calder appeared untroubled by this revelation. He said, "I had a very interesting talk with Mrs. King-Bassett."

"I bet. Did she tell you she thought I was a prize bastard?"

"Yes."

Albert Rivers burst into a hearty guffaw of laughter which drew glances of whole-hearted disapproval from the bridge players.

"That's what I like about you, Corker. You tell the truth. Waiter! What's your tipple?"

"Scotch and water."

"And you, Colonel?"

"Nothing more for me, thank you."

"Oh, come along, Colonel. It won't do you any harm. Bring us three large whiskies. In fact, it'll save a lot of time in the long run if you bring the bottle."

"The bottle, sir?"

"The bottle, Moxon. The whole bottle, and nothing but the bottle."

The waiter shot a sideways look at Colonel Crofter but, getting no help there, pottered off. Albert stretched himself even more comfortably in his chair and prepared to ride one of his favourite hobby-horses. "As I was saying, it always seems odd to me that we have to mix up militarism and science."

"This happens," said Colonel Crofter, "to be a military establishment."

"Sure, Colonel. But you don't parade your scientists in the morning." Rivers threw his head back and roared out, "Scientists form fours. By the right. Quick march."

One of the bridge players said angrily, "This is impossible. We'll have to move." They carried the table and chairs into the next room as Moxon arrived with the whisky.

The two beer drinkers had left and the port drinker had fallen asleep over his crossword. Mr. Calder knew very well that if he himself made the least move to depart Colonel Crofter would take himself off as well. As long as he stayed, the colonel, as his host, had to stay too. He watched Rivers pouring out the drinks. A double for each of them, and pretty nearly half a tumbler for himself. Mr. Calder reckoned that this one would do the trick.

"Let's face it, Colonel," said Rivers. "Cheers! Let's face it. You can't conduct scientific research by numbers. Science can't be drilled or court-martialled." He had added a little water and now knocked back nearly half the contents of the glass in three gulps. "Science is universal, and international."

"I hope you're bearing in mind," said Colonel Crofter, "that you've got to drive home tonight."

"I've got my car trained. It finds its own way home. What was I saying?"

Mr. Calder said, "You were telling us that science was international."

"I wonder why I said that?"

"At a guess, you were going to say that since science was international, it no longer observes national boundaries. That the days when nations conducted their own private, selfish scientific research were over, and that the results of one should be freely communicated to all."

The room was very quiet. Rivers seemed to be thinking. The cool and cautious part of his mind was fighting with the fumes of the whisky. Colonel Crofter sat watching him, his grey eyes weary.

Rivers said, "I don't think I like you."

"That makes it mutual."

"You're a crafty old bastard. You've been leading me on. I'm going home."

"It's time we all went home," said the colonel. They got up. Rivers seemed to be steady enough.

"You're not going to waste that lovely drink, surely," said Mr. Calder.

Rivers glared at him, picked up the glass, swallowed what was in it, and put it back where he thought the table was. It fell on the carpet, without breaking. While the colonel was picking it up, Mr. Calder moved to the door. He didn't appear to hurry, but he wasted no time.

He had something to do.

Rivers' car was parked in front of his. It was pitch dark and he had to work quickly, making no mistakes. First he took something out of his own car; back to Rivers' car; back to his own car; back to the front steps again.

He was standing there, buttoning up his overcoat, when Rivers and the colonel came out. The cold night air seemed to be having less than its normal effect. Rivers was his jaunty self again. He said, "Good night, Colonel. Up guards and at 'em, as Wellington didn't say at the battle of Waterloo. Good night, Corker, you crafty old bastard."

"He's not often as bad as this," said the colonel apologetically.

"Don't apologise, it was a most enlightening evening."

"Do you think I ought to have let him have that last drink?"

"He had so much alcohol in his blood-stream already that I don't suppose it made the slightest difference."

"He's got to get home." They heard the car start. "Luckily it's fairly straightforward." The car started to move. "And there isn't likely to be a lot of traffic about."

"One," said Mr. Calder softly, "two, three, four."

"I beg your pardon?"

"Five, six, seven."

"That corner's a nasty turn – ditch the other side."

"Eight, nine."

"Slow down, you bloody fool. He'll never –"

"Ten."

There was an appalling crash. The colonel and Mr. Calder started to run.

"At the adjourned inquest," said the news commentator, "on the well-known scientist and bridge player, Albert Rivers, Inspector Walsh said that, in view of the evidence that the car drove straight out into the main road without making any attempt to slow down or turn, he could only surmise that, at some stage, Rivers had completely lost consciousness. Enquiries are still proceeding. A further outbreak has been reported from the Egyptian Military Research Station at Al-Maza. Victims include the Director, Professor Fawazi. Amongst other alarming symptoms, he has lost all the hair on his body, and his skin has wrinkled and turned bright yellow –"

"For goodness sake," said Mrs. Trumpington, "turn that thing off."

4

The Peaceful People

"We call ourselves," said Lord Axminster, "the Peaceful People, and we are gathered here tonight to testify by our presence, our belief in the rightness, the cumulative force and the inevitable ultimate success of the cause we all have at heart, the cause of world peace. It *must* prevail.

"There will be setbacks. No cause worthy of the name has ever succeeded without encountering, and overcoming, the opposition of bigotry, self-interest and indifference. These are dragons to be slain and we will slay them, not grudging the mortification, and the wounds, the toil and the discomfort . . ."

The chair on which Mr. Behrens was seated had, he concluded, been designed by a sadist. Its seat was not only hard, but knobbly in all the wrong places. It was tilted at an angle which threw you forward, but so short that it gave no real support to the thighs.

". . . But I will detain you no longer with blasts from my feeble trumpet. The object of our gathering is an exchange of ideas. A cross-fertilisation of mind with mind. After we have heard the report of our International Secretary, Reverend Bligh, of the Unitarian Church of Minnesota, and have considered the financial statement produced by our hard-working treasurer, Mr. Ferris, we will be pleased to deal with the many questions which must, I feel sure, be agitating your minds."

Reverend Bligh plunged straight into business. "Support for our movement," he said, "continues to be global. In the period since we last met together, messages of encouragement, and donations, have been received from Algeria, Anatolia, the Andaman Islands, Bahrain, Bangkok, Barbados, Botswana . . ."

The raised edge of the seat dug into the femoral artery, cutting off the blood supply and causing agonising pins and needles.

". . . Venezuela, West Germany, Yucatan and Zanzibar. In the light of such universal support we should be wrong to consider ourselves as lonely fighters. We must feel ourselves to be, as it were, the advance guard of a great invisible army with banners, marching as to war." Feeling, perhaps, that this was an unhappy metaphor, he added, "A war for peace," and sat down; whereupon Mr. Ferris, armed with a bundle of documents, reeled off a quantity of figures.

The young man in horn-rimmed spectacles on Mr. Behrens' left woke up and started to make notes. Pins and needles was succeeded by complete paralysis of the lower leg.

Question time kicked off with an enquiry from a lady who had a nephew in Tanzania; touched on devaluation (dealt with by Mr. Ferris), the Church's role (a sitter for Reverend Bligh), and the iniquities of the Government (blocked by Lord Axminster, whose peerage was political). It did not take them long to reach Vietnam.

A tall man, with insecure false teeth, managed to ask, "Would the platform expound to us its proposals with regard to the unhappy conflict at present decimating the peaceful people of Vietnam?"

"Certainly," said Lord Axminster. "Our proposal is that the fighting should cease at once."

"On a more concrete plane," said the young man with horn-rimmed spectacles, "how is it proposed that this solution with which we all, of course, agree, should actually be attained?"

"It will be attained automatically, and immediately, when the United States withdraws its armed forces from the country."

When the applause had subsided, Mr. Behrens rose to his feet and said, "Would it be proposed that the South Vietnamese forces should also withdraw from the country?"

"Certainly not," said Lord Axminster. "The Vietnamese of the South would lay down their arms and embrace their brothers from the North in fraternal friendship."

Renewed applause.

When the meeting finished, Mr. Behrens got out as fast as the state of his legs would allow.

He had spotted a familiar-shaped head of grey hair in the front row. When its owner emerged into the foyer, Mr. Behrens had his back turned and was examining one of the campaign posters. He allowed the grey-headed, red-faced figure to get ahead of him, and followed. A taxi cruised past. The man ignored it, and strode on. Evidently he had a car parked somewhere. Mr. Behrens secured the taxi. He said to the driver, "If I was leaving here by car for the West End which way would I have to go?"

The driver meditated. He said, "You're bound to go over the railway bridge. Carnelpit. All one way, see."

"Excellent," said Mr. Behrens. "Get to the railway bridge and draw up."

"Want me to follow someone?"

"That's the idea."

"Police?"

"Special Constable."

"You look a bit old for a policeman."

"They're so short of men these days," said Mr. Behrens sadly. "They have to call up anyone they can get hold of."

It was an interesting chase. The grey-haired man was a bad-tempered driver, and took a lot of chances with traffic lights and other motorists, but the taxi-driver stuck to him with the ease of an expert angler playing a fresh fish. They finished up, fifty yards apart, outside a house in Eaton Terrace. Mr. Behrens noted the number, and signalled the taxi-driver to keep going. Once they were round the corner, he re-directed him to the Dons-in-London Club. He had a long report to write.

Two hundred miles to the north, in the industrial outskirts of a Midland town, a different sort of meeting was taking place. A couple of hundred men, mostly in overalls or old working clothes, were crowded into the small open space in front of the main gates of the Amalgamated Motor Traction Company's factory. Since it was the lunch hour, many of them were eating sandwiches out of small dispatch cases, but all were listening to the speaker.

"Punchy" Lewis had a jerky, but forceful delivery. He had learned the value of short simple sentences, and his timing was expert. Lord Axminster could have learned a lot from him.

"And who gains from this lovely arrangement? Who actually gains from it? I'll tell you one thing. *We* don't. And if *we* don't, who does? You don't need to be a genius at mathematics to work that out. Who gains?"

"*They* do," shouted the crowd.

Mr. Lewis smiled down on his listeners. "You heard what they call it! They call it a new deal. That's not what I call it. I call it a crook deal. A deal with a stacked pack. And shall I tell you who's champion at stacking cards?" Pause for effect. "The bloody Yanks!"

There was a roar from the crowd.

Mr. Calder, who was standing inconspicuously at the back, found it difficult to tell whether the applause was a tribute to the speaker's timing, or whether there was genuine warmth in it.

"That's what I said. The bloody Yanks." Lewis turned his head towards the building behind him, and shouted, "And I hope you heard *that* in the board room." Swinging round on the meeting, and lowering his voice to a conversational level, he added, "What we've had plenty of since these Yanks took over is trouble. A big hand-out of trouble. Now they want us to crawl in and lick their boots and say, Thank you for a lovely new deal. If you want to do that, I don't."

Mr. Calder became aware of movement behind him. The workers who wanted to get back because the lunch-break was over were forming up in some sort of order at the rear of the crowd, which blocked the way. Lewis saw them, too.

"I notice some of our mates," he said, "hanging round the back there, waiting to crawl in. That's why we're holding our meeting right here. Because if they want to crawl in, they'll have to crawl past us and we can see them do it."

There were police there too, Mr. Calder noticed, in plain clothes as well as in uniform. Leading them was a super-intendent, with the beefy red face and light blue eyes of a fighter. He pushed his way through the crowd and made for Lewis.

He said, "Stand back. Clear the way there. If these men want to get in, you've got no right to stop them."

Over the growing crowd noises, Lewis could be heard shouting, "We've got our rights under the law. We're picketing this gate. Peaceful picketing."

The superintendent said, "Take that man." And pandemonium broke loose.

Mr. Calder had every intention of keeping out of trouble. He started to back away. As he did so, someone tripped him from behind. He put his hands out to save himself, and received a violent blow in the middle of the back. Until that moment he had assumed that the hustling was accidental. Now he knew better. Instead of trying to turn, he let himself go, falling across the trampling legs like a scrum-half checking a forward rush. Two men tripped over him, and he pulled a third man's legs from under him, squirmed onto his hands and knees, and crawled to temporary safety behind this human barricade.

As he scrambled to his feet he could hear the police whistles shrilling for reinforcements. A crash proclaimed that the platform had gone down. Mr. Calder waited no longer. He scuttled off towards the side road, where he had left his car.

When he got there, he saw that there was going to be more trouble. A van had been parked across the nose of his car and two men were sitting in it, watching him.

He said, "Would you mind moving that van? I want to get out."

The men looked at each other, then climbed slowly out, one each side of the cab. They were big men. One of them said, "What's the hurry, mate? You running away or something?" The other laughed and said, "Looks as if someone's been roughing him up already."

"That's right. And if he doesn't mind his manners, he may be in for more."

Mr. Calder said, "I'm getting tired of this." He opened the door of his car. Rasselas came out and looked at the men, lifting his lip a little as he did so. Mr. Calder indicated the man on the right and the dog moved towards him, his yellow eyes alight. The man stepped back quickly. As he did so, Mr. Calder hit the second man.

It was not a friendly blow. It was a left-handed short-arm jab, aimed low enough to have got him disqualified in any ring. As the man started to double up, Mr. Calder slashed him across the neck with the full swing of his right arm, hand held rigid. The man went down and stayed down. Mr. Calder then transferred his attention to the other man, who was standing quite still, his back against the van, watching Rasselas.

"You can either move the van," said Mr. Calder, nursing his right hand, which had suffered in the impact, "or have your wind-pipe opened up."

"You would appear to have been in the wars," observed Mr. Fortescue. "That's a remarkably pairfect example of a black eye that you have. How did you acquire it?"

Mr. Calder said, "I was trodden on. By a plain-clothes policeman, actually."

"I trust you weren't attempting to assault him."

"I wasn't attempting to do anything, except keep out of trouble. I was tripped from behind, hit as I went down, and trampled on."

"Accidents will happen."

"There was nothing accidental about it. I was on the edge of the crowd, minding my own business. But someone had spotted me. There were two more of the heavy brigade waiting for me by my car. Luckily I had Rasselas with me, and that evened things up."

"I see. And what was your impression of the meeting?"

"Manufactured, for public consumption. A very skilled piece of stage management, by people who knew their job backwards. A couple of hundred genuine strikers, at least twenty professional agitators, and an equal number of reporters, who'd been tipped off beforehand that something was going to happen, and were ready with cameras and notebooks to record it for posterity."

"It may not prove," said Mr. Fortescue, "that having reporters there was really such a good idea. The police impounded all the photographs they'd taken. I have copies here. Is there anyone you recognise?"

Mr. Calder looked at them. Some of them seemed to have been taken from a window overlooking the scene, and showed the whole crowd. Others were close-ups, taken by photographers in the mêlée itself. There was a fine shot of the platform going down and Punchy Lewis jumping clear.

"Is that Superintendent Vellacott on the ground?"

"It is indeed. He was very roughly handled and is in the Infirmary now. He's still on the danger list."

Mr. Calder had carried one of the photographs over to the window to examine it. He said, "There are one or two faces here I seem to recognise."

"Indeed, yes. Govan, Patrick, Hall . . ."

"An all-star cast. What are they doing with them?"

"They're being held. The chief constable would like to charge them. He's very sore about his superintendent. I've tried to persuade him that it would be unwise. They'll make a public show out of the trial. If they're convicted, they're martyrs. If they're acquitted, they're heroes."

Mr. Calder was still intent on the photographs. "That's me," he said. "You can just see my foot sticking out." He picked up another one. "What beats me is, who puts the money up for a show like this. Twenty top-class agitators, at twenty-five pounds apiece. And they wouldn't get Punchy to come from South Wales for less than a hundred quid."

"Part, at least, of their funds come from a liberal and philanthropic body known as the Peaceful People. You may have seen their manifestos in the press."

"I have indeed. I thought they were a harmless and woolly-minded lot of intellectual pinks."

"Behrens has attended six of the public meetings in the last two months. He found them excessively boring."

"*My* meeting wasn't boring!"

"Last night he thought he recognised Sir James Docherty in the audience. He followed him home, to check up. It was him."

"Odd place to find our current Shadow Foreign Secretary."

"Sir James is an odd man," said Mr. Fortescue.

He said the same thing to the Home Secretary, that afternoon.

Mr. Fortescue had served six Home Secretaries, and the present incumbent was the one he admired most; a thick Yorkshireman, sagging a little now, but still showing the muscle and guts that had brought him up from a boyhood in the pits.

He said, "If things go wrong for us at the next election, Fortescue, he'll be one of *your* new bosses. I wish you luck with him. He was here this morning, complaining about some Customs officer who'd dared to open his bag when he was coming back from one of his trips to Paris. Asked me to discipline him. I refused, of course. Don't let's talk about Sir James. I want to hear about the riot."

"Calder was in the crowd. He confirms what we'd suspected. It was a put-up job. Aimed at the American management."

"Motive?"

"Anti-Americanism is the easiest platform for any rabblerouser today."

"The easiest, *and* the most dangerous," said the Home Secretary. "An open split between ourselves and the Americans would benefit the Russians enormously. And the Chinese still more. Who were behind this show? Do we know?"

"It was paid for, if not actually run, by the action committee of the Peaceful People. The main body is respectable, above board, and full of public figures. It holds meetings, writes to the papers, and collects funds, which it hands over to its action committee, without much idea, I would suspect, of how the funds are going to be used."

"The tail wagging the dog, eh? They'd want more than casual money to finance the sort of national pressure they keep up."

"Yes," said Mr. Fortescue. "I fancy they're getting regular subsidies."

"Where from?"

"I'd very much like to find out. But it's not going to be easy. Some organisations are easy to penetrate. But not this particular committee. It's too closely integrated. The members all know each other personally. They've worked together for years. If we tried to slip anyone in, it would simply be asking for trouble. The sort of trouble Calder ran into at the meeting."

He told the Home Secretary about it. The Yorkshireman said, "Aye, they're a rough crowd. What do you suggest?"

"We shall have to tackle it from the outside. Slower, but more certain. The first thing is to trace the money. It comes from somewhere abroad. Regularly, and in largish amounts. The Bank of England is confident that it's not done by credit transfer. This money actually comes in. It's brought in, physically. If we knew how, it'd be a start. Either the money would lead us to the man, or the man to the money. When we've got proof, we'll let the Peaceful People know exactly how they're being used. They won't like it. And they'll stop financing the committee. Without money they can't function."

The Home Secretary had listened to his exposition in silence; a silence which continued after Mr. Fortescue had finished. At last he said, "I don't have to tell you that things are moving very fast in international politics at the moment. Personally, I'm not unhopeful. The outcome might be very good. On the other hand, it might be very bad. And the smallest thing could tip the balance. So don't take too long."

The offices of William Watson (Paris) Limited, Importers and Exporters, are in a small street running south from the Quai des Augustins. The head of the firm is a Mr. Mackenzie, but should you ask to see him, you will invariably find that he is on sick leave. You will be invited to return in a week's time.

If you know the form you refuse to be put off, and enquire instead for his deputy, Mr. Rathbone. Mr. Behrens evidently knew the form. He was shown into an outer office and was passed, after scrutiny by a severe, grey-haired lady, into the inner sanctum where a surprisingly youthful Mr. Rathbone was trying his hand at a French crossword puzzle.

When the preliminaries had been concluded, he said, "Your last signal stirred things up a bit, I can tell you. Do you mind explaining what's happening?"

Mr. Behrens said, "It's a long story. Four men were pulled in after a strike meeting in the Midlands. A Welshman called Lewis, and three others. They had some trouble with them."

"Was that when the superintendent got kicked?"

"That's right. Well, they found money on all of them. New notes, in sequence. And it was hot money. Part of the proceeds of two bank jobs pulled by the Barron gang last year. But – and this was the odd part – we knew for certain, because we'd had a squeak, that the loot had left the country. It was taken across the Channel on the night of the robbery, and was out of the country before the thing broke. It was cached somewhere here, in Paris, until the heat cooled off. Then it was offered, discreetly, for sale. At a heavy discount, of course. Three months ago the Chinese bought the lot."

"So that's why you asked us to keep an eye on their Trade Commission."

"That's right. We thought it might give us a lead."

"Well, we've got something for you. Whether it's a lead or not, I don't know. You'll have to tell me."

Mr. Rathbone went across to a cabinet labelled "Export Samples", unlocked it, and extracted a folder.

"The only thing we've noticed which is in the least bit odd, is that one of their chauffeurs has been paying regular visits, after dark, to a small place called the Hôtel Continental. It's a moderate-sized dump in the Place Languedoc. Not too expensive, much used by business men from England, civil servants coming to conferences, Government delegates, and folk of that type. The sort of place where they serve bacon and eggs for breakfast without being asked."

"And what does the chauffeur do when he gets there?"

"He disappears into the kitchen. What happens after that, we haven't been able to find out."

"Possibly he has a girl friend among the kitchen staff."

"Maybe. When he's not being a chauffeur, he's a colonel in the Chinese Army, so I think it's unlikely."

"Even colonels have human feelings," said Mr. Behrens. "But I agree. There might be something in it. Could you get a list of all the guests – particularly English guests – who have stayed at the Continental during the past six months?"

Mr. Rathbone extracted a list from the folder and said, "Your wishes have been anticipated, sir. It goes back to January."

Mr. Behrens studied the list. Two names on it, which occurred no less than four times, appeared to interest him.

★

The prison interview room was quiet and rather cold. Punchy Lewis, in custody, looked a smaller, less magnetic figure than Punchy Lewis on a platform. His thin white face was set in obstinate lines. He said, "It's bloody nothing to do with you where I got the money from. It's not a crime in this country to own money, or have they passed some law?"

"If you don't realise the spot you're in," said Mr. Calder, "it's a waste of time talking to you." He got up and made for the door. A policeman was sitting outside it, his head just visible through the glass spy-hole.

"No-one's persuaded me I'm in a spot," said Lewis. "I didn't do anything. If the police charge in while I'm speaking, and get roughed up, they can't blame me. I didn't incite anyone. Every word I said's on record. I've got nothing to be afraid of."

Mr. Calder perched on the corner of the table, like a man who is in two minds whether to go or stay. He sat there for a long minute while Lewis shifted uneasily in his chair. Then he said, "I don't like you. I don't like the people you work for. And if I didn't want something out of you personally, I wouldn't lift a finger to help you. But that's the position. You've got one piece of information I want. It's the only thing you've got for sale. And I'll buy it."

"Talk straight."

"You think you're going to be charged with incitement or assault, or something like that. You're not. The charge is receiving stolen goods. And you'll get five or seven for it."

"The money, you mean? Talk sense, man. I didn't know it was stolen."

"That's not what the police are going to say. Do you know where that money came from? It was lifted from a bank by the Barron gang last year."

"And just how are they going to show I knew that?"

"Be your age. They've already got two witnesses lined up who saw Charlie Barron handing it to you in a Soho club."

"It's a lie."

"All right," said Mr. Calder calmly. "It's a lie. But it's what they're going to say all the same. They don't like having their chaps kicked on the head. They're funny that way."

"The bloody coppers," said Lewis. He thought for a moment and then added, "They'd do it, too."

Mr. Calder got up. He said, "I haven't got a lot of time to waste. Do we deal or not?"

"What's the proposition?"

"I want to know where that money came from. Who gave it to you. When and where and how. Details I can check up. You give me that, and the charge of receiving goods goes out of the window."

Sir James Docherty said to his wife, "I'm afraid I'm off on my travels. It's Paris again."

"Oh dear," said Lady Docherty. "So soon."

"Needs must, when public duty calls. Is there any more coffee in that pot?"

"I can squeeze another cup. Who is it this time?"

"I've got semi-official talks with de Bessières at the Quai d'Orsay. There are occasions . . ." Sir James dropped two lumps of sugar into his coffee ". . . when the French Government finds it easier to make unofficial suggestions to a member of the Opposition than to the Government. Then they can disclaim them if things don't work out."

"I'm sure they like talking to you because they know that you'll be Foreign Minister as soon as the electorate comes to its senses."

"Maybe," said Sir James. "I'll be taking Robin with me."

A faint shadow crossed Lady Docherty's face.

"Do you really think you ought to, James?" she said. "He's been away such a lot. Four times to France, and those trips to the Midlands . . ."

"My dear," said Sir James, "you're talking as though they were holiday jaunts. He's not wasting his time, you know. He's studying political economy. And what better way to study political economy than to see it in action? When he comes to France with me, he meets important people. People who matter. He can see the wheels of international politics turning. When he goes to the Midlands, it's with an object. To study these industrial strikes at first hand."

"Those terrible strikes. Why do they do it?"

"You mustn't assume," said Sir James, scooping the sugar out of the bottom of the cup with his spoon, "that the faults are all on one side. The managements can be quite as bloody-minded as the workers. More so, sometimes. Particularly the American ones."

In the next forty-eight hours, a lot of apparently disconnected activities took place. Mr. Calder spent the time working as a porter in Covent Garden, helping to load the lorries of an old friend of his in the fruit trade. His spare time was divided between betting shops and public houses, neither of which are in short supply in that neighbourhood. The money he made in the former he spent in the latter.

Mr. Behrens, who had reserved a room at the Hôtel Continental in the Place Languedoc, spent his time making friends with the hotel staff.

Young Robin Docherty had a prickly interview with his class tutor at the London School of Economics. The tutor said that if Robin spent all of his time running errands for his father in the Midlands and trotting across to Paris with him in the intervals, he was most unlikely to complete the scholastic side of his studies satisfactorily.

The Home Secretary answered two questions and three supplementaries about the strikes and disturbances which were paralysing the motor industry. And Mr. Fortescue attended to the customers at the Westminster Branch of the London and Home Counties Bank, granting one overdraft and refusing two.

To him, on the third day, came Mr. Calder.

Mr. Calder said, "What Lewis told us has been checked. I don't know how the money gets into this country from France, but as soon as it does get here it's taken to a betting-shop in Covent Garden. The action committee meets in the back room of a pub, just down the road. It's on their instructions that the cash payments are handed out from the bookmakers. That's as far as I've been able to get. I can't get any closer to these people. Some of them know me."

Mr. Fortescue considered the matter, rotating a silver pencil slowly in his hand as he did so. Then he said, "If you've evidence that stolen money is passing through this betting-shop, there should be no difficulty about getting permission to listen in to their telephone."

"You ought to get some useful tips from the course," said Mr. Calder.

Mr. Fortescue did not smile. His eyes were on his pencil. "Some sort of arrangements must be made for the reception of the money."

"That probably takes place after the shop's shut. There's a back entrance."

"No doubt. What I mean is, they must know when to expect the money, and who's going to bring it. If we could find that out, we could put our finger on the courier. Then we might be able to track back, from him, to the person who brings it across the Channel. We shall have to do it very carefully."

"You will indeed," said Mr. Calder. "These boys have got eyes in the backs of their heads."

It was exactly a week later when Mr. Fortescue called, by arrangement, on the Home Secretary and made his report.

He said, "When you gave us permission to listen in to that betting-shop, we started to make some real progress. It was the calls after hours that interested us. They were very guarded and they came through different intermediaries, but we were able to trace them back to their ultimate source."

"To the carrier of the money?"

"To his house."

"Excellent. Who is the man?"

"The owner of the house," said Mr. Fortescue, with a completely impassive face, "is Sir James Docherty."

For a moment this failed to register. Then the Home Secretary swung round, his face going red. "If that's a joke . . ." he said.

"It's not a joke. It's a fact. The point of origin of these messages is Sir James' house in Eaton Terrace. Sir James also happens to be a member – a founder member – of the Peaceful People. Taken alone, I agree, neither of these facts is conclusive."

"Taken together, they're still inconclusive. You told me that the Peaceful People were backing their action committee with money. The messages might have been about that."

"They might have been," said Mr. Fortescue, "but they weren't. They had nothing to do with the official business of the society at all. And here are two other facts. One of my men has been making enquiries in Paris. He has established that there is a regular courier service between the Chinese Trade Commission and the Hôtel Continental. *Which happens to be Sir James' regular pied-à-terre in Paris.* Add to that the fact that Sir James' visits are usually arranged at official level. And that this enables him to bring in his valise, which is said to carry official papers, under the diplomatic exemption arrangements."

The Home Secretary said, "Do you really believe, Fortescue, that a man in Sir James' position would lend himself to smuggling currency – a criminal manoeuvre?"

"Whether I believed it," said Mr. Fortescue cautiously, "would depend, in the last analysis, on my estimate of Sir James' character."

The Home Secretary turned this reply over in his mind for a few moments. Then he grunted and said, "He's a loud-mouthed brute, I agree. And I loathe his politics. But that doesn't make him a crook."

"I am told that he is something of a domestic tyrant. I would not assert that he beats his wife, but she certainly goes in considerable awe of him. His only son, Robin, has been forced to study political economy, and is dragged round at his father's chariot wheels, no doubt destined to be turned into a junior model in due course."

"And that's our next Foreign Secretary. A Palmerstonian Fascist, with a taste for gun-boat diplomacy. What do you want to do? Tap *his* outgoing calls?"

"Yes. And have his mail opened. And have him watched, day and night, in England and in France. If he's our man he'll slip up sooner or later, and we've got to be there to catch him when he falls."

"*If* he's our man," said the Home Secretary. "And if he isn't, by any chance, and if he finds out what we're doing – there'll be an explosion which will rock Whitehall from end to end."

"So I should imagine."

"The first head that will roll will be mine. But make no mistake about it, Fortescue. The second will be yours."

The young Customs officer at Heathrow Airport produced a printed form and said, "You know the regulations, sir?"

"Since I have travelled backwards and forwards to Paris some twelve times this year," said Sir James Docherty, "I think you may assume I have a nodding acquaintance with the regulations. Yes."

"And have you made any purchases while you were abroad?"

"None whatever."

"Or acquired any currency?"

Sir James looked up sharply and said, "I don't *acquire* currency when I travel. I spend it."

"I see, sir. Then would you mind opening this valise?"

"I would mind very much."

"I'm afraid you must, sir."

"Perhaps you would be good enough to examine the seal on the lock. I take it you are capable of recognising an embassy seal?"

"Yes, sir."

"And perhaps you would also read this note from our ambassador, requesting you to confer the customary exemption from search on this bag, which, I might add, contains important diplomatic documents."

The Customs officer glanced at the letter and handed it to the thick-set man in a raincoat who was standing beside the counter. This man said, "I'm afraid, sir, that I have an order here, signed by the Home Secretary, over-riding the ambassador's request."

"And who the hell are you?"

"My name's Calder."

"Then let me tell you, Mr. Calder . . ."

"I think we ought to finish this in private."

Sir James started to say that he was damned if he would, realised that he was shouting and that people were starting to look at him, and resumed his public relations manner.

"If you wish to continue this farce," he said in a choked voice, "by all means let us do it in private."

"But it wasn't a farce," said Mr. Calder. "There was £2,000 in fivers, stowed away flat at the bottom of his valise."

"What explanation did he give?"

"He was past rational explanation. He screamed a bit, and stamped and foamed at the mouth. Literally. I thought he might be having some form of fit."

"But no explanation?"

"I gathered, in the end, that he said someone must have been tampering with his baggage. Frame-up. Police state. Gestapo. That sort of line."

"I see," said Mr. Fortescue. He said it so flatly that it made Mr. Calder look up.

"Is something wrong, sir?"

"I gather," said Mr. Fortescue, "that Sir James managed to persuade our masters that we have made a very grave mistake."

"But, good God! I *saw* the notes. We all did. How does he suggest they got there?"

"He suggests," said Mr. Fortescue sadly, "that Behrens put them there. I am seeing the Home Secretary in an hour's time. I rather fear that we may be in for trouble."

"Incredible though it may seem," said the Home Secretary, "it really does appear that the one person who can't have put the money there was Sir James himself – unless he bribed half the ambassador's private staff."

"What exactly happened?"

"Our ambassador had a highly confidential document – a memorandum in the General's own hand – and Sir James offered to act as courier. The Head of Chancery put the document in Sir James' valise – which was almost empty, as it happens – saw it sealed, and handed it to the ambassador's secretary, who took it back to the hotel and himself saw it locked up in Sir James' bedroom. The secretary didn't leave the hotel. He stayed there, lunched with young Robin, and the two of them escorted the valise to the airport."

"And what was Sir James doing all this time?"

"Sir James was having lunch with our ambassador, the French Minister of the Interior, and the French Minister of the Interior's wife."

"How exactly is it suggested that the notes got into the valise?"

"There's no mystery about that. Microscopic examination of the seal – what was left of it – shows that it had been removed, whole, with a hot knife and refixed with adhesive. Probably during the lunch-hour."

"And it's suggested that Behrens did that?"

"He was at the hotel."

"So were two hundred other people."

"You don't think, Fortescue, that he might – just conceivably . . . thinking he was being helpful?"

Mr. Fortescue said, "I have known Behrens for thirty years, Home Secretary. The suggestion is ludicrous." After a pause he added, "What is Sir James going to do?"

"He's been to the PM. He wants the people responsible discovered, and dealt with."

Mr. Fortescue smiled a wintry smile. He said, "I do not often find myself in agreement with Sir James, but that sentiment is one with which I heartily concur. I shall need to make an immediate telephone call to Paris."

"I'm afraid you won't catch Behrens. He's on his way back at this moment."

"Excellent," said Mr. Fortescue. He seemed to have recovered his good humour. "Excellent. We may need him. The person I wished to speak to was the ambassador's private secretary. Perhaps your office could arrange it for me? Oh, and the manager of the Hôtel Continental. Then we must have Behrens intercepted at the airport and brought straight round to Sir James' house, to meet me there."

"You're going to see Sir James?"

"I have really no alternative," said Mr. Fortescue genially. "In his present mood he would certainly not come to see us, would he?"

*

Sir James was at ease, in front of his drawing room fire, the bottom button of his waistcoat undone, a glass of port in one hand, an admiring audience of two, consisting of wife and son, hanging on every word.

"And it might have come off," he said, "if I hadn't been wide awake and, I admit it, had a bit of luck. I could have been in a very awkward spot."

"And now it's them who are on the spot," said Robin with a grin.

"In the old days," said Lady Docherty, "they'd have had their heads cut off."

"Even if they don't lose their heads, I think we can ensure that the people concerned lose their jobs. I'm seeing the PM again tomorrow. I wonder who *that* can be?"

"I'll go," said Robin. "The girl's out. What if it's the press?"

"Invite them in. The wider the publicity this deplorable matter receives the better for . . ." he was going to say "my chances at the next election," but changed it to ". . . the country."

Robin came back, followed by two men. "I don't think it *is* the press," he said. "It's a Mr. Fortescue and a Mr. Behrens."

"I see," said Sir James coldly. "Well, I've nothing much to say to you that can't be said, in due course, in front of a tribunal of enquiry, but if you've come to apologise, I'm quite willing to listen. No, stay where you are, my dear. And you, Robin. The more witnesses we have, the better."

"I agree," said Mr. Behrens.

"Kind of you."

"It would be appropriate if your son were to remain, since most of what I have to say concerns him." Mr. Fortescue swung round on the boy, ignoring Sir James. "I've just spoken to the ambassador's private secretary in Paris. He tells me that you were away from the luncheon table for nearly half an hour. Making a long-distance call, you said. Why did you lie?"

"Don't answer him," said Sir James. But the boy also appeared to have forgotten about his father. He said, in his pleasant, level voice, "What makes you think it was a lie, sir?"

"I know it was a lie, because I've talked to the hotel manager, too. He tells me that no long-distance call, in or out, was recorded during that period. On the other hand, Behrens here saw you leave the dining room. He followed you up to the bedroom, saw you go in and heard you lock the door."

"And who do you suppose," fumed Sir James, "is going to believe your tame *agent provocateur?*"

"Well, Robin," said Mr. Fortescue, "if you weren't telephoning, what were you doing?"

Sir James jumped up and forced himself between them. "I'll deal with this," he said. "If you think you can shift the blame on to my son, on manufactured evidence . . ."

"Don't you think he might be allowed to speak for himself?"

"No. I don't."

"He'll have to, sooner or later."

"Unless you can produce something better than the word of your own spy, he's not going to have to answer anything at all."

"Oh, there's plenty of evidence," said Mr. Fortescue mildly. "Robin's been a member of the action committee of your society for two years — that's right, isn't it, Robin? I would surmise that during all that time he's been using your diplomatically protected luggage to bring back funds for the committee."

"Lies," said Sir James in a strangled voice.

"He has also taken a personal part in a number of demonstrations. He was up in the Midlands last week . . ."

"Collecting information for me."

"No doubt. He also put in some time kicking a police superintendent. Have you the photographs, Behrens? The *Mail* shows it best, I think."

Sir James glared at the photograph. "A fake!"

Robin said, "Oh, stop fluffing, Dad, of course it isn't faked. How could it be?"

There was a moment of complete silence, broken by Lady Docherty who said, "Robin" faintly.

"Keep out of this, Mother."

Sir James had recovered his voice. He said, "Your mother has every right . . ."

"Neither of you," said Robin, silencing his parents with surprising ease, "have any rights in the matter at all. I'm twenty-one. And I know what I'm doing. You talk about violence and ruthlessness, Dad. But that's all you ever do. You and your Peaceful People. Talk. I don't believe . . ." a faint smile illuminated his young face, ". . . that you've ever actually hit anyone in your life. Really hit them, meaning to hurt. Have you?"

But Sir James was past speech. "Well I have, and I'm going to go on doing it, because if you truly believe in something, that's the only way you're going to make it happen – in your own life-time anyway. By breaking the law and hurting people, and smashing things. The Negroes in America have seen it. And young people all over the world. They're just beginning to see it. Don't talk. Kick out."

Mr. Fortescue said, "I take it that includes kicking people when they're on the ground."

"Of course," said Robin. "It's much easier to kick them when they're lying down than when they're standing up. Why not?"

"I left that to Sir James to answer," said Mr. Fortescue, some time later, to the Home Secretary. "He's a politician and used to answering awkward questions."

5

The Lion and the Virgin

Mr. Calder first met Colonel Garnet in 1942 in the Western Desert.

The colonel, who had commanded an Armoured Regiment with such dash that it had lost most of its tanks, was doing a stand-in job as GSO2 at Corps. He had acquired the reputation of turning up more often at the dangerous end than was usual with staff officers. Nevertheless it did surprise Mr. Calder to see him at that particular time and place; seeing that the Infantry Regiment to which he was attached was about to do one of the things which infantry regiments dislike greatly. It was due, in five minutes' time, to advance over a stretch of open desert which was certainly registered by enemy mortars and was probably full of anti-personnel mines.

Colonel Garnet had engaged Captain Calder in a learned discussion on modern theories of artillery support, whilst Captain Calder kept an anxious eye on his watch. When the whistle blew, and he climbed cautiously out of the line of slit trenches, he was staggered to observe that the colonel was climbing out with him. It appeared that there were some additional observations on artillery support which he had not had time to finish, and that he saw no reason that these contributions to military thought should be lost. "Just exactly," as Mr. Calder said afterwards to his CO, "as though we were out for an afternoon stroll. And the odd thing is that the mortars didn't open up, and if there were any mines we, at least, didn't tread on them. In fact, we had remarkably few casualties. When we reached our objective, he said, 'Well I must get back, I suppose. Can't stand about all day gossiping.'" "He's quite mad," said the CO. "That's why he's collected two DSOs already."

Later on, Colonel Garnet went to Burma and finished up with a Brigade and a second bar to his DSO. His rise after that was steady, if not spectacular, and it was generally felt that he had reached his limit as GOC Southern Command, when he was unexpectedly appointed Vice-Chief of the Defence Staff. This was not, normally, a very exacting job, but became so when his Chief, Air Marshal Elvington, had to retire to a nursing home with a heart condition, brought on, it was rumoured in Whitehall, by his attempts to cope with a government which thought that free wigs and dentures were more important than fighter aircraft.

The career of Arnold Litman had been a good deal less exciting. A member of the merchant banking family, with offshoots on both sides of the Atlantic, he had entered politics in the late forties, had captured a marginal seat in the 1951 election, and had risen in his party's counsels by a mixture of financial shrewdness and political tact. Why he should have been made Under-Secretary of State for War was far from clear. But once installed in office he had delighted his master by abolishing several ancient and expensive regiments.

His only known indiscretion had been his marriage to Rebecca, a dreamy girl, with a weakness for picking up fads and a habit of discussing them with the press. In a private citizen this would not have mattered. In the wife of a public man it could, and did.

Sue Garnet read the article, first to herself, and then to her father, over the breakfast table. It was headed, "The Lion and the Virgin" and started: "In a special interview given to *Daily News* man Frank Carvel yesterday, Mrs. Litman, wife of recently appointed Under-Secretary for War, Arnold Litman, gave it as her view that all great wars were likely to break out between late July and early September. She pointed out that it was at this period that the two most exciting signs in the Zodiac come into conjunction. Leo and Virgo, the Lion and the Virgin. It could hardly be a coincidence, she said, that every major war in history had started at this time. The Under-Secretary refused to comment on this remarkable prediction."

"Bloody fool," said General Garnet.

"Which?"

"Both of them."

"What could he have done except refuse to comment?"

"Not asked the brute into the house."

"I expect his wife did the asking."

"I don't doubt it. She's a stupid bitch."

"Daddy!"

"He's not stupid, though. I'm beginning to think he's a crook."

Sue Garnet was hardened to her father's methods of discourse and argument. These, as she had warned Terence Russel when he became her father's military secretary and her fiancé, resembled a machine gun firing on fixed lines interspersed with casual grenade-throwing. But even she was taken aback by this last comment.

She said, "You can't really mean that."

"Can't I," said the General, decapitating his second breakfast egg with the same zeal and expertise that he had once decapitated a Japanese officer with his own Samurai sword. "What about that fight we had last month with the Americans over the ground-to-air ballistic missile? Our prototype was years ahead of theirs and a bloody sight cheaper. So why did we have to give them the contract?"

"Well, why did we?"

"If you want my guess it's because Litman, or his associates, have got a big holding in the American company."

"If you can prove it," said Sue, "you ought to do something about it. If you can't you ought to be jolly careful about saying it. After all, he's your boss."

"My boss," said the General, "is the Queen, and not a jumped-up jack-in-office who'll probably be Deputy Postmaster General next time they re-shuffle the Cabinet. Dammit, where's Terence. I want to see those papers before the meeting."

"He's *your* secretary. You ought to know where he is."

"He's your fiancé. You ought to keep him up to the mark, the idle young beggar. What are you laughing at?"

"I saw his last confidential report. You said that he was a keen and promising young officer."

"Are you aware, Miss," said the General, filling his mouth with toast, "that you can be prosecuted under the Official Secrets Act for disclosing the contents of a confidential document?"

"And did you know," said Sue unrepentantly, "that you can be cashiered for leaving them lying about? You never lock anything up. Anyone could read them. Our char might be an agent of an enemy Secret Service."

The idea so tickled the General that he roared with laughter whilst trying to swallow the last piece of toast. In the middle of this complicated situation, the telephone rang.

The General listened, spluttered, listened some more, and then said, "All right. I'll be there." And to Captain Terence Russel, who had hurried in carrying a briefcase, "The meeting's postponed."

"I heard," said Russel. He was a large blond young man, who wore his service dress with the swagger expected of a cavalry officer. "The emergency meeting's at the Foreign Office. You're to go in quietly by the Charles Street entrance, not the Downing Street one. I've laid on a car."

Mr. McAlister, the head cashier at the Westminster Branch of the London and Home Counties Bank, greeted Mr. Calder and Mr. Behrens as old friends and explained that the Manager, Mr. Fortescue, was engaged, but would be free soon.

"What's happened to the stockmarket, Mac?" said Mr. Behrens.

"We've all been asking ourselves the same thing. Fifteen points down yesterday and twenty-five over the weekend. We haven't seen anything like it since August 1939. Ah, there's his light. He's disposed of his visitor. Go straight in."

Mr. Calder had sometimes wondered how Mr. Fortescue disposed of visitors whose identities he wished to conceal. One never saw them come out. He concluded that there was either a hidden door in the chocolate-coloured pottery panelling behind his desk, or an oubliette in the floor.

"I've not much time," he said to them. "I have to be at the Foreign Office at eleven. If you have been reading your papers you must have seen what is happening."

"You could hardly miss it, could you?" said Calder. "What are we supposed to do about it? Soothe the shattered nerves of Lombard Street."

"The reactions of the City," said Mr. Fortescue coldly, "are not a cause of alarm. They are a symptom of it. The real reason for their uneasiness is that Interstock has started selling heavily."

"Interstock?"

"I'm not at all surprised that you haven't heard of them, Calder. They take pains to avoid the limelight. They're a group of people, based in Switzerland, who handle much of the floating money of the world. Their funds come mainly from Kuwait, Abu Dhabi, the Argentine, Greece and South Africa. They are very large sums of money indeed, and Interstock's job is to keep them in an optimum state of investment. This means reasonably high interest rates. But above all – absolute safety."

"And they're selling us short, are they?"

"They're not selling us short. They're selling us out."

"Where's the money going?"

"Most of it to Canada."

"What on earth's got into them?"

"That is exactly what we have to find out. The most probable explanation is that someone has deliberately started a scare. There could be financial as well as political reasons for it. There's a lot of money to be made on a falling market, if you happen to know when it's going to stop falling."

Mr. Behrens said, "I have a war-time acquaintanceship with Grover Lambert. I understand he's the London representative of Interstock. But it's a fairly casual connection. Even if I could get in to see him, I can't think I'd get much of an answer if I just said, 'Why are you selling us out?'"

"I've often found a direct question gets a direct answer."

"Only if backed by force. In some countries, no doubt, the authorities would string him up by his thumbs and prod him with a white-hot knitting needle until he volunteered the desired information. But we can't do that here."

"No," said Mr. Fortescue. "No." His listeners thought they detected a note of disappointment in his voice.

★

Arnold Litman said to his wife, "I don't think you quite realise what you've done. I had to make a personal explanation to the Cabinet this morning. It was accepted. As far as they're concerned, this particular episode is over. But people aren't going to forget about it. In politics, it's fatally easy to pick up labels. Look at Winston and Tonypandy. In a few months' time no one's going to remember precisely what happened. But I shall be permanently labelled as an alarmist."

Rebecca Litman said, "I'm terribly sorry, my darling. But was I really to blame?"

"What do you mean?"

"When I told that young man that I thought war was coming, was it *me* talking? I did wonder."

"For God's sake –"

"Do you think someone was using me as a mouth-piece? Speaking through me. These things do happen."

"And who do you think was speaking through you?"

"It's a wild idea. But it did occur to me that it might have been you. After all, if war was coming, you'd know about it, wouldn't you?"

Litman had stopped pretending to smile, and his blue-grey eyes were as cold as the snow-fed lakes of his fatherland. He said, "I suppose you haven't by any chance passed on *that* interesting idea to the papers, too?"

"Oh, Arnold. As if I would."

Litman said, "No. I don't think even you would be stupid enough to do a thing like that."

Terence Russel and Sue Garnet were sitting on a bench in St. James's Park, watching the ducks. They were discussing the crisis, too.

"Daddy's been very funny lately," said Sue. "You know he promised me a month in Florence. The thing was practically fixed. Now he's back-pedalling. It's almost as though he doesn't want me out of his sight. In case anything starts."

"Nothing's going to start," said Terence flatly.

"Well, that's a comfort," said Sue. "If anyone knows, you ought to."

"I'm only a junior captain."

"Said he modestly. You also happen to be a military secretary to someone who is notoriously the least security minded officer in the three services. Daddy doesn't just leave confidential papers in taxis. He discusses their contents with the taxi-driver."

Terence grinned, and said, "If you're not going to go to Florence, why don't we get married?"

"Right away?"

"As soon as possible."

"Have we got enough money?"

"I've a feeling we shall manage all right."

"Well," said Sue, "it would be rather nice."

Mr. Calder had not found General Garnet as hard to approach or as difficult to talk to as he had anticipated. The General had not pretended to remember him, but had greeted him as a former comrade in arms. He had also, clearly, seen his DMI file and was quite willing to talk.

"What we really want to know, sir," said Mr. Calder, remembering Mr. Fortescue's dictum about direct questions, "is whether there really is a chance of someone pressing the button, or whether the whole thing's a manufactured scare."

The General paused before answering. Then he said, "When I was a young soldier I was told that an ounce of demonstration was worth a pound of explanation. I was just about to make a visit of a routine nature. If you will come with me, I will try to convince you that, although a nuclear war could start at any moment it is extremely unlikely that it will do so."

The staff car took them westward towards Holborn, and stopped in a quiet side street. The General unlocked a metal grille which led into a small concrete yard. On the other side of the yard was an insignificant looking concrete building, the size of a large tool-shed. Using a second key, the General unlocked the door of this, and Calder saw that it housed a lift. They stepped inside. The General pressed a button, and the lift started slowly to descend.

"How far does this go down?" said Mr. Calder.

"A hundred and fifty feet. The people who built them had to

get through the London clay and into the rock."

"There's more than one, then?"

"There are six in the London area and eight in the home counties. Here we are. Good morning, Sergeant-Major! This is Mr. Calder. You have his clearance?"

"Just came through by telephone, sir. Shall I open up?"

"Please."

The sergeant-major evidently released some switch under his hand, and a steel partition behind him slid up. He then rose to his feet, saluted the General punctiliously, and ushered him and Mr. Calder in, remaining outside.

Mr. Calder's first reaction was disappointment. He saw that the General was smiling.

"Well," he said, "what did you expect?"

"I don't really know," said Mr. Calder. "Masses of complicated machinery. Shining steel. Winking lights."

"You've been reading too much science fiction. This is a communication centre. The machinery it controls is all over the place. The Norfolk coast, Dartmoor, the lochs of Scotland. This place is in contact with them all. Triple cable, buried in concrete. That set of telephones links with the Defence Ministry and the PM. The other lines are to service headquarters. And to Strike Force."

"And the system is in operation?"

"Naturally. The exchanges at the other end are permanently manned."

"And either of us could give the order for a nuclear attack right now?"

"I could. You couldn't," said General Garnet with a grin which emphasised rather than softened the fact that he was talking about the possible destruction of millions of human beings. "There's a code-word which has to precede the order. It's changed every day. There are ten people at any one time who know it."

"Nine too many," said Mr. Calder.

"Perhaps. It's a question of immediacy. Suppose the enemy started a conventional air raid. Enough to block roads and cause confusion. If only two or three men knew the word for launching

Counterstrike, they might none of them, temporarily, be in a position to do it. And ten minutes could make all the difference."

Mr. Calder thought that it was one of the most disturbing conversations he had ever had. He was not a man who suffered much from nerves, but the smallness of the room, the enormous physical presence of the General and the hundred and fifty feet of earth on top of him were bringing on the symptoms of claustrophobia.

He said, "You talk about the enemy, General. Had you anyone in mind?"

"Naturally. I mean the Chinese."

This forthright statement took Mr. Calder aback even further.

"Do you think they would?"

"I put the point to Litman at the meeting this morning. Do you know what he said? He said, 'Their civilisation is two thousand years older than ours. Why would they want to destroy the world?' The only answer I could think of was a rude word of one syllable beginning with 'b'." The General rocked with sudden laughter at the recollection, then said, more seriously, "Of course they'd do it. The moment they were convinced it would pay them. They're logical. A damn sight more logical than we are in the West. They know that the only thing which counts in world politics is results. Legality and illegality don't come into it. That's a conception confined to a country with laws. It cuts no ice in the international sphere, because in that sphere, there are no laws. If the Chinese could blast the rest of us off the face of the earth *and get away with it*, they'd do it tomorrow. The rate they're growing they'd repopulate the world quick enough on their own."

"But they can't get away with it?"

"Not as long as Counterstrike is manned here and in the States. Our detection apparatus are far more sophisticated than theirs. We could wipe them out, every mother's son of the thousand million of them. If not by direct blast, inevitably by nuclear fall-out."

"Do you know," said Mr. Calder, "this seems to me to be about the most dangerous thing I've ever heard of. Ten men know the code-word. If one of them was a traitor, or even a fool, he could start a nuclear holocaust."

"He'd have to get down here first."

"If I had the keys, I could do it easily enough. I'd simply step out of the lift and shoot the sergeant-major."

"That wouldn't get you very far. Did you notice that he didn't get up when I came in?"

"Yes. It seemed rather curious."

"He was making quite sure of our identity. He'd been given instructions from the Ministry of Defence to let the two of us in. If anyone turned up without that instruction – even me – he wouldn't let them past. And he was sitting with his hand on a spring loaded lever. If he let it go, the door into here would have been permanently locked. And I mean permanently. It would need a breakdown squad to get it open."

"I see," said Mr. Calder, thoughtfully.

"The situation is becoming ludicrous," said Mr. Fortescue. "None of our normal Intelligence agencies know anything. The international situation generally has never been quieter."

Mr. Calder said, "Things seem to be hotting up in China."

"Internally, yes."

"I see the legation has been attacked again. They caught the First Secretary in the street and beat him up."

"I'm very sorry for the First Secretary. But it doesn't alter the situation. Someone, for some inexplicable reason, has made up their mind that we are going to be subjected to a nuclear attack. And – possibly by accident, but more likely deliberately – they've allowed the news to leak out. With the result that the pound is under severe pressure, the bottom has fallen out of the stock market, and now the allies are beginning to get worried. The American ambassador saw the PM yesterday."

"And everyone," said Mr. Calder, "is damn certain who's responsible. If it wasn't for the law of libel the papers would print what's being said in every club in London. That Litman started the rumour – helped by that pea-brained wife of his – so that his friends in the City and in Wall Street could make a killing on a bear market. *And it's got out of hand.*"

"You realise that we've no option. We've got to do something about it," said the General.

"I'm not sure what you mean," said Litman.

"You've read Foster's report, I take it."

"Yes. I don't necessarily agree with it."

"Foster says that the attacks on British lives and property have now reached a point where it goes far beyond casual hooliganism."

"As I said, I've read the report."

"He thinks it's an organised campaign, designed to provoke retaliation, which could, in turn, be used by the Chinese as an excuse for hostile action."

"I'm afraid I don't agree with him."

"For God's sake," said the General savagely. "What do you know about the Chinese?"

"At first hand, nothing."

"Well I do. I've fought with them, as nominal allies, in Burma. They're treacherous bastards. Do you realise that they – or some friend of theirs," as the General said this he put both hands on the desk and his knuckles showed white, "have fixed things so that an actual *date* for their attack is now on everyone's lips? July 17th."

Litman said, "*If* this is a deliberate plot, which I don't believe, why on earth would they warn us of when to expect the blow?"

"The oldest trick in war. Get your opponents' eyes fixed on one particular date. Then hit him the day before. A nuclear attack on this country will start on July 16th. I am completely certain of it."

When the General had gone, Arnold Litman's hand went out to the green telephone on his desk, which carried the direct line to Downing Street. He hesitated for a long time before he picked it up.

"Our instructions," said Mr. Fortescue to Mr. Behrens, "have been changed. They are now categorical, and quite clear. We are to find out *by any means we choose to employ*, from what source Interstock first received information that a nuclear attack was possible." He paused, and repeated, "By any means."

"A few days ago," said Mr. Behrens, "I contrived to run into Grover Lambert. Our acquaintanceship dates from 1940, when we worked together at Blenheim. I suggested that we might have dinner one night at the Dilly. I told him he would meet some of his old friends. Sands-Douglas and Happold particularly. He jumped at the idea."

"Then I suggest," said Mr. Fortescue, "that the reunion takes place as soon as possible. Today is July 10th. We haven't a lot of time."

As old Mr. Happold explained to Grover Lambert over the port in the small private dining room, the Dilly club was a very useful *pied-à-terre* for impoverished senior members of Oxbridge and the Bar. Having been handsomely endowed by that eccentric millionaire, Professor Goodpastor, it could afford to limit both its charges and its membership.

"It is open to all senior members of Oxbridge, I suppose," said Grover Lambert.

"In theory," said Mr. Behrens, "it's open to anybody. There's only one limitation. *All* the existing members have to approve a new nomination."

"That must make it rather a close circle."

"It's very cosy," agreed Commander Sands-Douglas. He was large, red-faced, and had a mop of snowy-white hair, in curious contrast to Mr. Happold who looked like a very old snapping turtle. "The hard-core are people who worked together in Intelligence during the war. Most of them came from the Universities and the Bar. Incidentally, it makes you eligible – if you could stand the food."

"It was fairly plain," agreed Grover Lambert politely. "But more than compensated for by the wine. I think that Corton was the finest I've ever drunk. By the way, didn't I recognise your wine waiter?"

"Applin. Sergeant Applin when you were at Blenheim."

"Circulate the port, Behrens," said Mr. Happold. "It's taken root in front of you."

As Grover Lambert took up the decanter his hand slipped and he put it down, spilling a few drops.

"I'm sorry," he said. "Stupid of me. It must be the heat."

"It is warm," agreed Mr. Behrens, studying his guest's face, which was red and sweating. "Would you like to sit outside for a moment?"

Sands-Douglas said, "Let me give a hand," and both men helped Grover Lambert carefully to his feet, supporting his weight between them. That weight became heavier as his knees buckled and his eyes turned glassy.

"Put him on the sofa," said Behrens.

"I thought for one terrible moment," said Mr. Happold, "that he was going to upset the port. How long have we got?"

"The stuff would normally knock him out for fifteen minutes. Then he'd start to come round with nothing worse than a shocking hangover."

"Better lock the door," said Sands-Douglas. "Applin wouldn't let anyone in, but you can't be too careful. What next?"

"What I'm going to do," said Mr. Behrens "– prop his head up, would you, Happold – is to put a regulated dose of scopalaminedextrin into him. It should wake him up enough to make him talkative, but not enough to remember things afterwards."

"Inject him, you mean."

"Good heavens, no," said Mr. Behrens. "What's he going to think if he wakes up with his arm full of holes? It might get the club a bad name. No, the modern method is to inhale it." He was breaking a capsule under Grover Lambert's nose as he spoke. "It's quicker, and more effective that way."

The unconscious man's eyelids fluttered. Mr. Behrens perched on the couch beside said in a loud voice, "Wake up, Lambert. You are Lambert. Grover Lambert."

"I am Grover Lambert," said the man sleepily.

"You work for Interstock."

"I work for Interstock."

"Your directors have told you to sell your British holdings."

"Sell British holdings."

"Why? Why are you to sell British holdings?"

"War. Because of war."

"Who told you war was coming?"

"Who told me war was coming."

"Who told you?" said Mr. Behrens, very sharply.

The young man behind the counter in the travel agency looked superciliously at Mr. Calder, and said, "I'm afraid we aren't allowed to give information about other customers."

Mr. Calder leaned forward across the counter, and spoke without heat. He said, "You have a telephone. That is the private number of Scotland Yard. You can ring it, if you wish, and ask for Extension 05. That is Commander Elfe, head of the Special Branch. He will confirm my authority."

"Well –" said the young man, uncertainly.

"But if you hold me up for more than five minutes, I will have this branch closed for a week whilst we investigate your reasons for obstructing the police."

"I'm sure I didn't mean to be obstructive."

"Then answer my question."

The young man turned to a filing cabinet behind him. His hand was shaking slightly as he pulled out a folder and opened it. He was not the first man to find Mr. Calder unnerving. He said, "General Garnet booked the tickets through this agency two days ago."

"For his daughter?"

"Yes. Air travel. London to Montreal. Montreal to Ottawa. Rail to Pettawawa. That's quite a small place, outside Ottawa. I believe it used to be an army camp."

"Singles," said Mr. Behrens. "Not returns."

"That's right. We thought it a bit odd."

"It would have been odder still if he had booked her a return ticket," said Mr. Calder and left the shop without further comment.

Mr. Fortescue looked at the calendar on his desk. It was held by a large white china cat, with a blue ribbon round its neck, and it showed July 16th. He glanced at his watch, picked up one of the telephones on his desk and dialled a number. The voice at the other end said, "CMP Duty Officer."

"Please fetch Colonel Jackson."

It took a few minutes to find Colonel Jackson.

Mr. Fortescue said, "Colonel Jackson? Fortescue here. Send an officer and a sergeant – the officer must be of the rank of captain or above to detain Captain Terence Russel. He's military secretary to General Garnet. You'll find him in his room at the Defence Ministry. The charge will be under the Official Secrets Act. I'll have the details in your office by the time you bring him back."

"Good afternoon, Sergeant-Major," said the General. "You look worried. Nothing amiss with your family, I hope?"

"No sir. Not that I know of."

"I'm glad to hear it. Now, if you wouldn't mind –?"

The sergeant-major looked even more worried, but remained seated his right hand out of sight down by his side. He said, "You know the drill, sir. I'm not allowed to let anyone in, even yourself, sir, until I've had a telephone call from headquarters."

"Quite right. But this is a surprise visit. To keep you on your toes."

"I see, sir."

"Then unless you think I'm an enemy agent in disguise, perhaps you'll be good enough to open the door."

"I can't do it, sir."

"Are you questioning my order?"

"Not without authority."

The General smiled, a ferocious grin which lifted his upper lip and showed a fine pair of incisor teeth. He said, "You have a telephone by your left hand, Sergeant-Major. Perhaps you'd care to ring my assistant, Captain Russel. You have his number. Well, what is it?"

"It's the lift, sir. It's just gone up. I expect this will be your authorisation."

The General said thoughtfully, "Ah. Yes. I expect it is. That will save us all a lot of trouble, won't it?"

After that they waited, in silence, for what seemed to both of them to be an uncomfortably long time before the lift reappeared and Mr. Calder stepped out of it. He said to the General, "I'm sorry I'm late. My car got held up in the traffic." And to the sergeant-major, "There seems to have been some break in the line between the Ministry and this post. They thought the General might have some trouble in getting in, and sent me after him with a written authority."

The sergeant-major read the document carefully right through, and then said slowly, "I see, sir. Yes. That clears everything up. I'll unlock the door."

"After you, General," said Mr. Calder.

The door closed behind them as silently as it had opened. The General sat down on the edge of the table, with his back to the door, swung one leg a couple of times as though to shake the stiffness out of it, and said, "Now, perhaps, Captain Calder, you will be good enough to tell me the truth. Since no one knew I was coming here, how could they have sent you after me, with a written authority?"

Mr. Calder was standing, his feet apart, his arms hanging down at his sides. It was an attitude of apparent, but deceptive relaxation.

He said, "I took the liberty of following you, General. As soon as we found out you were planning to send your daughter away to Canada. Even before that, some of the things you've been doing and saying have been worrying your superiors."

"My superiors are a lot of weak-kneed old women who'd be scared if you came up behind them and said 'boo'."

"They haven't got a row of medals for gallantry, I agree."

"I'm not talking about gallantry. I'm talking about guts. A few years ago, we wouldn't have allowed a crowd of half-educated Chinese reds to jump us. But then, at that time the war machine was being run by Churchill. Not by a long-haired Lithuanian pimp."

"What do you think Churchill would have done?"

"What I'm going to do. Hit them first, and hit them for keeps. And no one is stopping me. I take it you can see this."

Mr. Calder said, sadly, "Yes, General, I can see it. A .415 automatic. In my opinion, the best weapon the British army ever produced."

"You're on top-secret Defence Ministry premises. You got in

here by telling lies. I should be entirely justified in shooting you. And I will if I have to. You understand?"

"Perfectly, General."

"Then proceed. You say I've been worrying my superiors. How?"

"It wasn't only you. Your military secretary, Captain Russel, has been under arrest since midday. He has already admitted that some weeks ago, he communicated to an acquaintance in the City, a Mr. Grover Lambert of Interstock, the view that this country would be at war with Communist China before the end of July."

"Nonsense."

"It's been confirmed by Mr. Lambert. He – er – happened to let it out after a very good dinner at my club."

"Why would anyone listen to what a captain said?"

"In the ordinary way, of course, they wouldn't. But Captain Russel was able to quote certain facts and figures in a private memorandum you had written for the Cabinet. Written, but not, I think, yet delivered. You really should have been more careful with such a potentially inflammatory document."

"Continue," said the General. He was smiling in a way which Mr. Calder found disturbing.

"What happened then, might have been funny if it hadn't been so bloody dangerous. In the eighteenth century, I understand, this country went to war because a Captain Jenkins had his ear cut off. We very nearly went to war because Captain Russel wanted to get married. He was innocent enough to think that his communication to Lambert would cause a sharp, but temporary fall in the market. His naïve scheme was to buy at the low point and then revive the market by telling Lambert that it was all nonsense, when he could sell at a handsome profit. I think he rather fancied himself as a financier. In fact, he was a babe-in-arms playing with high explosive. He had started a chain reaction, which he had no hope of stopping.

"What happened then, is that the Chinese took fright. They don't understand a free press. When a senior war minister's wife foretold war in July, and the big boys started selling their British holdings, they reckoned they could read the signs. They got frightened, and they got angry. They still didn't really believe we would attack them, but if we did, they are going to be ready to hit back."

"I've always been told that you chaps had vivid imaginations," said the General. "You've made up a very good story. It might even convince a weak-kneed pacifist like Litman. But it doesn't convince me. You're completely wrong. This whole business started in China. It was worked out by them, from beginning to end, like a game of chess. Move and countermove. I'm not a chess-player. That's why I'm going to kick the board over, before we get to check-mate. Do you think you can stop me?"

Mr. Calder was trying to do three things at once. He was keeping the whole of his apparent attention on the General, whilst watching the door which had started to open very slowly, and trying to work out certain angles and possibilities.

The General had picked up the telephone. Still keeping Mr. Calder carefully covered, he lifted the receiver, and spoke into it. "Counterstrike Headquarters. General Garnet speaking, Codeword 'Cromwell'. Action immediate. Full scale. I'll give you the count-down. Ten-Nine-Eight –"

The door was open now and the sergeant-major was inside the room. He knew exactly what to do, because Mr. Calder had written it all down on the paper he had given him and he had now had time to counter-check it by telephone.

"Seven-Six-Five-Four –"

Mr. Calder noticed that sensibly, he had taken his shoes off, and was moving in stockinged feet. The overhead strip-lighting would throw no shadow.

"Three-Two-One."

The sergeant-major whipped one arm round the General's throat from behind. As his gun went up, Mr. Calder went forward in a dive for his knees.

They could neither of them have done it by themselves, but together they managed it. When they had lashed his hands and feet, the General spat in Mr. Calder's face, and said genially, "It must be a comfort to you to know that you're too late. Nothing can stop it now."

★

"Do you think," said Mr. Fortescue, "that he realised that the telephone had been disconnected?"

"I don't think so," said Mr. Calder. "But it's always difficult to know what a madman does grasp and what he doesn't."

"When did you realise he was mad?"

"In 1942," said Mr. Calder. "But I didn't realise how far it had gone. However, I'm very glad he didn't shoot me at that particular moment."

"Why at that moment?"

"I had an urgent telephone call to make to my stockbroker. You remember what you told us. There's a good deal of money to be made on a falling market if you happen to be the only person who knows that it's going to stop falling."

6

The African Tree Beavers

Like many practical and unimaginative men Mr. Calder believed in certain private superstitions. He would never take a train which left at one minute to the hour, distrusted the number twenty-nine, and refused to open any parcel or letter on which the stamp had been fixed upside down. This, incidentally, saved his life when he refused to open an innocent-looking parcel bearing the imprint of a book-seller from whom he had made many purchases in the past but which proved, on this occasion, to contain three ounces of tri-toluene and a contact fuse. Mr. Behrens sneered at the superstition, but agreed that his friend was lucky.

Mr. Calder also believed in coincidences. To be more precise, he believed in a specific law of coincidence. If you heard a new name, or a hitherto unknown fact, twice within twelve hours you would hear it again before a further twelve hours was up. Not all the schoolmasterly logic of Mr. Behrens would shake him in this belief. If challenged to produce an example he will cite the case of the Reverend Francis Osbaldestone. The first time he heard the name was at eleven o'clock at night, at the Old Comrades Reunion of the Infantry Regiment with which he had fought for a memorable eight months in the Western Desert in 1942. He attended these reunions once every three years. His real interest was not in reminiscence of the war, but in observation of what had taken place since. It delighted him to see that a motor transport corporal, whom he remembered slouching round in a pair of oily denims, should have become a prosperous garage proprietor and that the orderly room clerk, who had sold places on the leave roster, had developed his talents, first as a bookmaker's runner and now as a bookmaker; and that the God-like company sergeant-major should have risen no higher than commissionaire in a block of flats at Putney, who would be forced, if he met him in ordinary life, to call his former clerk "sir".

Several very old friends were there. Freddie Faulkner, who had stayed on in the Army and had risen to command the battalion, surged through the crowd and pressed a large whisky into his hand. Mr. Calder accepted it gratefully. One of the penalties of growing old, he had found, was a weak bladder for beer. Colonel Faulkner shouted, above the roar of conversation, "When are you going to keep your promise?"

"What promise?" said Mr. Calder. "How many whiskies *is* this? Three or four?"

"I thought I'd get you a fairly large one. It's difficult to get near the bar. Have you forgotten? You promised to come and look me up."

"I hadn't forgotten. It's difficult to get away."

"Nonsense. You're a bachelor. You can up-sticks whenever you like."

"It's difficult to leave Rasselas behind."

"That dog of yours? For God's sake. Where do you think I live? In Hampstead Garden Suburb? Bring him with you. He'll have the time of his life. He can chase anything that moves, except my pheasants."

"He's a very well-behaved dog," said Mr. Calder, "and does exactly what I tell him. If you really want me –"

"Certainly I do. Moreover I can introduce Rasselas to another animal-lover. Our rector. Francis Osbaldestone. A remarkable chap. Now get your diary out, and fix a date –"

It was at ten o'clock on the following morning when the name cropped up next. Mr. Calder was stretched in one chair in front of the fire, his eyes shut, nursing the lingering remains of a not disagreeable hangover. Mr. Behrens was in the other chair, reading the Sunday newspapers. Rasselas occupied most of the space between them.

Mr. Behrens said, "Have you read this? It's very interesting. There's a clergyman who performs miracles."

"The biggest miracle any clergyman can perform nowadays,"

said Mr. Calder sleepily, "is to get people to come to church."

"Oh, they come to *his* church, all right. Full house, every Sunday. Standing room only."

"How does he do it?"

"Personal attraction. He's equally successful with animals. However savage or shy they are, he can make them come to him, and behave themselves."

"He ought to try it on a bull."

"He has. Listen to this. *On one occasion a bull got loose and threatened some children who were picnicking in a field. The rector, who happened to be passing, quelled the bull with a few well-chosen words. The children were soon taking rides on the bull's back.*"

"Animal magnetism."

"I suppose if you'd met St. Francis of Assisi you'd have sniffed and said 'animal magnetism'."

"He was a saint."

"How do you know this man isn't?"

"He may be. But it would need more than a few tricks with animals to convince me."

"Then what about miracles? *On another occasion the rector was woken on a night of storm by an alarm of fire. The verger ran down to the rectory to tell the rector that a barn had been struck by lightning. The telephone line to the nearest village with a fire brigade was down. The rector said, 'Not a moment to lose. The bells must be rung.' As he spoke the bells started to ring themselves.*"

Mr. Calder snorted.

"It's gospel truth. Mr. Penny, the verger, vouches for it. He says that by the time he got back to his cottage, where the only key of the bell chamber is kept, and got across with it to the church, the bells had *stopped* ringing. He went up into the belfry. There was no one there. The ropes were on their hooks. Everything was in perfect order. At that moment the brigade arrived. They had heard the bells, and were in time to save the barn."

Mr. Calder said, "It sounds like a tall story to me. What do you think, Rasselas?" The dog showed his long white teeth in a smile. "He agrees with me. What is the name of this paragon?"

"He is the Reverend Francis Osbaldestone."

"Rector of Hedgeborn, in the heart of rural Norfolk."

"Do you know him?"

"I heard his name for the first time at about ten o'clock last night."

"In that case," said Mr. Behrens, "according to the fantastic rules propounded and believed in by you, you will hear it again before ten o'clock this evening."

It was at this precise moment that the telephone rang.

Since Mr. Calder's telephone number was not only ex-directory but was changed every six months, his incoming calls were likely to be matters of business. He was not surprised, therefore, to recognise the voice of Mr. Fortescue, Manager of the Westminster Branch of the London and Home Counties Bank, and other things besides.

Mr. Fortescue said, "I'd like to see you and Behrens, as soon as possible. Shall we say, tomorrow afternoon?"

"Certainly," said Mr. Calder. "Can you give me any idea what it's about?"

"You'll find it all in your *Observer*. An article is about a clergyman who performs miracles. Francis Osbaldestone."

"Ah!" said Mr. Calder.

"You sound pleased about something," said Mr. Fortescue suspiciously.

Mr. Calder said, "You've just proved a theory."

"I understand," said Mr. Fortescue, "that you knew Colonel Faulkner quite well, in the Army."

"He was my company commander," said Mr. Calder.

"Would you say he was an imaginative man?"

"I should think he's got about as much imagination as a No. 11 bus."

"Or a man who would be easily deluded?"

"I'd hate to try."

Mr. Fortescue pursed his lips primly, and said, "That was my impression, too. Do you know Hedgeborn?"

"Not the village. But I know that part of Norfolk. It's fairly primitive. The Army had a battle school near there during the war. They were a bit slow about handing it back, too."

"I seem to remember," said Mr. Behrens, "that there was a

row about it. Questions in Parliament. Did they give it back in the end?"

"Most of it. They kept Snelsham Manor, with its park. After all the trouble at Porton Experimental Station they moved the gas section down to Cornwall, and transferred the Bacterial Warfare Establishment to Snelsham, which is less than two miles from Hedgeborn."

"I can understand," said Mr. Calder, "that Security would keep a careful eye on an establishment like Snelsham. But why should they be alarmed by a saintly vicar two miles down the valley?"

"You are not aware of what happened last week?"

"Ought we to be?"

"It has been kept out of the press. It's bound to leak out sooner or later. Your saintly vicar led what I can only describe as a village task force. It was composed of the members of the Parochial Church Council, and a couple of dozen of the villagers and farmers. They broke into Snelsham Manor."

"But, good God," said Calder, "the security arrangements must have been pretty ropy."

"The security was adequate. A double wire fence, patrolling guards and dogs. The village blacksmith cut the fence in two places. A farm tractor dragged it clear. They had no trouble with guards, who were armed with truncheons. The farmers had shotguns."

"And the dogs?"

"They made such a fuss of the vicar that he was, I understand, in some danger of being licked to death."

"What did they do when they got in?" said Behrens.

"They broke into the experimental wing, and liberated twenty rabbits, a dozen guinea-pigs and nearly fifty rats."

Mr. Behrens started to laugh, and managed to turn it into a cough when he observed Mr. Fortescue's eyes on him.

"I hope you don't think it was funny, Behrens. A number of the rats had been infected with Asiatic plague. They *hope* that they recaptured or destroyed the whole of that batch."

"Has no action been taken against the vicar?"

"Naturally. The police were informed. An inspector and a

sergeant drove over from Thetford to see the vicar. They were refused access."

"Refused?"

"They were told," said Mr. Fortescue gently, "that if they attempted to lay hands on the vicar they would be resisted – by force."

"But surely –" said Mr. Behrens. And stopped.

"Yes," said Mr. Fortescue. "Do think before you say anything. Try to visualise the unparalleled propaganda value to our friends in the various CND and peace groups if an armed force had to be despatched to seize a village clergyman."

Mr. Behrens said, "I'm visualising it. Do you think one of the more enterprising bodies – the International Brotherhood Group occurs to me as a possibility – might have planted someone in Hedgeborn. Someone who is using the rector's exceptional influence –"

"It's a possibility. You must remember that the Bacterial Warfare Wing has only been there for two years. If anyone *has* been planted, it has been done comparatively recently."

"How long has the rector been there?" said Mr. Calder.

"For eighteen months."

"I see."

"The situation is full of possibilities, I agree. I suggest you tackle it from both ends. I should suppose, Behrens, that there are few people who know more about the IBG and its ramifications than you do. Can you find out whether they have been active in this area recently?"

"I'll do my best."

"We can none of us do more than our best," agreed Mr. Fortescue. "And you, Calder, must go down to Hedgeborn immediately. I imagine that Colonel Faulkner would invite you?"

"I have a standing invitation," said Mr. Calder. "For the shooting."

Hedgeborn has changed in the last four hundred years, but not very much. The church was built in the reign of Charles the Martyr and the Manor in the reign of Anne the Good. There is a village smithy, where a farmer can still get his horses shoed. He can also buy diesel oil for his tractor. The cottages have thatched roofs, and television aerials.

Mr. Calder leaned out of his bedroom window at the Manor and surveyed the village, asleep under a full moon. He could see the church, at the far end of the village street, perched on a slight rise, its bell-tower outlined against the sky. There was a huddle of cottages round it. The one with a light in it would belong to Mr. Penny, the verger, who had come running down the street to tell the rector that Farmer Alsop's farm was on fire. If he leaned out of the window Mr. Calder could just see the roof of the rectory, at the far end of the street, masked by trees. Could there be any truth in the story of the bells? It had seemed fantastic in London. It seemed less so in this forgotten backwater.

A soft knock at the door heralded the arrival of Stokes, once the colonel's batman, now his factotum.

"I was to ask if you'd care for anything before you turned in, sir. Some biscuits, or a nightcap?"

"Certainly not," said Mr. Calder. "Not after that lovely dinner. Did you cook it yourself?"

Stokes looked gratified. "It wasn't what you might call hote kweezeen."

"It was excellent. Tell me, don't you find things a bit quiet down here?"

"No, sir. I'm used to it. I was born here."

"I didn't realise that," said Mr. Calder.

"I saw you looking at the smithy this afternoon. Enoch Clavering's my first cousin. Come to that, we're mostly first or second cousins. Alsops and Stokes and Vowles and Claverings."

"It would have been Enoch who cut down the fence at Snelsham Manor?"

"That's right, sir." Stokes' voice was respectful, but there was a hint of wariness in it. "How did you know about that, if you don't mind me asking? It hasn't been in the papers."

"The colonel told me."

"Oh, of course. All the same, I do wonder how *he* knew about Enoch cutting down the fence. He wasn't with us."

"With *you*," said Mr. Calder. "Do I gather, Stokes, that you took part in this – this enterprise?"

"Well, naturally, sir. Seeing I'm a member of the Parochial Church Council. Would there be anything more?"

"Nothing more," said Mr. Calder. "Good night."

He lay awake for a long time, listening to the owls talking to each other in the elms.

"It's true," said Colonel Faulkner next morning. "We are a bit inbred. All Norfolk men are odd. It makes us just a bit odder, that's all."

"Tell me about your rector."

"He was some sort of missionary, I believe. In darkest Africa. Got malaria very badly, and was invalided out."

"From darkest Africa to darkest Norfolk. What do you make of him?"

The colonel was lighting his after-breakfast pipe, and took time to think about that. He said, "I just don't know, Calder. Might be a saint. Might be a scoundrel. He's got a touch with animals. No denying that."

"What about the miracles?"

"No doubt they've been exaggerated in the telling. But – well – that business of the bells. I can give chapter and verse for that. There only *is* one key to the bell chamber. I remember what a fuss there was when it was mislaid last year. And no one could have got it from Penny's cottage, opened the tower up, rung the bells *and* put the key back without someone seeing him. Stark impossibility."

"How many bells rang?"

"The tenor and the treble. That's the way we always ring them for an alarm. One of the farmers across the valley heard them, got out of bed, spotted the fire, and rang through for the brigade."

"Two bells," said Mr. Calder thoughtfully. "So one man *could* have rung them."

"If he could have got in."

"Quite so." Mr. Calder was looking at a list. "There are three people I should like to meet. A man called Smedley."

"The rector's warden. I'm people's warden. He's my opposite number. Don't like him much."

"Miss Martin, your organist. I believe she has a cottage near the church. And Mr. Smallpiece, your village postmaster."

"Why those three?"

"Because," said Mr. Calder, "apart from the rector himself, they are the only people who have come to live in this village during the past two years – so Stokes tells me."

"He ought to know," said the colonel. "He's related to half the village."

Mr. Smedley lived in a small dark cottage. It was tucked away behind the Viscount Townshend public house, which had a signboard outside it with a picture of the Second Viscount looking remarkably like the turnip which had become associated with his name.

Mr. Smedley was old and thin, and inclined to be cautious. He thawed very slightly when he discovered that his visitor was the son of Canon Calder of Salisbury.

"A world authority on monumental brasses," he said. "You must be proud of him."

"I'd no idea."

"Yes, indeed. I have a copy somewhere of a paper he wrote on the brasses at Verden, in Hanover. A most scholarly work. We have some fine brasses in the church here, too. Not as old or as notable as Stoke d'Abernon, but very fine."

"It's an interesting village altogether. You've been getting into the papers."

"I'd no idea that our brasses were *that* famous."

"Not your brasses. Your rector. He's been written up as a miracle worker."

"I'm not surprised."

"Oh, why?"

Mr. Smedley blinked maliciously, and said, "I'm not surprised at the ability of the press to cheapen anything it touches."

"But *are* they miracles?"

"You'll have to define your terms. If you accept the Shavian definition of a miracle as an act which creates faith, then certainly, yes. They are miracles."

It occurred to Mr. Calder that Mr. Smedley was enjoying this conversation more than he was. He said, "You know quite well what I mean. Is there a rational explanation for them?"

"Again, it depends what you mean by rational."

"I mean," said Mr. Calder bluntly, "are they miracles, or conjuring tricks?"

Mr. Smedley considered the matter, his head on one side. Then he said, "Isn't that a question which you should put to the rector? After all, if they *are* conjuring tricks, he must be the conjurer."

"I was planning to do just that," said Mr. Calder, and prepared to take his leave. When he was at the door, his host checked him by laying a clawlike hand on his arm. He said, "Might I offer a word of advice? This is not an ordinary village. I suppose the word which would come most readily to mind is – primitive. I don't mean anything sinister. But being isolated, it has grown up rather more slowly than the outside world. And another thing –" Mr. Smedley paused. Mr. Calder was reminded of an old black crow, cautiously approaching a tempting morsel and wondering whether he dared to seize it. "I ought to warn you that the people here are very fond of their rector. If what *they* regarded as divine manifestations were described by *you* as conjuring tricks, well – you see what I mean."

"I see what you mean," said Mr. Calder. He went out into the village street, took a couple of deep breaths, and made his way to the post-office. This was dark, dusty and empty. He could hear the postmaster, in the back room, wrestling with a manual telephone exchange. He realised, as he listened, that Mr. Smallpiece was no Norfolkman. His voice suggested that he had been brought up within sound of Bow Bells. When he emerged, Mr. Calder confirmed the diagnosis. If Mr. Smedley was a country crow, Mr. Smallpiece was a Cockney sparrow.

He said, "Nice to see a new face around. You'll be staying with the colonel. I 'ope his aunt gets over it."

"Gets over what?"

"Called away ten minutes ago. The old lady 'adder fit. Not the first one neither. If you ask me, she 'as one whenever she feels lonely."

"Old people are like that," agreed Mr. Calder. "Your job must keep you very busy."

"Oh I am the cook and the captain bold and the mate of the *Nancy* brig," agreed Mr. Smallpiece. "I work the exchange –

eighteen lines – deliver the mail, sell stamps, send telegrams and run errands. 'Owever, there's no overtime in this job, and what you don't get paid for you don't get thanked for." He looked at the clock above the counter which showed five minutes to twelve, pushed the hand on five minutes, turned a card in the door from "Open" to "Closed" , and said, "Since the colonel won't be back much before two, what price a pint at the Viscount?"

"You take the words out of my mouth," said Mr. Calder. As they walked down the street, he said, "What happens if anyone wants to ring up someone whilst you're out?"

"Well, they can't, can they?" said Mr. Smallpiece.

When the colonel returned – his aunt, Mr. Calder was glad to learn, was much better – he reported the negative results of his enquiries to date.

"If you want to see Miss Martin, you can probably kill two birds with one stone. She goes along to the rectory most Wednesdays, to practise the harmonium. You'll find it at the far end of the street. The original rectory was alongside the church, but it was burned down about a hundred years ago. I'm afraid it isn't an architectural gem. Built in the worst style of Victorian ecclesiastical red brick."

Mr. Calder, as he lifted the heavy wrought-iron knocker, was inclined to agree. The house was not beautiful. But it had a certain old-fashioned dignity and solidity. The rector answered the door himself. Mr. Calder had hardly known what to expect. A warrior ecclesiastic in the Norman mould? A fanatical priest, prepared to face stake and faggot for his faith? A subtle Jesuit living by the Rule of Ignatius Loyola in solitude and prayer? What he had not been prepared for was a slight nondescript man with an apologetic smile who said, "Come in, come in. Don't stand on ceremony. We never lock our doors here. I know you, don't I? Wait! You're Mr. Calder, and you're staying at the Manor. *What* a lovely dog. A genuine Persian deerhound of the royal breed. What's his name?"

"He's called Rasselas."

"Rasselas," said the rector. He wasn't looking at the dog, but was staring over his shoulder, as though he could see something of interest behind him in the garden. "Rasselas." The dog gave a rumbling growl. The rector said, "Rasselas," again, very softly. The rumble changed to a snarl. The rector stood perfectly still, and said nothing. The snarl changed back into a rumble.

"Well, that's much better," said the rector. "Did you see? He was fighting me. I wonder why?"

"He's usually very well behaved with strangers."

"I'm sure he is. Intelligent too. Why should he have *assumed* that I was an enemy. You heard him assuming it, didn't you?"

"I heard him changing his mind, too."

"I was able to reassure him. The interesting point is, why should he have started with hostile thoughts. I trust he didn't derive them from you. But I'm being fanciful. Why should you have thoughts about us at all. Come along in, and meet our organist, Miss Martin. Such a helpful person, and a spirited performer on almost any instrument."

The opening of an inner door had released a powerful blast of Purcell's overture to *Dido and Aeneas*, played on the harmonium with all stops out.

"Miss Martin. MISS MARTIN."

"I'm so sorry, rector. I didn't hear you."

"This is Mr. Calder. He's a war-time friend of Colonel Faulkner. Curious that such an evil thing as war should have produced the fine friendships it did."

"Good sometimes comes out of evil, don't you think."

"No," said the rector. "I'm afraid I don't believe that at all. Good sometimes comes in spite of evil. A very different proposition."

"A beautiful rose," said Miss Martin, "can grow on a dunghill."

"Am I the rose, and Colonel Faulkner the dunghill, or vice-versa?"

Miss Martin tittered. The rector said, "Let that be a warning to you not to take an analogy too far."

"I have to dash along now, but please stay, Miss Martin will do the honours. Have a cup of tea. You will? Splendid."

Over the teacups, as Mr. Calder was wondering how to bring the conversation round to the point he required, Miss Martin did it for him. She said, "This is a terrible village for gossip, Mr.

Calder. Although you've hardly been down here for two days people are already beginning to wonder what you're up to. Particularly as you've been – you know – getting round, talking to people."

"I am naturally gregarious," said Mr. Calder.

"Now, now. You won't pull the wool over my eyes. I know better. You've been sent."

Mr. Calder said, trying to keep the surprise out of his voice, "Sent by whom?"

"I'll mention no names. We all know that there are sects and factions in the Church who would find our rector's teachings abhorrent to their own narrow dogma. And who would be envious of his growing reputation."

"Oh, I see," said Mr. Calder.

"I'm not asking you to tell me if my guess is correct. What I do want to impress on you is that there is nothing exaggerated in these stories. I'll give you one instance which I can vouch for myself. It was a tea party we were giving for the Brownies. I'd made a terrible miscalculation. The most appalling disaster faced us. *There wasn't enough to eat.* Can you imagine it?"

"Easily," said Mr. Calder with a shudder.

"I called the rector aside, and told him. He just smiled, and said, 'Look in that cupboard, Miss Martin.' I simply stared at him. It was a cupboard I use myself for music and anthems. I have the only key. I walked over and unlocked it. And what do you think I found? A large plate of freshly cut bread and butter, and two plates of biscuits."

"Enough to feed the five thousand."

"It's odd you should say that. It was the precise analogy that occurred to me."

"Did you tell people about this?"

"I don't gossip. But one of my helpers was there. She must have spread the story. Ah, here is the rector. Don't say a word about it to him. He denies it all, of course."

"I'm glad to see that Miss Martin has been looking after you," said the rector. "A thought has occurred to me. Do you sing?"

"Only under duress."

"Recite, perhaps? We are getting up a village concert. Miss Martin is a tower of strength in such matters –"

"It would appear from his reports," said Mr. Fortescue, "that your colleague is entering fully into the life of the village. Last Saturday, according to the *East Anglia Gazette*, he took part in a village concert in aid of the RSPCA. He obliged with a moving rendering of the 'Wreck of the Hesperus'."

"Good gracious," said Mr. Behrens. "How very versatile."

"He would not, however, appear to have advanced very far in the matter I sent him down to investigate. He thinks that the rector is a perfectly sincere enthusiast. He has his eye on three people, any one of whom *might* have been planted in the village to work on him. Have you been able to discover anything?"

"I'm not sure," said Mr. Behrens. "I've made the round of our usual contacts. I felt that the IBG was the most likely. It's a line they've tried with some success in the past. Stirring up local prejudice, and working it up into a national campaign. You remember the school children who trespassed on the missile base at Loch Gair and were roughly handled?"

"Were alleged to have been roughly handled."

"Yes. It was a put-up job. But they made a lot of capital out of it. I have a line on their chief organiser. My contact thinks they *are* up to something. Which means they've got an agent planted in Hedgeborn."

"Or that the rector is their agent."

"Yes. The difficulty will be to prove it. Their security is rather good."

Mr. Fortescue considered the matter, running his thumb down the angle of his prominent chin. He said, "Might you be able to contrive, through your contact, to transmit a particular item of information to their agent in Hedgeborn?"

"I might. But I hardly see –"

"In medicine," said Mr. Fortescue, "I am told that when it proves impossible to clear up a condition by direct treatment, it is sometimes possible to precipitate an artificial crisis which *can* be dealt with."

"Always bearing in mind that if we do precipitate a crisis, poor old Calder will be in the middle of it."

"Exactly," said Mr. Fortescue.

It was on the Friday of the second week of his stay that Mr. Calder noticed the change. There was no open hostility. No one attacked him. No one was even rude to him. It was simply that he had ceased to be acceptable to the village. People who had been prepared to chat with him in the bar of the Viscount Townshend now had business of their own to discuss when he appeared. Mr. Smedley did not answer his knock, although he could see him, through the front window reading a book. Mr. Smallpiece avoided him in the street.

It was like the moment, in a theatre, when the iron safety-curtain descends, cutting off the actors and all on the stage from the audience. Suddenly, he was on one side. The village was on the other.

By the Saturday, the atmosphere had become so oppressive that Mr. Calder decided to do something about it. Stokes had driven the colonel into Thetford on business. He was alone in the house. He decided, on the spur of the moment, to have a word with the rector.

Although it was a fine afternoon, the village street was completely empty. As he walked, he noted the occasional stirring of a curtain, and knew that he was not unobserved, but the silence of the early autumn afternoon lay heavily over everything. On this occasion he had left a strangely subdued Rasselas behind.

His knock at the rectory door was unanswered. Remembering the rector saying, "We never lock our doors here," he turned the handle and went in. The house was silent. He took a few steps along the hall, and stopped. The door on his left was ajar. He looked in. The rector was there. He was kneeling at a carved prie-dieu, as motionless as if he had been himself part of the carving. If he had heard Mr. Calder's approach, he took absolutely no notice of it. Feeling extremely foolish, Mr. Calder withdrew by the way he had come.

Walking back down the street, he was visited by a recollection of his days with the Military Mission in war-time Albania. The mission had visited a remote village, and had been received with the same silent disregard. They had usually been well received, and it had puzzled them. When he returned to the village some months later Mr. Calder had learned the truth. The village had caught an informer, and were waiting for the mission to go before they dealt with him. He had heard the details of what they had done to the informer, and although he was not naturally queasy, it had turned his stomach.

That evening Stokes waited on them in unusual silence. When he had gone, the colonel said, "Whatever it is, it's tomorrow."

"How do you know?"

"I'm told that the rector has been fasting since Thursday. Also that morning service tomorrow has been cancelled, and Evensong brought forward to four o'clock. That's when it'll break."

"It will be a relief," said Mr. Calder.

"Stokes thinks you ought to leave tonight. He thinks I shall be all right. You might not be."

"That was thoughtful of Stokes. But I'd as soon stay. That is, unless you want to get rid of me."

"Glad to have you," said the colonel. "Besides, if they see you've gone, they may put it off. Then we shall have to start all over again."

"Did you contact the number I asked you to?"

"Yes. From a public call-box in Thetford."

"And what was the answer?"

"It was so odd," said the colonel, "that I was afraid I might get it wrong, and I wrote it down." He handed Mr. Calder a piece of paper.

Mr. Calder read it carefully, folded it up, and put it in his pocket.

"Is it good news or bad?"

"I'm not sure," said Mr. Calder. "But I can promise you one thing. You'll hear a sermon tomorrow which you won't forget."

When the rector stepped into the pulpit his face was pale and composed, but it was no longer gentle. Mr. Calder wondered how he could ever have considered him nondescript. There was a blazing conviction about the man, a fire and a warmth which lit up the whole church. This was no longer the gentle St. Francis. This was Peter the Hermit, "whose eyes were a flame and whose tongue was a sword".

He stood for a moment, upright and motionless. Then he turned his head slowly, looking from face to face in the crowded congregation, as if searching for support and guidance from his flock. When he started to speak it was in a quiet, almost conversational voice.

"The anti-Christ has raised his head once more. The Devil is at his work again. We deceived ourselves into thinking that we had dealt him a shrewd blow. We were mistaken. Our former warning has not been heeded. I fear that it will have to be repeated, and this time more strongly."

The colonel looked anxiously at Mr. Calder, who mouthed the word, "Wait."

"Far from abandoning its foul work at Snelsham Manor, I have learned that it is not only continuing, but intensifying it. More of God's creatures are being imprisoned in its cells and tortured by methods which would have showed the Gestapo. In the name of science, mice, small rabbits, guinea-pigs and hamsters are being put to obscene and painful deaths. Yesterday a cargo of African tree beavers, harmless and friendly little animals arrived at this – at this scientific slaughterhouse. They are to be inoculated with a virus which will first paralyse their limbs, and then cause them to go mad with pain, and finally to die. The object of the experiment is to hold off the moment of death as long as possible –"

Mr. Calder, who was listening with strained attention to every word, had found it difficult to hear the closing sentence and realised that the rector was now speaking against a ground-swell of noise, which burst out suddenly into a roar. The rector's voice rode over the tumult like a trumpet.

"Are we going to allow this?"

A second roar crashed out with startling violence.

"We will pull down this foul place, stone by stone. We will purge what remains with fire. All who will help, follow me."

"What do we do?" said the colonel.

"Sit still," said Mr. Calder.

In a moment they were alone in their pew with a hundred angry faces round them. The rector, still standing in the pulpit, quelled the storm with an uplifted hand. He said, "We will have no bloodshed. We cannot fight evil with evil. Those who are not with us are against us. Enoch, take one of them. Two of you the other. Into the vestry with them."

Mr. Calder said, "Go with it. Don't fight."

As they were swirled down the aisle, the colonel saw one anxious face in the crowd. He shouted, "Are you in this too, Stokes?" The next moment they were in the vestry. The door had clanged shut and they heard the key turn in the lock. The thick walls, and nine inches of stout oak cut off the sounds. They could hear the organ playing. It sounded like Miss Martin's idea of the Battle Hymn of the Republic. A shuffling of feet. A door banging. Then silence.

"Well," said the colonel. "What do we do now?"

"We give them five minutes to get to the rectory. There'll be some sort of conference there, I imagine."

"And then?"

Mr. Calder had seated himself on a pile of hassocks, and sat there, swinging his short legs. He said, "As we have five minutes to kill, maybe I'd better put you in the picture. Why don't you sit down?"

The colonel grunted, and subsided.

Mr. Calder said, "Hasn't it struck you that the miracles we've been hearing about were of two different types?"

"Don't follow you."

"One sort was simple animal magnetism. No doubt about that. I saw the rector operating on Rasselas. Nearly hypnotised the poor dog. The other sort – well, there's been a lot of talk about them, but I've only heard any real evidence of two. The bells that rang themselves and the food that materialised in a locked cupboard. Isolate them from the general hysteria, and what do they amount to? You told me yourself that the key of the vestry had been mislaid."

"You think someone stole it. Had it copied?"

"Of course."

"Who?"

"Oh," said Mr. Calder impatiently, "the person who organised the other miracle of course. I think it's time we got out of here, don't you?"

"How?"

"Get someone to unlock the door. I notice they left the key in it. There must be some sane folk about. Not all the farmers were in the church."

The colonel said, "Seeing that the nearest farm likely to be helpful to us is a good quarter of a mile away, I'd be interested to know how you intend to shout for help."

"Follow me up that ladder," said Mr. Calder, "and I'll show you."

The rector said, "Is that clear? They'll be expecting us on the southern side, where we attacked before. So we'll come through the woods, on the north. Stokes, can you get the colonel's Land-Rover up that side?"

"Easily enough, rector."

"Have the grappling irons laid out at the back. Tom's tractor follows you. Enoch, how long to cut the wire?"

"Ten seconds."

This produced a rumbling laugh.

"Good. We don't want any unnecessary delay. We drive the tractors straight through the gap and ride in on the back of them. The fire raising material will be in the trailers behind the rear tractor. The Scouts can see to that under you, Mr. Smedley."

"Certainly, rector. Scouts are experts at lighting fires. If we start upwind, that should give you time to get the animals out before it takes hold."

"Excellent. Now, the diversion at the front gate. That will be under you, Miss Martin. You'll have the Guides and Brownies. You demand to be let in. When they refuse, you all start screaming. If you can get hold of the sentry, I suggest you scratch him."

"I'll let Matilda Briggs do that," said Miss Martin. "She'll enjoy it."

Enoch Clavering touched the rector on the arm and said, "Listen." Then he went over to the window and opened it.

"What is it, Enoch?"

"I thought I heard the bells some minutes ago, but I didn't like to interrupt. They've stopped now. It's as it was last time. The bells rang themselves. What does it signify?"

"It means," said the rector cheerfully, "that I've been a duffer. I ought to have seen that the trap-door to the belfry was padlocked. Our prisoners must have climbed up, and started clapping the tenor and the treble. Since they've stopped I imagine someone heard them and let them out."

Miss Martin said, "What are we going to do?"

"What we're not going to do is lose our heads. Stokes, you've immobilised the colonel's car?"

Stokes nodded.

"And you've put the telephone line out of communication, Mr. Smallpiece?"

"Same as last time."

"Then I don't see how they can summon help in under half an hour. We should have ample time to do all we have to."

"I advise you against it," said Mr. Calder.

He was standing in the doorway, one hand in his pocket. He looked placid, but determined. Behind him they could see the great dog, Rasselas, his head almost level with Mr. Calder's shoulder, his amber eyes glowing.

For a moment there was complete silence. Then a low growl of anger broke out from the crowded room. The rector said, "Ah, Calder. I congratulate you on your ingenuity. Who let you out?"

"Jack Collins. And he's gone in his own car, to Thetford. The police will be here in half an hour."

"Then they will be too late."

"That's just what I was afraid of," said Mr. Calder. "It's why I came down as fast as I could, to stop you."

There was another growl, louder and more menacing. Enoch Clavering stepped forward. He said, "Bundle him down into the cellar, rector, and let's get on with it."

"I shouldn't try it," said Mr. Calder. His voice was still peaceful. "First, because if you put a hand on me this dog will have the hand off. Secondly, because the colonel's outside in the garden. He's got a shot gun, and he'll use it if he has to."

The rector said, gently, "You mustn't think you can frighten us. The colonel won't shoot. He's not a murderer. And Rasselas won't attack me. Will you, Rasselas?"

"You've got this all wrong," said Mr. Calder. "My object is to prevent *you* attacking us. Just long enough for me to tell you two things. First point, the guards at Snelsham have been doubled. They are armed. And they have orders to shoot. What you're leading your flock to isn't a jamboree, like last time. It's a massacre."

"I think he's lying," said Mr. Smedley.

"There's one way of finding out," said Mr. Calder. "But it's not the real point. The question which really matters – what our American friends would refer to as the sixty-four thousand dollar question is – have any of you ever seen a tree beaver?"

The question was so unexpected that it fell into a sudden pool of silence.

"Come, come," said Mr. Calder. "There must be some naturalists here. Rector, I see the *Universal Encyclopaedia of Wild Life* on your shelf. Would you care to turn its pages and give us a few facts about the habits of this curious creature."

The rector said, with half a smile of comprehension on his face, "What are you getting at, Mr. Calder?"

"I can save you some unnecessary research. The animal does not exist. Indeed, it could not exist. Beavers live in rivers, not in trees. The animal was invented by an old friend of mine, a Mr. Behrens. And having invented this remarkable animal, he thought it would be a pity to keep it all to himself. He had news of its arrival at Snelsham passed to a friend of his, who passed it on to a subversive organisation, known as the International Brotherhood Group. Who, in turn, passed it to you, rector, through their local agent."

The rector was smiling now. He said, "So I have been led up the garden path. *Sancta simplicitas!* Who is this agent?"

"That's easy. Who told you about the tree beavers?"

There was a flurry of movement. A shout, a crash, and the sound of a shot.

"It is far from clear," said Mr. Calder, "whether Miss Martin intended to shoot the rector or me. In fact Rasselas knocked her over and she shot herself. As soon as they realised they had been fooled, the village closed its ranks. They concocted a story that Miss Martin, who was nervous of burglars, was known to possess a revolver, a relic of the last war. She must have been carrying it in her handbag, and the supposition was that, in pulling it out to show to someone, it had gone off and killed her. It was the thinnest story you ever heard, and the Coroner was suspicious as a cat. But he couldn't shake them. And after all, it *was* difficult to cast doubt on the evidence of the entire Parochial Church Council supported by their rector. The verdict was accidental death."

"Excellent," said Mr. Fortescue. "It would have been hard to prove anything. In spite of your beavers. How did the rector take it?"

"Very well indeed. I had to stay for the inquest and made a point of attending Evensong on the following Sunday. The church was so full that it was difficult to find a seat. The rector preached an excellent sermon, on the text, 'Render unto Caesar the things that are Caesar's'."

"A dangerous opponent," said Mr. Fortescue. "On the whole, I cannot feel sorry that the authorities should have decided to close Snelsham Manor."

7

Signal Tresham

"You are my Member," said Colonel Mounteagle.

"Indeed, yes," said Mr. Pocock, sipping nervously at the glass of sherry which the colonel had thrust onto him when he arrived.

"You represent my interests in Parliament."

"Yours, and other people's."

"Never mind about other people. It isn't other people's land this feeder road is going to ruin. It's my land."

"That's one way of looking at it," agreed Mr. Pocock. "But you have to bear in mind that by taking the pressure off the road between your lodge gates and the roundabout, a number of people with houses on that stretch will be relieved of the heavy flow of traffic just outside their front gates. Danger to children –"

"Irrelevant," said the colonel. "People who buy houses on the main road must expect to see a bit of traffic. That's not the point. When a road is going to invade the privacy of a land-owner – is going to trespass across *his* fields – he *must* be allowed some say in the matter. That's right, isn't it?"

"Up to a point."

"Right. Have some more sherry." Without allowing Mr. Pocock to say yes or no he refilled his glass. "Now, you've got a chance to do what's needed. You've drawn a place – third place, I believe – in the ballot for private members' bills. I've told you what's wanted. A simple three- or four-clause bill saying that where a new road is planned the land-owners affected by it will have a right to veto it. If there are several of them, the verdict to be by a straight majority. That's democratic, isn't it?"

"In a way," said Mr. Pocock. He wished he could dispose of the sherry, but if he drank it too quickly he was going to choke.

"But one has to look at the other side of the coin. The new road will be a great benefit to a number of householders."

"Including you."

"Yes. It's true that my present house happens to be on that stretch of road. But I hope you don't impute –"

"I don't impute anything," said the colonel. "I state facts. Mine is the only property which is going to be invaded, and that means that I am the only person directly concerned."

He gazed out of the window. From where he stood he could see, across two fields, the line of hedge which marked the main road – a thick hedge of well matured beech. What he now had to face was the thought of a road, a loathsome snake of tar macadam, giving right of access to every Tom, Dick, and Harry with a stinking motorcar or a roaring motorcycle, violating lands which had been in the Mounteagle family for two and a half centuries. Was it for this that they had fought Napoleon, Kaiser William, and Hitler, that one Mounteagle had fallen in the breach at Badajoz, and another in the sodden wastes of Passchendaele, that he himself –?

He looked down at his left hand from which three of the middle fingers were gone. Mr. Pocock, not fancying the expression on his face, managed to swallow most of the sherry in his glass.

"It may not be easy to push such a bill through," said the colonel. "But it's a chance. And maybe your last chance to settle this matter without bloodshed."

"Metaphorically, I hope you mean," said Mr. Pocock with a nervous smile.

"I'm not in the habit of talking in metaphors," said the colonel. "If you put me with my back to the wall, I shall fight."

"And, oh dear," said Mr. Pocock to his wife that evening, "I've got a feeling he meant it."

"You can't possibly promote an anti-social bill of that sort."

"If I did, it would be the end of me, politically. And it wouldn't get a second reading. It would be laughed out of Parliament, and me with it."

"Then," said his wife, "what's the difficulty? You just say no."

"You didn't see his face," said Mr. Pocock.

★

"When I was in India," said Mr. Fortescue, "there was a saying that all sappers were mad, married, or Methodist. Colonel Mounteagle is a bachelor, and a staunch upholder of the established Church."

"So he must be mad," said Mr. Calder.

When Mr. Fortescue, Manager of the Westminster Branch of the London and Home Counties Bank, wished to make contact with Mr. Calder or Mr. Behrens, both of whom lived in Kent, he would convey a message to them that their accounts were causing him concern. The precise form of the message indicated the gravity of the situation. On this occasion it had been of very moderate urgency, and directed to Mr. Calder only.

"Madness is an imprecise term," said Mr. Fortescue. He steepled the tips of his fingers and looked severely at Mr. Calder over his glasses.

"If you mean, is he certifiably insane, the answer must be in the negative. But his conduct in recent months has been causing concern in certain quarters. A number of my people have, as you know, succeeded in establishing themselves in positions of some confidence in IRA cells in this country. One of my people has managed to become friendly with Michael Scullin."

Mr. Calder knew that the people referred to were very brave men who took their lives into their hands every day of the year. He also knew that the systematic penetration of IRA groups was one of the ways in which bomb outrages were kept within manageable limits.

He said, "Scullin? He's their electronics expert, isn't he?"

"One of them. He specialises in detonation by remote control, and devices of that sort. He learned his trade in Russia."

"I'm surprised that we don't take steps to abate him."

"On the whole it is more useful to keep him under observation. It can produce surprising results – as it has on this occasion. It seems that recently he has been paid substantial sums of money by a certain Colonel Mounteagle for what I can only describe as a refresher course in the use of high explosive."

"A refresher course?"

"Certainly. As a young officer, in 1945, Mounteagle had a considerable reputation. He was a member of the task force charged with clearing the mouth of the Scheldt, and blowing up the submarine pens. They were jobs which had to be done against time, and this involved the acceptance of risks. There was a procedure by which unmanned barges filled with explosive could be directed into the underground pens and exploded. The danger lay in the variety of underwater devices which had first to be brought to the surface and dismantled. It was while he was engaged in this work that the colonel lost three fingers of his left hand – and gained an immediate DSO."

"He sounds quite a lad," said Mr. Calder. "Do we know what is leading him to a renewed interest in the forces of destruction?"

"He is annoyed with the authorities for wishing to build a road across his park and with his local MP for failing to introduce a private bill to stop them."

Mr. Calder thought for a moment that Mr. Fortescue was joking, then realised that he was serious. He said, "What sort of reprisals do you think he might be intending?"

"He could be laying a number of booby traps in his park. Alternatively, or in addition, he may be planning to blow up the MP concerned, a Mr. Pocock. Two nights ago Mr. Pocock was awakened by mysterious noises. He telephoned the police. When they arrived they found that the door of his garage had been forced. From the garage an unlocked door leads into the house."

"I see," said Mr. Calder. "The colonel sounds like a determined character. Perhaps Mr. Pocock would be wise to press on with his bill."

Mr. Fortescue said, "I think we must take a hand. The loss of an occasional Member of Parliament may not be a matter of concern, but we don't want some innocent bulldozer driver destroyed. I suggest you make yourself known to the colonel. His address is Mounteagle Hall, Higham. He is managing director of his own family firm, The Clipstone Sand and Gravel Company. It is on the river, north of Cooling. I will alert Behrens as to the position, but I imagine you will be able to handle this yourself."

Mr. Calder's methods were usually simple and straightforward. On this occasion he put on his oldest clothes, armed himself with a fishing rod, and sat down to fish at a point just outside the boundary fence of the Clipstone Sand and Gravel Company. Soon after he had started, a man came out of a gate in the fence and stood watching him. From his appearance and walk he was an ex-naval type, Mr. Calder guessed. At this moment he succeeded in hooking a sizable fish.

This served as a convenient introduction, and Mr. Calder was soon deep in conversation with Chief Petty Officer Seward. He mentioned that he was putting up for a few days at the local pub. Seward agreed that the beer there was drinkable, and that he might be down there himself after work.

By ten o'clock that evening, in the friendly atmosphere of the saloon bar, Mr. Calder had learned a good deal about the Clipstone Sand and Gravel Company and its owner.

"He's all right," said Seward. "I mean, you don't find many like him nowadays. He knows what he wants, and he likes to get his own way, no messing about. But if he likes you, he'll do anything for you."

"And if he doesn't like you?"

"If he doesn't like you," said Seward with a grin, "you clear out quick. We had a chap once who set himself up as a sort of shop steward. Wanted to get us unionised. The colonel soon put a stop to it."

"How did he manage to do that?"

"Threw him in the river."

"I see," said Calder thoughtfully.

"I don't say he would have got away with it in the usual outfit, but we're more a sort of family business. All ex-service. We've even got our own fleet."

Mr. Calder had seen the neat row of grey metal barges anchored to the jetty.

"Lovely jobs," said Seward. "Self-powered. One man can handle them easily. Built to ferry stuff ashore on the beaches at D-day. Picked them up from the Crown Agents after the war. Most of our stuff – sand and aggregate, that is – goes up by river. And they bring back timber piling and iron sheeting. When we're opening a new section of quarry we have to blanket off each section as we go –"

He expounded the intricacies of the quarryman's job, and Mr. Calder, who always liked to learn about other people's work, listened with interest.

He said to Mr. Behrens when he met him three days later – "Mounteagle's a real buccaneer. The sort of man who used to go out to India in the seventeenth century and come back with a fortune and a hobnailed liver. But he's running a very useful outfit, and his men swear by him."

"Would he be capable of blowing up a Member of Parliament?" said Mr. Behrens.

"Think nothing of it. He chucked a shop steward into the river."

On the following Sunday Mr. Calder paid a visit, by appointment, to the modest villa residence of Alfred Pocock, MP. It stood, with five similar residences, on the far side of the road which skirted Colonel Mounteagle's park. He found Mr. Pocock at home, alone and depressed. He said, "I've sent my wife away to stay with her mother. She didn't want to go but I thought it would be safer."

"Much safer," said Mr. Calder. "I take it the explosives experts have given your house a clean bill of health."

"They poked around with some sort of machine which reacts to explosives. They didn't find anything."

"I expect it was just a reconnaissance. The colonel's a methodical man."

"He's a public menace," said Mr. Pocock indignantly. "I'm told that the workmen who should have started on the new road a week ago have refused to proceed without police protection."

"I'm not sure that policemen would be much use. What they need is a military reconnaissance screen, armed with mine detectors."

"Then the colonel should be arrested."

"And charged with what?"

Mr. Pocock gobbled a bit, but could think of no answer to this. Mr. Calder said, "I suppose you couldn't make some sort of gesture? Have this bill he wants printed, and given a first reading.

Since you're convinced it wouldn't get any further, no real harm would be done."

"It would be the end of my political life."

"If I had to make a choice between the ending of my political life and the ending of my life, I know which alternative I would select. But then, I'm a natural coward."

Mr. Pocock, his voice rising as it did when he was excited or alarmed, said, "It's a scandal. We should all be given the fullest possible protection against menaces of this sort. It's what we pay our rates and taxes for and we're entitled to expect it."

"Having me on your side," said Mr. Calder, "is what you might call a tax bonus."

Mr. Pocock was not appeased. He shook hands coldly when his visitor left. Mr. Calder, also, was silent. He was reflecting that maybe the trouble with England was that it was run by people like Mr. Pocock and not by people like Colonel Mounteagle.

His next object was to meet the colonel. Since he could hardly march up to the front door and introduce himself, this was a question of manoeuvre and good luck. He was early afoot on Monday morning and found two young men with white poles, a steel tape, and a theodolite on the road verge just south of the manor's great gates – high columns, each surmounted by a stone eagle poised to swoop.

As he stopped to talk to them a car swept out of the entrance. The colonel, who was driving, spotted the men, pulled up, and got out. The men looked apprehensive. The colonel was smiling. He said, "Getting ready for the great day, lads?"

"That's right, Colonel."

"The day when the first bulldozer drives through my hedge."

"That won't be us, Colonel. That's not our job."

"Someone's got to drive it. Can't do it by remote control." A thought struck him. "Come to think of it," he said, "when I was doing a similar sort of job during the war, we *did* use remote control. But that was ships, not bulldozers. No. As I said, someone will have to drive it." The colonel's smile widened. "Give him a message from me, lads. What he'll need is not police protection. He'll need insurance for his widow."

The colonel swung round and seemed to notice Mr. Calder for

the first time. He said, "Are you in charge of this mob?"

"Certainly not," said Mr. Calder. "I just happened to be passing."

"You don't look to me like someone who happened to be passing. You look to me like a spy. This is war. And you know what happens to spies in war." The smile appeared again. "They get shot."

It was the smile that convinced Mr. Calder. The colonel was neither eccentric nor in any way admirable. Whether he was mad or not was a nice point. What was certain was that he was very dangerous.

"We put a tap on both telephones," said Mr. Fortescue. "The one from the house and the one from the factory. We picked up an interesting exchange yesterday afternoon. The colonel was speaking to a young friend of his, also ex-Army, it seems. A man called David Cairns. Cairns is assistant manager at an open-cast coal site at Petheridge, above Reading. Their coal goes down by river to the power stations at Battersea and Rotherhithe."

"And the colonel is ordering coal?"

"He is ordering explosives. A ton of slurry explosive. Stable, but extremely powerful. It is used in open-cast mining. And in quarrying."

"So the colonel has a legitimate reason for ordering it?"

"Certainly. And used in small quantities, under careful control, it can be perfectly safe. When I asked one of our Home Office experts what the effect would be of detonating a ton of it, he said that no one in his senses would do such a thing. When I pressed him he said it would blow a crater, roughly the size of a football field, perhaps twenty foot deep."

Mr. Calder started to say, "Is there any reason to suppose –" but Mr. Fortescue interrupted him sharply. He said, "There were two further points. The colonel is fetching this load himself. He will take one of the barges upstream tomorrow. A run of nine to ten hours. The loading will be done when he arrives. He has also ordered a quantity of timber, which will be stowed on top of the explosive. To keep it firmly in position, he said. No doubt a wise precaution. He plans to spend the night on the boat and start back early the following morning. I think it would be a good idea if you supervised the shipment. But I confess I shall feel much happier when the whole of this particular cargo is safely stowed in the explosives store of the Clipstone Sand and Gravel Company."

"Me, too," said Mr. Calder.

There was a jetty at Petheridge, connected by a private railway with the loading bay at the open-cast colliery. A concrete track ran alongside the line. The colonel, who must have made an early start, tied up at the jetty at four o'clock. Mr. Calder, who had come by road and had not needed to hurry, was ensconced in a thicket of alder and nettles at the far end of the jetty.

He awaited developments with interest.

The timber arrived first, by rail. The explosive, packed in wooden boxes, followed in a lorry, driven by a youngish man with the stamp of a cavalry officer, whom the colonel greeted as David, and whom Mr. Calder assumed to be Cairns.

The wooden boxes were man-handled by the train crew and lowered into the barge. Nobody seemed unduly worried by their explosive potential, but Mr. Calder noticed that they were not treated roughly. Once they were safely stowed, a small crane was brought into operation and this was used to sling on board the timber baulks, which had evidently been cut to length and which fitted snugly over the boxes.

By the time the loading was finished, evening was closing in. The train clanked off, and the colonel said something which Mr. Calder was too far away to hear but which seemed to be an invitation to Cairns to come on board. He had been squatting among the nettles for three hours without achieving anything except cramp. Nothing much would happen before the barge started downstream at first light. Mr. Calder's ideas turned to a drink and dinner. He got stiffly to his feet. He could see Cairns and the colonel standing in the lighted bridge house. He eased his way along the jetty in the hope that he might pick up what they were saying.

What the colonel was saying was, "I bet you don't know what this box of tricks does."

Cairns said, "You lose your bet, Colonel. Almost the only interesting thing I did in the Army was the long electronics course I took at Rhyl. It's an automatic steerer. Come to think of it, that must have been the sort of thing you used when you were blowing up those submarine pens."

"Roughly the same apparatus," said the colonel. "Roughly. But it was a good deal more primitive in those days."

If Cairns had noticed the expression on the colonel's face, he might have cut short the conversation at this point. As it was, he had moved on to a second box that was beside the auto steerer and linked to it. Peering down at it he said, "This looks like a repeater. What would you need a repeater for?"

He put out one hand to touch the dial. The colonel said, in the tone of voice he might have used to a recalcitrant subaltern, "Don't touch that."

Cairns's head jerked back. He seemed suddenly to realise that something was wrong.

He said, "Do you mean that this repeater's already set? What on earth are you playing at?"

"That's none of your business."

Cairns was getting angry too. He said, "It is my business. You've got enough of my explosive on this craft to blow a hole in the home counties. And you've got an automatic steerer linked to a pre-set repeater. Unless you're prepared to tell me what you're playing at, I think I ought to report this to the police."

"You'll do nothing of the sort," said the colonel calmly. "I'll have no Tresham here." His hand came out of his pocket with a gun in it.

Calder was close enough by now to hear this, but not close enough to stop what followed. His feet were on the gangplank when the colonel shot Cairns through the heart, caught him as he fell, and heaved him over the side of the bridge and into the river. Hearing Mr. Calder coming up the iron steps onto the bridge he swung round and shot him, once in the head and once in the body, and threw him overboard as well.

Then he put the gun back into his pocket, turned about, and descended into the cuddy. He was breathing a little faster, but otherwise showed no particular sign of emotion. His hand, as he poured himself a whisky from a bottle in the bulkhead cupboard, was steady as a rock.

The first shot had creased Mr. Calder, ploughing a long furrow along the side of his head above the ear and rendering him temporarily unconscious. He had twisted as he fell, so that the second shot went into the right side of his chest, deflecting from the ribs and coming out under his right shoulder blade.

The fall into the chilly November waters of the Thames brought him round. He could use his legs, and with difficulty, his left arm. He realised that he was losing blood fast.

He let himself go with the current, kicking feebly towards the right bank, because he remembered that the towpath was on that side.

An eternity of cold and increasing pain.

Then he felt himself grounding on the gravel foreshore. Above him was a low wall of what seemed to be concrete sacks. He realised that he was incapable of climbing it and getting out onto the towpath.

He lay on his back and shouted.

The first passer-by was a young girl. She took one look down at Mr. Calder and scampered away. The next one, twenty interminable minutes later, was a policeman.

Mr. Behrens reached Reading Infirmary just before midnight. He was shown into a bleak reception office where he kicked his heels for ten minutes. His temper was wearing thin when a young doctor came in, accompanied by a policeman whom Mr. Behrens recognised – Superintendent Farr of the Reading police.

The superintendent said, "As soon as we knew it was Calder we got in touch with your office. They said, put the silencers on. Have you any idea what this is all about?"

"Why don't we ask Calder? He might be able to tell us."

"He won't tell you anything," said the doctor. Then he noted the expression on Mr. Behrens' face.

"Sorry," he said. "I didn't mean that. He's not dead yet, and with a bit of luck we'll keep him that way. But he's lost a lot of blood. And lying about on the river bank in this weather can't have helped. I've put him under, and he'll have to stay that way for the time being."

"How long will that be?"

"The longer the better for him," said the doctor.

Mr. Behrens recognised the finality of this. He said to Farr, "Can *you* tell me anything? We're all of us totally in the dark. It may be important."

"All I can tell you is that one of my men found him on the river bank, whistled up an ambulance, and got him in here. It was when they were going through his wallet that they found his 'I' card with the special instructions on it, and got hold of me."

"Did he say anything before you put him under? Anything at all?"

"Not really," said the doctor. "If I'd known it was going to matter I might have listened more carefully." Men who were brought in with two bullet wounds in them and were important enough to bring the head policeman round at midnight were something new in his experience. "He did mention two names, though – several times over. One was Cairns and the other, I think, was Tresham."

"Tresham?" said Mr. Fortescue thoughtfully, when Mr. Behrens spoke to him on the telephone. "I seem to remember a man of that name. Tresham or Trencham. He was a Norfolk fisherman. He gave a lot of help to German agents landing by submarine on the east coast."

"And was Calder involved?"

"He was at Blenheim at the time. He could have been."

"Then this might have nothing to do with Mounteagle. It might be a revenge killing. By Tresham's son perhaps."

"I don't think," said Mr. Fortescue precisely, "that this is a case in which it would be wise to jump to conclusions. What about Cairns?"

"He's a bachelor. We've telephoned his digs. No answer. The police are sending a car round."

Mr. Fortescue digested this news in silence for some seconds. Then he said, "I'll look into the Tresham case. And I'll arrange for the police to monitor Mounteagle's barge as it goes down-stream tomorrow. There's a lot to do. I suggest you go home and get some sleep. Be at the Bank by nine tomorrow morning."

Mr. Behrens went back home to the Old Rectory in the sleepy Kentish village of Lamperdown, and he lay on his bed, but he did not go to sleep. The answer to a lot of their problems was under his hand, if only he could close his fingers on it.

The deceptive light of false dawn was in the sky, and the first cocks were beginning to crow across the valley when Mr. Behrens got up, pulled on his dressing gown, and made his way downstairs, walking quietly, so as not to wake his aunt, who shared the house with him and was a light sleeper.

He switched on the reading lamp in his study and searched the shelves for the book he wanted. In the end he found it among a complete set of the works of Charles Dickens.

"Are you suggesting," said Mr. Fortescue, "that Colonel Mounteagle intends to blow up the Houses of Parliament?"

"That's right."

"And you found this in *A Child's History of England*?"

"It was the only book I could lay my hand on quickly," said Mr. Behrens apologetically.

It was not yet six o'clock in the morning but Mr. Fortescue was dressed in the pinstripe trousers and black coat appropriate to a senior bank official. Also he had shaved, which was more than Mr. Behrens had done. He turned his attention to the book and read it once again.

"'*Lord Mounteagle, Tresham's brother-in-law, was certain to be in the House; and when Tresham found that he could not prevail upon the rest to devise any means of sparing their friends, he wrote a mysterious letter to this Lord and left it at his lodging in the dusk, urging him to keep away from the opening of Parliament.*' So Tresham has nothing to do with our Norfolk fisherman?"

"Nothing at all. Tresham is probably something Calder heard the colonel saying when he shot Cairns."

"Then you think Cairns is dead?"

"I'm afraid so."

"The whole thing is unthinkable. Totally unthinkable. And yet –"

Now that he was getting used to it, Mr. Fortescue seemed to be finding the idea of the wholesale destruction of the legislature more interesting than shocking. "An outrageous idea. How would one set about it?"

"It's some sort of automatic pilot with a receiver at the other end to guide it."

"Then has something been planted in the House?"

"I fancy the receiver will be going there tonight. In Pocock's car. That would be what the colonel was up to when Pocock heard burglars."

"How could he be certain that Pocock would be there tonight?"

"It's the debate on Common Market finance. His pet subject. He'll be there early and stay late."

"Well, we can soon see if you're right. We'll call on Pocock. And we'll take Brackett with us. If he finds this gadget in Pocock's car, do you know, I shall be almost inclined to believe you."

"He could hardly have chosen a more appropriate day for it," said Mr. Behrens. The calendar on Mr. Fortescue's desk had not yet been turned from the previous day. It showed November 4th.

An hour later, as the milkman and the postman were delivering their wares, three men stood in Mr. Pocock's garage and watched the fourth at work. Major Brackett, who looked like a dyspeptic bloodhound and was the top electronics expert in the Ministry of Defence, was lying on his back under the car. He said, "It's here all right. Wired onto one of the cross-members. A very neat job."

He eased his way out, stood up, and wiped a drop of oil from his nose.

"That's all right then," said Mr. Fortescue. "All we have to do is switch it off." And when Brackett said nothing, "Well, isn't it?"

"I'm afraid not," said the Major sadly. "Once this jigger's set and on beam, if you turn it off, or interfere with it in any way, you activate the switch at the other end, and your barge load goes up."

*

"I think, Major," said the Home Secretary, "that if you could explain, in terms simple enough to be understood by someone like myself who knows nothing about electronics, then we might be able to see our way more clearly."

Apart from Major Brackett, his audience consisted of the Police Commissioner, the head of the Special Branch, Commander Elfe, Chief Superintendent Baker in charge of River Division, and Mr. Fortescue. Mr. Behrens was sitting unobtrusively in the background.

"Well," said the major, "there are a number of different ways of detonating explosives at a distance."

"As we know," said Elfe grimly.

"The simplest is a pair of linked sets. Master and slave, we call them. The master emits an impulse which increases in strength as the two sets come together. When they are a predetermined distance apart the stronger 'kills' the weaker one. This throws a switch, and the explosive goes up."

"I'm with you so far," said the Home Secretary.

"It can be linked to an automatic steering device. We've developed one recently, on the ranges at Bovington. It steers an old tank filled with explosive into an enemy strong point and detonates it when it gets there. In fact, if Mounteagle has managed to get hold of the latest box of tricks, there's an additional jigger which not only keeps the tank on a predetermined course but allows it to side-step obstacles. It's done with an 'eye' – a photo-cell connected with a microprocessor that registers changes of light striking the cell and takes the appropriate action."

"Does that mean that Mounteagle need never go on board at all? Suppose he's fixed the slave set to go off at – what? Fifty yards? That would be about the distance from the edge of the embankment to the car park under the House. Then he could leave it to steer itself downstream."

"I doubt he'd do that," said Baker. "The barge would call too much attention to itself, zig-zagging down the river like a pin-ball. He'll surely take it down as far as he can by manual steering – at least until it's dark. Any time after that, I agree, he could leave it to its own devices."

For a moment the men in the room were silent. They were

watching a steel craft, packed with enough explosive to tear the top off a mountain, sliding downstream in the darkness, steering under bridges, avoiding other boats, obedient only to the beckoning of its master in Parliament.

The Home Secretary said, "Where is it now?"

The Commissioner said, "Our last report was Bell View Lock below Runnymede. The colonel was certainly on board then. He was making about four miles an hour." He was studying a map that Baker had produced. "Say it's dark by seven. If he keeps up that speed he'd be ten miles above Westminster by then."

"The tide'll be against him when he gets below Teddington," said Baker. "He won't make more than three miles an hour after that."

Everyone did some mental arithmetic.

Elfe said, "Then H-hour could be either side of ten o'clock."

"Is there any chance," said the Home Secretary, "of getting someone aboard *after* the colonel's left and reverting to – what did you call it? – manual steering."

"If you tried that," said Brackett, "you'd almost certainly send the whole lot up. No. I'm afraid there's only one answer. Put the master set from Pocock's car into a police launch and lead the barge out to sea. Safe enough if the launch keeps two hundred yards ahead. Have an experienced man in charge."

"I'll take it myself," said Baker. "That is," he added with a grin, "if the major will come with me in case of any – er – technical hitches."

"I was afraid you were going to say that," said Brackett, looking sadder than ever.

"Very well, gentlemen," said the Home Secretary briskly. "That seems to be the best plan. You have total authority to clear the river of craft, and take any other precautionary measures you think necessary. I assume that Mounteagle plans to bolt abroad. You'll take the usual steps to block the exits."

The Commissioner said, "It occurs to me, Home Secretary, that if we succeed in taking the barge out to sea and destroying it, we shall have very little real evidence left. Suppose he decides to brazen it out."

"He'll have to brazen out one murder and one attempted murder," said Mr. Fortescue coldly. "Calder recovered sufficiently an hour ago to tell us what happened at Petheridge."

"When you're dealing with a madman," said the Home Secretary, "it's impossible to predict what he'll do."

Mr. Behrens disagreed, though he felt it was hardly his place to say so. He thought he knew exactly what the colonel was planning to do.

At ten o'clock that night Mr. Behrens was sitting, alone, on a bench on a hilltop on the northern fringe of London. In front of him, and below him, a million lights twinkled through the misty darkness. There were smaller lights, which were windows and lamp standards and motorcars, and larger lights which were bonfires. The nearest was a quarter of a mile below the point where he was sitting. He could see the dark figures congregated round it like priests at a ritual burning, and he could see, lashed to a stake on top, the grotesque parody of Guy Fawkes, the first great pyrotechnic.

A rocket sailed up into the sky and burst in clusters of red and yellow lights.

Mr. Behrens had chosen this particular place because he had remembered something Mr. Calder had once told him and he was convinced that Colonel Mounteagle, if he avoided immediate capture, would come there too.

A bronze plaque, set in a stone pillar beside the bench, was the reason for his certainty.

"Parliament Hill Fields," it said, "so named because the conspirators who, in the year 1605, planned to blow up the Houses of Parliament, escaping to the north, halted their horses at this spot to observe the outcome of their device."

With his strong sense of history, the colonel must surely come to that spot to observe the outcome of his own more powerful and sophisticated device.

Mr. Behrens was wondering exactly what the colonel had planned to do, and what he would have done but for the unfortunate contretemps at Petheridge. There were several ways in which he might have escaped detection. On the supposition that the original barge would be destroyed beyond any possibility of identification, he needed only to have a duplicate ready filled with explosive, of which he had no doubt already accumulated a stock at his works, waiting for him below Tower Bridge. He could then proceed quietly on his way with this and turn a bland face of innocence to the world. Suspicion, yes. But proof would turn on a number of imponderables, such as whether they could prove the acquisition by the colonel of the self-steering device.

It was at this moment that Mr. Behrens heard a car draw up and stop on the road above him. A door slammed. Footsteps came crunching down the cinder track towards the seat. Mr. Behrens had never met the colonel, but he had been shown photographs of him, and in the dying light of the rocket he had no difficulty in recognising him.

The colonel stood for a long minute, in silence, staring down at the scene below. Mr. Behrens stood up, and the movement caught the colonel's eye. He turned his head.

"A magnificent spectacle, is it not?" said Mr. Behrens.

The colonel grunted.

"But I fear that the main attraction has been cancelled. Owing, you might say, to a technical hitch. When it does take place, it will be some miles offshore, and with a very limited audience."

The colonel was motionless, a black figure outlined against the night sky. When he spoke his voice sounded quite easy. He said, "Who are you, little man?"

"I doubt if this is really a moment for introductions," said Mr. Behrens. "I am a very old friend of one of the men you shot last night. Not Cairns, the other one."

"The Government spy."

"I suppose that's as good a description as any."

"And what do you propose to do about it?"

The colonel had swung round now, but both his hands were visible, hanging idle by his side. Mr. Behrens moved towards him until he was quite close, watching the colonel's hands all the time.

He said, "It seemed to me that there was only one logical end to this matter, Colonel. You come up here to witness the success of your plan. Being disappointed in its failure – we may assume by now, I think, that it has failed – you decide to take your own life."

So saying, Mr. Behrens shot Colonel Mounteagle neatly through the heart. He had removed the silencer from his gun, being confident that the noise of the shot would arouse no interest on this particular night. He stooped over the crumpled body, pressed the muzzle against the entry point of the bullet, and fired again. Then he wiped the gun carefully and pressed it into the colonel's right hand.

A salvo of rockets soared up into the sky, and burst almost overhead with a loud crack and a shower of silver rain.

8

The Mercenaries

It was eleven o'clock, on a fine February morning when Mr. Calder's car gave up the struggle and rolled to a halt on the outskirts of Winterbourne Vaisey.

Mr. Calder knew enough about cars to realise that whatever had happened needed expert attention. He was glad that the breakdown had occurred on the outskirts of a sizeable village. It looked the sort of place which might boast a garage.

He found both a garage and a helpful mechanic who ran him back in his own car to the stranded vehicle. Mr. Calder sat in the sun, smoked a cigarette, and waited for the verdict.

"It's the petrol pump."

"How long will it take to put right?"

"Depends. If I can fix it up, maybe two, three hours. If I can't, and you have to have a new pump, maybe two, three days."

Mr. Calder said "Humph", and started rearranging his plans in the light of alternative contingencies.

"I'll give you a tow back to the garage. Know more about it when we've got the pump off."

Half an hour later Mr. Calder, attended by his Persian deerhound Rasselas, was strolling down the main street of the village. The prognosis had been favourable. It seemed he might be able to resume his journey that afternoon. Meanwhile he had a telephone call to make, putting off a lunch appointment with a certain Brigadier Totton; and he had at least three hours to kill.

The delay was annoying, but not serious. For the last few days he had been touring round the home counties, talking to retired Army officers and Colonial policemen. He was engaged in tracing the early careers of the Croft brothers, Martin and Selby, a pair of middle-aged thugs who had been deported, by sea, from

Egypt and were on their way to England. What the Home Office wanted was evidence sufficient either to send them on somewhere else, or to put them straight into detention. All that he had discovered so far was that they were a tough and resourceful couple.

A woman from whom he sought directions said, after admiring Rasselas, "There's the Crown Inn, at the end of the High Street. A lot of motorists stop there. Or if you don't mind a bit of a walk, you could take the first lane to the right outside the village, that'll bring you down to the river. There's an old inn there. The Pike and Eels. Boating people and fishermen go there a lot in the summer, but it's quiet at this time of year."

Mr. Calder, who preferred anglers to motorists at any season of the year, thanked the lady and set off down the lane.

It went on for a long way, but at last it emerged on the towpath. The Thames is a quiet river in its upper reaches. Here it was still fairly broad, and was split by an island, which rode like a ship at anchor. Most of the island seemed to be occupied by a sprawling and pretentious house, with a big glassed-in balcony looking down stream.

Some millionaire's folly, thought Mr. Calder. Ugly, and out of place in these surroundings. Much more to his taste was the Pike and Eels, a two-storeyed clap-board building with a long garden which straggled along the river bank. At the far end of the garden a youth was planting something in a leisurely way. Potatoes? Surely too early for potatoes? Might be broad beans. Apart from him the place seemed to be dozing in the sun.

He approached a door which was labelled "Public Bar". The notice painted above it in faded letters announced that Samuel Garner was licensed to sell Beer, Wines and Spirits for Consumption on or off the Premises. The tell-tale bell fixed over the door fetched out a stout man in shirt-sleeves and braces from the back premises. Mr. Garner himself, no doubt.

"What can we do for you, sir?"

"A pint of your best bitter," said Mr. Calder, "and a bowl of water for Rasselas."

"Is that your dog?"

"That's Rasselas." The dog had looked up as Mr. Calder

spoke his name. "If he isn't allowed in here, I'll turn him out."

"That's all right, sir. I never mind dogs in here, so long as the other customers don't object. And seeing we haven't got any other customers in the bar right now, they can't very well object, can they?"

"Do you get many people here?"

"In the summer, when the boating parties are up and down the river, we get quite crowded. In winter, it's quiet."

Mr. Calder had been aware, for some time, of two things. The first was that they were not, whatever Mr. Garner might say, the only customers. The second was that Mr. Garner was uneasy.

In the far corner of the bar, down a couple of steps, was a door labelled "Private Bar". It was a thick door, built to maintain privacy. But he had been picking up a low rumble of dialogue from behind it. One voice, the deeper of the two seemed to be laying down the law. The second seemed to be protesting, though without much conviction, against having the law laid down. None of this would have interested Mr. Calder unduly. If people wished to carry on arguments in private bars that was their affair. What intrigued him was the noticeable and growing agitation of the landlord.

He said, "They seem to be having a bit of a debate in there. What is it? Two anglers arguing about who caught the biggest fish last season?"

"A friendly argument of that sort I expect, sir."

"Not so friendly," said Mr. Calder.

There had been a sudden flurry of movement. A crash of a table going over. A rush of footsteps. It sounded as if one of the debaters had made a dash for the door and had been headed off at the last moment.

Mr. Calder was now listening unashamedly.

He heard the second voice saying, "You've got no right –" and then, in a tone of panic which came clearly through the closed door, "Don't do it, please," followed by the sound of a blow.

Mr. Calder said, "It sounds to me as if the argument is getting out of hand. Do you think, perhaps, you ought to break it up?"

The landlord leaned forward, with both his arms on the bar,

and said, "If I was you, sir, I should just finish up that drink, and push off."

Up to that point Mr. Calder had had no intention of interfering. He had enough troubles of his own in the ordinary line of business not to wish to intervene in other people's quarrels. But the threat in the landlord's voice had annoyed him.

He said, "I think I'll have a look. Perhaps I shall have a calming influence on them. I'll tell them the story of the angler who caught Brighton Pier."

"I'm telling you, you can't go in there."

"Oh! Why not?"

"Major Porter won't like it. It's a private room, see. And he's reserved it."

"It's labelled 'Private Bar'. If your pub's open, all the bars in it are open to the public. That's the law."

"Law or no law –" began the landlord. But he got no further, because Mr. Calder had already moved across and opened the door.

There were three men in the private bar.

A red-faced, white moustached military character, dressed in a tight-fitting grey suit was standing in front of the fireplace, with his thumbs hooked in the arm-holes of a checked waistcoat. A young man wearing corduroy trousers and a pullover was sitting in a chair. He was sitting with his chin up and his head tilted back, the reason for this uncomfortable position being that the third man, standing behind the chair, had his hand enlaced in the youngster's hair, and was pulling his head back over the top rail.

"I don't know who the hell you are," said the red-faced man, "but get the bloody hell out of it, and shut the bloody door."

Mr. Calder said, "Good morning."

"Didn't you hear me? I said get the bloody hell out of it. And I'm not going to say it again."

Mr. Calder said, "I ought to warn you, Major. It is Major Porter, isn't it? The louder you shout, the more angry my dog gets. If he gets really angry, he'll probably eat a bit out of you."

"Naylor. Boot him out. And his dog with him."

Mr. Calder transferred his attention to the man behind the chair. During these exchanges he had not moved.

Now he released the boy's hair, and came forward cautiously, manoeuvring to avoid the legs of a table which had been knocked over.

"Naylor?" said Mr. Calder thoughtfully. "You were in D Division. Got booted out for taking bribes from street bookies. You're getting a bit old for this strong-arm stuff, aren't you?"

"Mr. Calder, ennit?"

Having made this discovery, he seemed even less anxious to come forward. He said, "I know this man, sir. He's a – well – he's sort of official, you see."

"I don't care if he's your Aunt Tabitha," said the major. "He's got no right in here. Remove him."

"The major's right," said Naylor, sidling up cautiously. "It's a private room. You'd better be off."

"How are you going to make me?" said Mr. Calder genially. "You're much too fat to fight."

"If you're afraid to tackle him alone," said the major, "I'll give you a hand."

"That you won't," said Mr. Calder. And to Rasselas, "Guard."

The great dog had moved like a shadow on springs, and was standing in front of the major, his lips lifted over long white teeth. Naylor made a tentative lunge at Mr. Calder, who dodged, caught the arm as it came past and pulled. The combined effect of the lunge and the pull swung Naylor half round. Mr. Calder chopped him, with economical force, at the point where his spine joined his skull. Naylor keeled over, hitting his head on the protruding table leg as he did so. The major's hand slid inside his open coat and came out with a gun in it. It was a quick, smooth move, but Rasselas moved even more quickly. His teeth sank into the major's hand. The gun dropped to the floor and Mr. Calder put his foot on it.

The major had given a brief cry as the teeth went in. Now he stood very still.

Mr. Calder picked up a linen runner from the sideboard, said "Loose" to Rasselas, who let go of the major's hand. Mr. Calder wrapped the runner round it to stop the spurt of blood. Then pulled the silk scarf off Naylor's neck as he lay on the floor, and tied it firmly round the runner.

Whilst he was doing all this, Mr. Calder was cursing himself, silently but steadily. He had committed an unpardonable offence. He had interfered in something which was not his business. Moreover he had made a mess. The nursery rule held good. If you make a mess, you clear it up.

He said, "That should hold until you get to hospital."

The major still said nothing. It was partly shock, Mr. Calder thought, but there was a lot of hatred in it too.

He said to the landlord, who had at last ventured into the room, "Major Porter has had a severe shock. Take him into the bar and fix him up with a brandy. And when you've done that come back here."

Mr. Garner looked at the man on the floor, looked at the man in the chair, looked at the major, who still said nothing, and finally looked at Mr. Calder.

"Get on with it," said Mr. Calder impatiently. "There's a lot to do."

He had picked up the gun from the floor, and was holding it, loosely wrapped in his handkerchief. The sight of the gun seemed to make up Mr. Garner's mind for him. He said, "Come on, then, Major," and led him out into the public bar.

Mr. Calder turned his attention to the young man, who seemed glued to the chair. He said, "I think you'd better clear off now. Have you got some transport?"

"Y-yes. My moped. It's in the y-yard."

"Then that's all right, isn't it?"

"Don't you want to know about – I mean – about me, and what they were doing?"

"If it's important, I'll find out later. You'd better go out the back way. That door probably leads into the yard."

"Y-yes. That would be best."

The young man stopped at the door. He seemed to have something on his mind. Then he said "Thank you," and went out, closing the door behind him.

Mr. Garner came back. He said, "That's a nasty wound."

"He shouldn't wave a gun around." Mr. Calder put it carefully in his own pocket. "My dog's funny that way. He doesn't like guns. They make him nervous."

Rasselas rumbled happily.

"It'll have to be seen to."

"Of course. A deep bite like that can be very dangerous. Has the major got a car?"

"He keeps his car here."

"Keeps it?"

"He couldn't keep it on the island, could he?"

That made sense. The major was exactly the sort of man to live in the sort of house he had seen on the island.

"Could you drive it?"

"I expect so."

"Then run him to the nearest hospital. The sooner they get an anti-tetanus injection into him the better. They'll probably want to keep him overnight. Have you got someone who could keep an eye on the place?"

"Ernie can do it."

He went to the door and shouted down the garden. Then he came back and said, "What about him?"

Naylor had turned over and groaned.

"He'll be all right," said Mr. Calder. "Just banged his head as he went down. Might be concussion. Nothing worse."

Mr. Garner said, "Look here. I don't know nothing about you. You come here. Stir up trouble. And now you're giving orders. This is *my* place."

"It's your place," said Mr. Calder softly, "and it's your licence. And if anyone found out that you'd allowed Major Porter and his hired thug to use your private bar to bully that young man, and if they knew that the major was carrying a gun, and had drawn it, and threatened a member of the public with it, then I think you might say good-bye to that licence."

Mr. Garner stood for a moment, in silence. Then he said, "All right. We'll do it your way."

As soon as Mr. Garner and the major had departed, Mr. Calder hoisted Naylor into a chair, fetched the brandy bottle from behind the bar and poured out a half-tumblerful. By the time Naylor had finished it he seemed to be himself again. The only mark on him was a large, purpling bruise on the side of his forehead.

Mr. Calder said, "Now, talk."

"I haven't got nothing to say."

"And I haven't got any time to waste," said Mr. Calder. "If you don't talk, I'll get my dog to chew off your fingers. He's had a taste of blood already this morning. He won't need much telling."

"You leave me alone."

"Guard," said Mr. Calder.

Rasselas jumped to his feet.

"All right, all right," said Naylor, hastily. "What do you want to know? Good dog. Sit down."

Rasselas advanced stiff-legged.

"It's all right," said Mr. Calder. "He won't actually start on you until I tell him to. The only thing is, once he does get going, I'm not sure that even I can stop him."

"Then don't let 'im get going. What do you want to know?"

"Just exactly what was going on here this morning."

When the landlord came back he found Mr. Calder playing darts with Ernie. Mr. Calder said, "Your other guest has gone. He won't come back. I've had two pints of beer, and Ernie found me some bread and cheese in the kitchen. Oh, and he's already won two pints off me at darts. If you'll tot it all up, I'll pay you and be off. And Ernie, if you wouldn't mind, I want a word in private with your boss."

Ernie grinned and departed to resume his gardening. He was a simple soul, but threw a good dart.

"What did you tell them at the hospital?"

"I told them what you said. That a man had come in with a dog, and the dog had thought the major was threatening him, and had bitten him."

"Did you mention my name?"

"I didn't mention it, because I didn't rightly know it. I heard that other man call you Corder, or something like that."

"Right," said Mr. Calder. "Now listen to me. This episode is finished. It's over and done with. Practically, you might say it never happened. If the major wants to take it any further that's up to him. My guess is he won't."

Here Mr. Calder underestimated Major Porter, but he was not to know this. Back in the village he found that his car was once again in working order. "Temporarily," said the mechanic. "You'll need a new pump soon, but it'll do for the moment." Mr. Calder thanked him, paid him and drove into Sonning. There was one more loose end to tidy up.

He found the young man, whose name was James Bird, half asleep in a chair in front of the fire in his lodgings. He said, "I got your address from that ape, Naylor. I want a few details from you. I gather that Major Porter is quite a lad. Owns a chain of betting shops, and at least three gaming clubs."

"Four, actually. The largest, and the most profitable, is the one on that island."

"And you know all about that because you're his accountant."

"One of his accountants. He uses several."

"And you ran into a bit of trouble."

"I was a fool. When the major invited me to come over and have a go I was rather flattered. Normally the only people who get invited to the island are his special friends, and people with a lot of money. I thought I understood the odds. I'd worked out a system."

"Oh, dear."

"All right. You can't kick me any harder than I've been kicking myself. I did make a bit of money – to start with."

"Then you started losing. How much?"

"In the end, just over eight hundred pounds. Of course, I hadn't got it. I gave them an IOU."

"And this morning's effort was Major Porter doing a bit of debt-collecting?"

"It wasn't just the money. He knew that was safe enough. He's only got to mention the matter to my firm, and I'd have got the sack on the spot. Anyway I'd made him an offer. Two hundred pounds, every three months, with interest at fifteen per cent. I could have managed that. Just."

"And he wouldn't accept it."

"It wasn't the money he was after. He said he'd tear up the IOU and forget about the debit if I did what he wanted. I look after the accounts for some of his betting shops. I do the annual audit. Well – you can guess."

"He wanted you to fiddle the books for him," said Mr. Calder brutally. "And you said you wouldn't, and he set Naylor onto you."

"He told me what Naylor was going to do. He said Naylor would knock out two or three of my teeth and fracture my jaw. I guess he'd have enjoyed watching it. He's that sort of man."

"And if I hadn't turned up, would you have said yes or no?"

Young Mr. Bird's face was crimson. In the end he said, "I think I might have said yes."

"Nasty either way," said Mr. Calder. "Just as well, perhaps, you didn't have to find out, wasn't it?"

Mr. Fortescue pursed his lips and said, "I am astounded that Calder should have behaved in such a stupid way."

"Yes," said Mr. Behrens.

When Mr. Fortescue was astounded in that tone of voice there was little point in arguing with him.

"A recruit to the service would have known better than to embroil himself with something which was not his concern."

The events at the Pike and Eels had been reported to him, as a matter of course, by Mr. Calder, though in a much abbreviated version; but Mr. Fortescue had had no difficulty in reading between the lines.

"Up to that point he had been doing some useful work. He had accumulated quite a comprehensive dossier on Martin and Selby Croft. They appear to be a pair of unscrupulous mercenary adventurers with a taste for violence and a flair for keeping out of trouble. Brigadier Rooke, who had had them as recruits in their para-corps days, writes" – Mr. Fortescue picked up one of the papers in front of him – " 'They had the making of first-class fighting men, but more trouble than they were worth. The best I can say about them is that they were attached to each other. On one occasion I know of, Martin saved Selby's life at some risk of his own.' " Hmph. "Major Sholto, who knew them in Rhodesia, says, 'You'd need wheels on your shoes to catch up with that pair.' What a curious expression. I wonder what he meant?"

Mr. Behrens, who knew that Mr. Fortescue understood exactly what Major Sholto meant, replied patiently. "He means that you'd have to move very fast to get ahead of them."

"We're ahead of them at this moment. They are docking at Tilbury tomorrow. The Egyptian authorities deported them by the slowest available ship. Which was thoughtful of them."

"Do we know why they were deported?"

"It appears that they shot a taxi-driver."

"Fatally."

"Fortunately for them, a flesh wound only. It involved them in the payment of compensation. They are not short of money."

"They sound quite a pair."

"They were on the losing side, in Tanzania, but removed themselves to America in time to avoid any unpleasant consequences. They lasted there for eighteen months, and then were deported on suspicion of being associated with various criminal activities. After that they spent some time in the Caribbean, allegedly running a cocoa plantation. There was some trouble about a labour dispute, and the use of unnecessary violence, and they moved on to Tunisia, where they were associated with the oil industry, although in what capacity I am not clear. Finally they gravitated to Egypt."

"It's all a bit vague, isn't it?" said Mr. Behrens. "Suspicion of association with criminals. Some trouble or other."

"As I told you, they are experts at avoiding specific charges."

"What are our instructions?"

"To keep an eye on them. To persuade them to behave whilst they are here. And to deport them as soon as they give us the least excuse to do so."

"If they are British, how can we deport them?"

"At some time in their career they acquired Panamanian citizenship."

"It sounds thin to me, but I suppose we could try. What is the immediate plan?"

"I want you to go to Tilbury and talk to them."

"I see," said Mr. Behrens.

"Normally it is the sort of assignment I should have entrusted to Calder, but in his present state of mind there's no saying what he might do. If they made some remark which annoyed him, he'd probably set that dog of his onto them."

"It sounds more like a job for the police."

"They have committed no offence in this country, as yet."

"Let's hope that their first one won't be an aggravated assault – on me."

"I'm sure you'll be able to make suitable arrangements."

"It's a funny thing, Mr. Berrings," said Martin Croft, "how people get ideas about us. They seem to think we're always roaring drunk and dripping with blood, or something like that. What they don't realise is we're just a pair of sober citizens. Isn't that right, Selby?"

"That's right."

The three of them were sitting in a small back room in a dockside pub at Tilbury which Mr. Behrens had hired for the occasion. He said, "You weren't entirely sober that night in Cairo."

"Ah, but we were provoked. Our moral sense was outraged."

"That's right."

"I mean, it's one thing for a taxi-driver to offer to sell you his sister. That's fair enough. But when he offers to sell you his mother! Anyone might let fly if they had a proposition like that made to them. You might yourself, Mr. Berrings."

"The situation is unlikely to arise. In any event, it's your intentions for the future, not your past, that I'm here to talk about."

Martin Croft looked at him thoughtfully. Fortyish, Mr. Behrens thought. Chunky. His wits about him. His younger brother was a malevolent lump. Both self-confident, with the confidence which came from coping successfully with various violent situations.

"You know," said Martin, "when you invited us in here for a little talk I thought, hullo, he's a copper. Then I thought, no. Can't be. Too old. So perhaps he's a reporter. Wants to buy our life stories. But I shall have to disappoint him."

"Oh, why? You must have had very interesting lives."

"The fact is, we've been paid too much, one way and another, *not* to publish them. It's one of the things I've found out in life Mr. –"

"Behrens."

"Mr. Berrings. Sometimes you get paid more for not doing things than for doing them. For instance, when Selby and me was in America there was this Senator – Hochstatter his name was – we was paid five thousand dollars each for not killing him. Which was funny, since we'd no idea of doing anything of the sort."

"Was that why you were deported?"

Martin looked disconcerted for a moment. He said, "Oh, you knew about that, did you?"

Selby said, abruptly, "Just who are you, mister?"

"You got something there, Selby. He isn't a copper, he isn't a reporter. So who is he?"

Mr. Behrens said, "I've been sent down by certain people who have an interest in seeing you behave yourselves."

"No one's got the right to put a finger on us. We're clean. Who are these people behind you? What do they want?"

"My instructions come from the Home Office, who are officially concerned with you because you've been the subject of at least one deportation order."

Selby lumbered to his feet. He said, "I've had enough of this bloody monkey-talk."

Martin Croft said, "Lay off, Selby. I want to get to the bottom of this. Why should anyone suppose we're *not* going to behave? Perhaps you can tell me that?"

Mr. Behrens took a deep breath. He said, "Your record speaks for itself. You've spent the last twenty years of your life peddling violence – in places where violence was appreciated. The message I'm trying to get through to you is this. There's no market for it here."

Martin Croft said, slowly, "I think you've got a nerve, coming down here, lecturing us, like we was a couple of naughty kids. What'd you do if I threw you through that window?"

"Is that a threat?"

"Take it any way you like. We've done more than that to people who've annoyed us. Remember that American reporter in Cuba, Selby? We took him by an ankle each and swung him against a tree. They were hours and hours picking his teeth out of the trunk."

Mr. Behrens said, in his gentlest voice, "I quite understand. And now you are threatening me with the same sort of violence."

"I wonder," said Martin equally softly, "what happens if we say yes?" He seemed to be listening. "Got men outside? Come rushing in? Search me and Selby? They won't find a thing."

"It's true you're not carrying guns at this moment," said Mr. Behrens. "But you both own them. Yours, Martin, is a P.38, number RN9688. Selby's is a Mauser. I can't tell you the number, because it's been filed off. The steward who carried them ashore for you has been arrested and charged. Whether he implicates you depends on how much he loves you – or how much you've paid him."

Silence descended again. The brothers seemed to sense, for the first time, something menacing in the spare, grizzled scholarly man in front of them.

At last Martin said, "Let him say what he likes, you've still got nothing you can pin on us." Selby growled his agreement.

"A little matter of threatening me with violence, wasn't there?"

"Two to one. Who's going to believe you?"

"If it comes to the point," said Mr. Behrens, "I expect they'll believe the tape recorder."

"Are you telling me you've got this place bugged?"

"Naturally. Why do you think I brought you in here?"

Martin got slowly to his feet. He looked at his brother. He said, "We've got work to do, Selby. We're going to take this bloody room to pieces and find that bloody recorder, and break it on this character's head."

"Waste of time," said Mr. Behrens. "Everything's gone straight through on the wire to London. It's probably been typed out in triplicate by now."

"You did that very nicely," said Mr. Fortescue. "I did wonder, for a moment, whether they would take a chance on it, and assault you. In a way that would have suited us very well."

"I was fairly sure they wouldn't," said Mr. Behrens. "They're not young tearabouts. They're middle-aged professionals. Even if they'd thought I was bluffing, they wouldn't have taken a chance on it. Incidentally, that steward wouldn't give them away. It wasn't just money. He was afraid of them."

"Thoroughly undesirable customers," said Mr. Fortescue. He sounded as though he was refusing them an overdraft at his bank.

"What do you plan to do next?"

"Calder has an idea about that."

"I did think," said Mr. Calder, "that it'd be a good idea if we put them somewhere where they'd have plenty of opportunities to get involved in trouble. Suppose we let them have a tip-off that Major Porter was looking for new talent. He sacked a rather ineffective muscle man called Naylor last week, so he's got at least one vacancy on his staff."

Mr. Fortescue thought about it. He said, "If it can be done discreetly, it might work well. We would, at least, know where they were. But I don't want any unnecessary violence."

Mr. Calder promised, meekly, that there would be no unnecessary violence. He knew that the episode of the Pike and Eels was neither forgotten nor forgiven.

Managing matters with discretion took time. Time to get the information, at fourth hand, to the Crofts. Time for them to vet the major and the major to vet them. It was on a fine morning in early May that they turned up at the Island Club to be given their instructions by Leo Harris, the major's chief of staff.

"In the ordinary way," he said, "it isn't a hard job. Most of the work's at night, when the tables are going. Perhaps someone loses money and gets a little bit upset about it. Or perhaps they've had too much to drink. Then you have to cool them off."

"Bounce them," said Martin. "That shouldn't be too difficult. What's amusing you, Selby?"

"He said, cool them off. All we've got to do is drop 'em in the river, right?"

"Certainly not," said Mr. Harris. "For the most part they are thoroughly respectable people. You put them in the motor launch, land them on the bank, and persuade them not to return."

"And that's all there is to it?"

"Not quite. There are the betting shops that have to be looked after. It's a cash trade, so no bad debts to be collected. But it does happen, sometimes, that one of the managers gets ideas. Puts the money in his pocket, not in the books. When the auditors spot anything like that, you and Selby pay the manager a visit –"

"And hold him upside down until the money runs out of his pockets."

"You've got the idea exactly."

It was nearly a fortnight before they saw the major, who'd been away on business. When he summoned them to his office, they noticed that his right hand was in a glove. He said to the Crofts, "Sit down. Harris has been giving me a good report on you. You seem to handle the work very competently."

"Well, you see, Major, it's the sort of job we've done in rougher places than this."

"I'm sure the routine work gives you no trouble at all. What I've got for you now, is a special job."

Martin looked at him speculatively. He said, "Special job, special pay?"

"Naturally."

"If there's someone you want done, it'll come expensive. Selby and me are aiming to keep our noses clean just now."

"Not someone. Something. There's a dog I want to have destroyed. A dangerous and savage dog. It attacked me the other day."

"Is that why you're wearing that glove?"

"Yes." The major removed the glove and Martin looked curiously at the hand. The print of Rasselas' teeth showed clearly on the back. "He severed two tendons. I've got the use of the hand back now. But it was painful."

"I'll say. It sounds the wrong sort of animal to mix with."

"I wasn't suggesting you mix with it. I've been making some enquiries. The animal belongs to a Mr. Calder. He lives in a cottage, two miles from the village of Lamperdown in Kent. I suggest –"

"That's all right, Major," said Martin. "Leave all the details to Selby. He's the marksman. Less you know about it the better."

At six o'clock in the morning, three days later, Mr. Behrens'
telephone rang in his bedroom at the Old Rectory, Lamperdown. Mr. Behrens sat up in bed, couldn't find his glasses,
swore, found his glasses, picked up the receiver and said,
"Hullo."

"It's me," said Mr. Calder.

"I guessed as much. What do you want now?"

"A little help," said Mr. Calder. "There's a man holed up in an
oak tree on the edge of the wood opposite my front door."

"How do you know?"

"Rasselas spotted him. He refused to let me open the front
door, and he's been 'pointing' him for the last five minutes."

"But you haven't actually seen him?"

"No. When I used my binoculars, I did think I spotted a slight
movement. What I guess he's done is knock a hole in the hollow
part of the trunk, and fixed his rifle up inside. That'd give him a
rest for the gun, and good cover."

"He sounds like an old hand," said Mr. Behrens appreci-
atively.

"That's why you'll need to take him very carefully."

"*I'll* need."

"Well, I can't come out. They may have the back covered
too."

"I haven't had breakfast yet."

"It won't take long," said Mr. Calder. "You know the back
path through the wood. All you've got to do is follow it, and you'll
come out right behind this joker."

Selby had reconnoitred the place the evening before and had
fixed up his hide before it was light. He was wearing a camouflage
jacket. He was a careful and experienced sniper. The range he
had estimated as two hundred yards. The telescopic sight was
focussed on the front door of the cottage, about eighteen inches
above the ground. He was happy to wait. Sooner or later the door
would open.

He tensed. The door had swung half open – showing a black
gap. Who would fill it first? Man or dog?

The voice behind him said, "Don't turn round too quickly."

Selby froze.

"Leave that rifle exactly where it is, and come out. What I've got here is a twenty-bore shot gun. It's got such a comfortable spread that I couldn't possibly miss you. Come out, and stand up."

"I know you," said Selby stupidly.

"We met at Tilbury, and had a short talk. I remember warning you against peddling your brand of violence in this country."

"Violence," said Selby. "Who's talking about violence? I came here to shoot a fox."

"In some parts of the country, that's regarded as worse than murder. Have you got a licence for that rifle?"

"What's it got to do with you?"

Keep him talking.

"Look," he said, "let's be reasonable about this, shall we?"

Get one step closer, then duck under the barrel and collar him round the legs. Would the old coot have the nerve to pull the trigger?

"I didn't mean any harm to you. Right? It's just a job I'm doing for a friend. As a matter of fact, it isn't a fox. It's a dog. A nasty dangerous animal."

"I shouldn't say anything to upset him," said Mr. Behrens.

Selby heard a slight sound and swung round.

Rasselas was standing just behind him. His nose was a few inches from Selby's leg, and he was grinning.

"Listen," said Martin Croft. "You've *got* to get him out."

He was trying to speak reasonably, but there was an undercurrent in his voice which Major Porter found disturbing. He had employed rough people before, but never anyone of quite this calibre.

He said, "They can't pin anything on him except the licence business. It'll only be a fine. I'll see it's paid."

"You don't understand, do you? You're not trying to understand. The way we've always worked is not to get mixed up with the law. Once they convict you of *anything* you've got a record. They've got your prints. You're pegged."

"Selby ought to have thought of that before he let himself be caught."

"Let himself?" Martin's voice went up. "Let himself nothing. He was doing your dirty work. A private grudge job."

"I chose him because I thought he could do a simple job. Not make a mess of it."

"When you talk like that," said Martin slowly, "I don't like you."

The major was not a fool. He knew when he had gone too far. He said, "There's no point in quarrelling. That won't get us anywhere. Tell me what you want me to do, and if it's reasonable, I'll do it."

"What you've got to do, is buy Selby out."

"Buy him?"

"That's right. Slip what's necessary to the top policeman or judge, and kill the case."

"You can't do it. Not in this country."

"Let me tell you," said Martin, "I've bought my way out of trouble in every bloody country I've ever operated in. The only difference is, some cost more and some cost less. Don't tell me they're so snotty-nosed in this country they don't know folding money when they see it."

The major considered the matter. Then he said, "First things first. Your brother's been committed for trial by the magistrates. They refused him bail. But they don't have the last word. There's an appeal to a judge in chambers. We'll do that next Monday. Get the best lawyers – a QC if necessary. It'll take a bit of organising. We'll have to put up two sureties. You can be one. I'll be the other."

"Now you're talking," said Martin.

"Fortescue doubts if we can hold him," said Mr. Behrens.

Mr. Calder said, "As soon as he gets bail, he and his brother will skip. They've probably got half a dozen different passports, and as many ways out."

"Which is exactly what we want."

"It's not what I want," said Mr. Calder, coldly. "I want Major Porter."

"You're taking this very personally."

"You seem to forget that he arranged to have Rasselas murdered."

Later that day he had a word with Superintendent Hadow, with whom he was on friendly terms, having known him when he was attached to the Special Branch.

"Certainly I've heard stories about this club," said Hadow. "Crooked play, and people being roughed up when they wouldn't pay up. The trouble is, nobody's ever been prepared to stand up in court and say so."

"But you'd like to shut the place up?"

"Certainly. Give me an excuse to take away its gaming licence, or even its drink licence, and it'd be dead."

"A bad case of disorderly conduct? Fighting? Use of firearms? Would that do it?"

"If it was reported to us."

"Suppose you actually heard it. You've got two police launches which make regular patrols. Next Monday, suppose one of them put me quietly on shore at the end of the island? Let's say at half past eight. Then they both cruise downstream, turn round and come back timing their arrival for exactly nine o'clock."

"And you think," said the Superintendent, "that if they did that, they might, at nine o'clock, just by coincidence, hear enough evidence of disorderly conduct to justify them investigating?"

"I'm a great believer in coincidences," said Mr. Calder.

At half past four on Monday afternoon Martin Croft came out of the High Court, into the Strand. He was accompanied by his solicitor and Mr. Mortleman, QC. He said, "Well, what do we do next?"

"Better come back to my Chambers and talk about it," said Mr. Mortleman.

The Chambers were in Queen Elizabeth Buildings and overlooked the Embankment.

"I've never known an application for bail more strenuously resisted," said Mr. Mortleman. "The charge is trespass when armed with a rifle for which no licence had been obtained. In simpler terms, you might call it poaching. A first offence, too. We offer them two sound sureties, who are prepared to deposit the money in court if necessary. If it had been you alone, Mr. Croft, if you'll excuse me saying so, they might have hesitated. You're no longer, I believe, a national of this country, and have no fixed residence here. But Major Porter is quite different. He's a substantial citizen, with a house, and a business."

"Then why did the beak say no?"

"He didn't say no. He agreed to adjourn the matter for a week so that the police could complete their enquiries. He didn't like doing it. And I'm quite certain that when we do come up next week he'll grant the application."

"That means Selby's got to stay inside."

"But only for a week."

"As long as that's all it is," said Martin.

When he came out of the building two men were waiting for him. They introduced themselves as detective sergeants and invited Martin, very politely, to accompany them back to Scotland Yard.

"What's it all about?" said Martin.

"Superintendent Knox would like to have a word with you."

"And who the hell is Superintendent Knox?"

"He's in charge of the police proceedings against your brother."

Martin thought about it. It occurred to him that possibly a deal was going to be offered.

Superintendent Knox came straight to the point. He said, "In court this afternoon your Counsel informed the Judge that the owner of the Island Club, Major Porter, was prepared to stand bail for your brother."

"That's right."

"We thought you ought to know that he's changed his mind."

"He's done *what*?" said Martin, his face going first red and then white.

"The message from the local station simply says that he's withdrawn his offer of bail. We thought you ought to know this, so that you can go down at once and sort it out."

"I'll sort it out," said Martin thickly. He looked at his watch. If he could find a taxi, he could just make the seven-fifty from Paddington.

On a fine summer evening business started early at the Island Club. When Martin got there just before nine o'clock, dusk had fallen. The lights were shining from the glassed-in balcony which looked downstream, and there was already a sizeable crowd round the gaming tables.

Martin came storming into the club. Leo Harris took one look at his face, and said, "What's up, Martin? How did it go up in court?"

"Never mind about the bloody court," said Martin. "I want a word with the major."

"I'm not sure —"

"And I want it *now*."

Harris could see that it was not a moment for argument. He said curtly, "You'll find him in his office," and went back into the gaming room.

Mr. Calder, who had been standing unobtrusively by the door, saw his chance. The moment that Harris's back was turned, he slipped into the passage way and followed Martin. As he did so, he looked down at the watch on his wrist. It showed two minutes to nine. The timing could not have been more exact.

As he reached the door of the office he heard the first explosion of anger from Martin and the Major's voice, also raised in answer.

He opened the door a few inches. The two men in the room were too engrossed to take any notice.

"If the police hadn't blown the gaff, I'd never have known, would I? Or not until next week. Then what was supposed to happen?"

"You're talking nonsense."

"Who am I supposed to believe? Them or you? You double-crossing bastard."

"Personally," said Mr. Calder, "I should believe the police. They're much more reliable."

Both men swung round. Mr. Calder had shut the door carefully behind him and was standing there, holding a gun in his gloved right hand.

The major said, "Who the hell are you? That's my gun. Put it down and get out."

He seemed more angry than frightened.

Mr. Calder said, "We've met before. If I'd brought my dog along, I imagine you'd recognise him. He became quite – er – attached to you."

The major said, "Take the gun from him, Croft. He's not got the guts to use it."

"No?" said Mr. Calder. His head was cocked, and he seemed to be listening. "I shouldn't bank on it." He raised the gun and took careful aim.

The first shot went through the glass of the window overlooking the river. The next shot hit Martin Croft in the upper part of his right arm. The third shot went into the ceiling.

The next moment the whole place seemed to be full of policemen.

"Ah," said Martin. "I've been waiting for you to put in an appearance."

He was propped up in bed, in a private room in the Reading General Infirmary, and looked reasonably comfortable.

"I've brought you some grapes," said Mr. Calder. "And some news. The police are holding Major Porter, on a charge of shooting at you with intent to kill. It's a very serious charge. It's his gun, registered in his name. If there are any prints on it, they'll be his. And they found it in the drawer of his desk."

"Of course they did. I saw you put it there."

"I told them," said Mr. Calder, without taking any notice of this interruption, "that I was a guest at the club. That I happened to be in the corridor, heard the sound of a violent quarrel, followed by shots and looked in. You were slumped in a chair with the blood dripping down your arm onto the floor. I saw the major hurriedly stowing the gun away in the drawer of his desk. His idea being, no doubt, to hide it before the police burst in."

"And that's your story?"

"That's my story," agreed Mr. Calder. "I'd be interested to know what yours was."

"I haven't told my story yet," said Martin with a grin. "Too shocked to answer any questions. Anyway, as one professional to another, I thought I'd have a word with you first."

"And what made you think that I was a professional?"

"When a man takes care to hit you in the one spot that doesn't signify a lot, *and winks at you when he's doing it*, I say to myself, he's a pro. He's planning a set-up. So I wait to see what it is."

Mr. Calder said, "I'm relieved that I didn't misjudge you. Here it is. If you tell the same story as I do, the major's got no chance. He'll get seven to ten years. And I'll get the charge against your brother withdrawn."

"I thought they were all bloody incorruptible."

"So they are. But it's sometimes possible to persuade the authorities that a certain course would be in the public interest."

"You were taking a quite unjustifiable risk," said Mr. Fortescue coldly.

"No risk, really, sir. I understand people like Martin Croft perfectly. We've got a lot in common, actually. Offer him a bargain which looks sensible all round and he'll take it every time. Debit side, a bullet in the arm. Credit, his brother let off the hook. Credit for us, the major put away for a long stretch."

"What will Martin do when he comes out of hospital?"

"I understand that he and his brother have been offered a job by a gambling syndicate in Mexico. Martin has already accepted. He says he finds England too dangerous."

9

Early Warning

"The trouble with Intelligence work nowadays," said Mr. Calder, "is that it has become obsessed with gadgets. In the old days, an operator who was told to obtain some piece of information went to the most likely source and, by the appropriate expenditure of cash or cunning –"

"Force or fraud," agreed Mr. Behrens sleepily.

"Exactly. He brought home the bacon. But how does your modern operator work? He sits on his backside all day, in a huge room –" Mr. Calder demonstrated the size of the room by spreading his arms and knocked a tobacco jar off the table. Fortunately it fell on top of Rasselas who was asleep on the floor beside his chair. Rasselas looked reproachful. Mr. Calder replaced the jar.

"A huge room, crammed with machines. Screens linked to radar trackers and listening posts, wireless sets in touch with patrolling spy planes and submarines, and bank upon bank of computers to digest and analyse and classify the unceasing flow of incoming information, most of it pointless –"

"Talking of banks," said Mr. Behrens who was listening to one word in ten of what Mr. Calder was saying, "I had a call from Fortescue this morning. He wants to see me tomorrow."

"Both of us?"

"No. Just me."

"Good. Rasselas and I have other plans for tomorrow."

The great dog thumped his tail in agreement. The July weather was much too fine to make the thought of London attractive.

"He said that it was a problem which called for the intellectual outlook."

"It's probably a new and even more complicated computer," said Mr. Calder.

Mr. Fortescue received Mr. Behrens in his sanctum, invited him to be seated, and said, "A fortnight ago the Home Secretary got a letter from Professor Wilfred Pitt-Hammersley of St. Ambrose College, Cambridge. It stated that Sir Boris Wykes is not Sir Boris Wykes at all, but an East German spy called Stefan Thugutt."

When Mr. Behrens had absorbed this extraordinary announcement he said, "I suppose the Home Secretary does get a lot of letters from cranks and maniacs."

"Would you describe Pitt-Hammersley as a crank or a maniac?"

"It's at least ten years since I met him. We worked together on the Jansen Enquiry. I thought he was a little eccentric, but certainly not crazy. He must be getting on now –"

"Seventy-four next April. It is true that when senescence sets in at one of our great Universities, it is apt to be overlooked."

"You mean that a lot of the dons are a bit off-beat, so one more doesn't stick out?"

"Do you know Sir Boris?"

"I know of him, of course. He's the Government whizz-kid in charge of our Early Warning System."

"Wykes," said Mr. Fortescue, "is not a kid. He was born in 1927 and is now forty-three years old. He is one of the most eminent experts in the country in the fields of radar and applied electronics. At present he is in charge, under the Chiefs of Staff Air Defence Committee, of the chain of Early Warning Stations in East Anglia which we operate in conjunction with the Americans."

"Then I can understand the alarm and despondency if there did happen to be any truth in Pitt-Hammersley's statement. But there isn't, is there? I mean, Wykes must have been doubly vetted before he was allowed anywhere near such a vital slice of our defences."

"Trebly. Once in the normal way, when he came to this country from Poland. His real name, by the way, is Wycech. He changed it to Wykes when he was naturalised in 1952. He was positively vetted when he came into Government service three years later and rechecked under the special procedure when he started working in Early Warning in 1960."

"Special procedure? That means that someone actually went to Poland and talked to relatives and friends?"

"Dick Raphael did it. It was one of the last jobs he did for us. He went to Sweden and Poland."

"Sweden?"

"Wycech's father was a Polish Army officer. He was one of the victims of the massacre at Katyn. Boris was sixteen at the time. His mother smuggled him away to Sweden. He spent the rest of the war working in the Nor-Jensen factory. The boy showed promise, even at that age, as an engineer and a scientist. As soon as the war was over he went back to Poland to look for his family, which consisted, as he thought, of mother, two older brothers and two nephews. It seems they were in Warsaw at the time of the abortive Bor-Komarowski rising. The four boys were shot by the Germans. The mother died of disease or malnutrition in a camp soon afterwards. Boris' only surviving relative was in England. Squadron-Leader Andreas Wycech, holder of the Polish Order of Merit and the British DSO and DEF."

"I thought the name rang a bell," said Mr. Behrens. "Didn't he lead the low-level raid on St. Nazaire?"

"He was a very gallant man," said Mr. Fortescue. "He was shot down in the last months of the war, in Italy. When young Boris found he had no family left in Poland, and made up his mind to come to England – that was at the end of 1946 – he was well received on account of his uncle's services to this country. He was awarded a visiting studentship at Oxford and produced a thesis on electronic detection which impressed everyone so much with its practical possibilities that it was at once put on the Restricted Index. The rest of Boris' history is public knowledge. Apart from a two-year attachment at Columbia he had never been out of England since. Certainly he has never shown any desire to revisit Poland."

So far Mr. Fortescue had been speaking without reference to his papers. Now he cast an eye down on the dossier in front of him.

"What else? He's a bachelor. He lives in a converted farm-house near Thetford, which is convenient for his work. His only close friends are intellectuals and scientists. His hobbies are punting and canoeing. He has no known vices, except hard work."

"In fact," said Mr. Behrens, "his life is an open book for all to read. And has been for a quarter of a century. Can anyone be taking this seriously?"

"We thought it right to inform the Americans. They have assigned one of their men to the job, Ebenezer Thom, who happens, fortunately, to be an expert in linguistics."

"How on earth does linguistics come into it?"

"Pitt-Hammersley is also a linguistics man. He holds the Dexter Chair of English Language and Literature and has managed to combine it with a study of the modern science of lingual interpretation."

"By computer?"

"Using a computer, certainly. Why?"

"Just a thought," said Mr. Behrens. "Please go on."

"In 1938 Pitt-Hammersley was a tutor at St. Ambrose, and this East German boy, Stefan Thugutt, studied under him. Pitt-Hammersley was so impressed by the quality of his work that he kept copies of everything Stefan wrote. The other day, he happened to be reading a collection of the scientific papers of Sir Boris Wykes, and says that he was immediately struck by certain stylistic and constructional similarities between them and the work of young Stefan. He submitted both sets of documents to a full computerised analysis, and decided that, without any doubt they came from the same hand."

"Although one lot of papers was written more than thirty years before the other."

"Your basic linguistic periphrases are, I understand, like your finger-prints. Once formed, they don't change with age."

"Didn't I read somewhere the other day that these linguistic boys had decided that Shakespeare didn't write half his own plays?"

"There are cranks at work in every scientific discipline," said Mr. Fortescue. "I have mentioned your name to the Warden, Dr. Lovell. He is very willing to lodge you at the college. Being vacation time there will not be many dons or students in residence. Professor Thom is there already. He will give you any necessary technical help. I understand, by the way, that he likes to be addressed as Ben."

Mr. Behrens was as nearly speechless as he had ever found himself in his dealings with Mr. Fortescue. He said, "You want me to go and stay at St. Ambrose's so that I can decide whether one of the senior dons is cuckoo?"

"That is, roughly, the position," agreed Mr. Fortescue blandly. "It is not, of course, the only step we are taking in the matter. I intend to send one of our men to Sweden and Poland to recheck Raphael's work."

"Send Calder," said Mr. Behrens. "He was telling me only yesterday that in *real* intelligence work legs were more useful than computers."

Dinner at the High Table had been agreeable, and six of them were now gathered companionably in the Warden's room cracking walnuts and sampling his port and madeira. On the Warden's right sat the massive Mrs. Hebrang, Professor of Far Eastern Languages; on his left Ebenezer Thom, a solemn Bostonian. On Mr. Behrens' right was the stooping, grey-haired figure of Professor Pitt-Hammersley, and opposite him Michael Mitos, bald and cheerful and understood to specialise in Eastern European languages.

The conversation, so far, had not been as alarming as Mr. Behrens had feared. It had dealt with the ballistics of fast bowling, the Government commission on monopolies, the comparative power of Trade Unions in England and America, on which Ben Thom had had some enlightening comments to make, and on fishing.

Michael Mitos was talking about fishing now. He said, "It has been ruined by your English upper classes with their passion for exercise. Fishing is intended by nature to be a static pursuit. You visualise the heron at the pool, motionless as the branch of an old tree? Only the English could have turned it into a game, where you race up and down the stream, hurling in a fly with the action of an over-arm bowler –"

"You mean that you fish with *bait*?" said the Warden. He sounded slightly horrified.

"Certainly, Warden. Sometimes a worm. Sometimes a piece of fat bacon. I sit on the landing stage at the foot of my garden. I watch the river flowing by. I think long thoughts about life. Occasionally a fish attaches itself to my hook. I reel it in, cook it and eat it."

"I agree," said Mrs. Hebrang, "that fishing bores, with their pet flies, are almost as bad as golf bores with their pet clubs, but that is not a criticism of the sport. It is a criticism of their own limited mentality."

Mr. Behrens had been devoting only half of his mind to the conversation. The other half was trying to work out how soon he could organise a private talk with Pitt-Hammersley without it appearing too obvious to the others. He was spared the trouble. As he rose to go Pitt-Hammersley said, "We were talking about Government commissions. You remember that affair we were engaged in together, Behrens?"

"The Jansen Enquiry?"

"Yes. I always wondered if anyone took any steps to implement our recommendations."

"In a number of details only, I believe."

"Perhaps you could join me in my room for a night-cap. I wouldn't want to bore everyone with such a specialised topic. Right? Come along then."

Pitt-Hammersley led the way to his room, lit the gas fire, emptied a chair by escalading a pile of books which were on it onto the floor, drew up a second chair and invited his guest to be seated. Then he said, "Of course, you don't want to talk about Jansen. What a silly man he was! You want to talk about my letter."

"Then the Warden has told you why I'm here?"

"No. But you're more famous than you think you are. I had dinner not long ago at the Dons-in-London, and Sands-Douglas pointed you out to me. I suppose the Home Secretary has had you sent down to see if I'm mad." Pitt-Hammersley emitted a cackle. "I've known Willie since he was up here himself. That was when he came back from the war. I've never had a high opinion of his mental powers, but I suppose a thick skin is more use in politics than a good brain. Right?"

Mr. Behrens said, "I should imagine that a certain mental agility is necessary if you are to survive in politics." He was glad that he was spared having to deal with Pitt-Hammersley's opening gambit. "Perhaps our best starting point would be if you could tell me something about Thugutt."

"Stefan, yes. For a young man he had an extraordinarily alert intelligence. I would suggest a subject. Not necessarily a scientific subject. He would write a paper on it. Anything I cared to suggest. It became almost a game between us. Chess? Claret? Incest? Breakfast foods? It was good practice for his English which was remarkably good already, although there were occasional Teutonic modes of thought which gave him away. You remember how dear old Quiller-Couch used to impress on his students the desirability of using Anglo-Saxon words in preference to their Romance equivalents. With Stefan it was the other way round. The hard, middle-German derivatives were natural to him. He felt he had to introduce occasional French stocks to decorate his prose. Like a bachelor buying a bunch of flowers to decorate his study, and not knowing quite how to arrange them."

"And it was these quirks of style which you identified in the writings of Sir Boris Wykes?"

"Not that alone. Good heavens no. My dear boy, linguistics isn't guess-work. It's a science."

"Most science is guess-work," said Mr. Behrens.

Pitt-Hammersley cocked his head on one side like an old turkey, and then said, "That is either a very sensible or a very stupid remark. Scientific discovery *starts* as guess-work. The rest of it is a series of co-ordinated efforts to limit alternative explanations for an observed phenomenon. When they have all been eliminated you have established a sequence of cause and effect."

Mr. Behrens was saved from having to answer this by the gas fire, which gave a soft 'pop' and went out. Pitt-Hammersley got to his feet, in the three or four distinct movements into which an old man divides a simple physical effort, turned the fire off, fed a coin into the meter and relit the fire.

"A sequence of cause and effect," said Mr. Behrens. "No money. No gas. No gas, no fire."

"Ah! but have you eliminated all the alternatives? There might have been air in the pipe. Eh? It happens sometimes. But in this case, I fancy you were right."

"You were saying that there are other similarities. Enough of them to establish a scientific correlation?"

"Enough of them to establish a strong *presumption*. A marked similarity of vocabulary. The computer identified one hundred and twenty-five comparatively uncommon words in both samples. But more conclusive than this was the similarity of rhythm. Even an inexpert musician would not confuse the rhythms of Bach and Mozart, would they now?"

"No, but he might confuse the rhythms of Bach and someone who was trying to imitate Bach."

"Perhaps. But people who write are unconscious of their own rhythm. There is therefore no question of deliberate imitation."

"I must accept your word for it," said Mr. Behrens. He was beginning to feel sleepy. "Tell me. What happened to Thugutt?"

"In 1939 when the authorities belatedly discovered that he was a German, he was interned. Typical bureaucratic stupidity. It turned a valuable friend into a dangerous enemy. Later he was sent over to Canada. The Canadian authorities allowed him to continue his studies at Toronto. It was there that he first seriously took up the study of electronics."

"And after the war?"

"I can tell you that he did not return here. I believe he went back to his home in East Germany and continued his studies, for a time, at Cracow University."

"A lot of East Germany," said Mr. Behrens thoughtfully, "had by that time been incorporated into Poland. If Thugutt *was* back there in 1946, he and Wycech *could* have met. I mean, the times and place roughly correspond."

Pitt-Hammersley looked at him over the top of his glasses. "So," he said, "I am not an old lunatic after all. Hey?"

"That's just what I'd like to be sure about," said Mr. Behrens. But this was to himself, when he was getting into bed.

★

"It was twenty-five years ago," agreed Mr. Calder, "but I sometimes find it easier to remember things twenty-five years ago than things which happened last week."

"That is true," said Olav Vinström. "Alas, the older we get the truer it becomes."

It had taken Mr. Calder two days of hard work to find Olav. There had been no difficulty about his initial contacts. His credentials had secured him co-operation from the General Director of the Nor-Jensen factory, but it was not the heads of the outfit that he wanted. They had been the people Dick Raphael had talked to in 1960. The General Director remembered Raphael. He had produced a photograph of Wycech and it had been compared with the photograph on his temporary identity card which had been filed away in the archives. The resemblance was reasonable enough. But it was not the photograph alone. Wycech – or Wykes, as he by then was – had furnished Raphael with a great number of names and nicknames, personal recollections and factory gossip, all of which Raphael had quickly checked.

Too quickly, perhaps, thought Mr. Calder. But in 1960 Raphael had been a sick man. He had died less than a year later. Was that why he had only spent one morning in Oslo and half a day in Warsaw? When the grey shadow is creeping up, other matters may become relatively less important.

What Mr. Calder had been looking for was a man who had worked with Wycech. Not necessarily alongside him, but in the same department. In the end he had found Olav Vinström. And Vinström had given him the lead he wanted.

"A nice boy, Boris," he said. "A good worker. He and his friend, Tadeus Rek. Both bright, intelligent lads."

"Tadeus was a close friend?"

"Certainly. They were both exiles from Poland. Boys of about the same age. Tadeus was a Danziger. I heard that he had gone back and was working in the shipyard."

Twenty-four hours later Mr. Calder was talking to Colonel Mauger, British Military Attaché at Warsaw, and an old friend. The colonel said, "I've made a few enquiries. Rek is certainly alive. Very much so."

"You mean that he's an important man now?"

"Not in the sense of being a prominent business man or politician. Far from it. On the face of it, he is no more than a workman. The sort of position he occupies in the shipyard would be called a chief shop steward. That is to say, it would be if they had unions and shop stewards. He is referred to as a 'man of confidence'. The man the management go to if they want rows settled quietly."

"Can you tell me anything more about him?"

"A little. He and Boris Wycech both came back from Sweden early in 1946, no doubt full of patriotism and anti-Russian feeling. By that time the old resistance fighters were split. One part of them wanted to parade the streets and drum up enthusiasm. They were easy meat for the Russians. The others went underground, and young Tadeus went with them. They had learned their lesson from Russian history. Keep your heads down and work through the workers. They grow in power every year. If ever there is a serious strike in Poland you can be sure the NSZ, as they are called, will be behind it."

"And Tadeus is one of their leaders?"

"Impossible to say. I do know that he has a personal reason to hate the Russians. In 1946 his brother was shot for his part in organising the pro-Anders revolt at Cracow University."

There had been something in Mr. Behrens' report about Cracow University. Mr. Calder groped for it, but lost it. He said, "Can you put me in touch with someone in Danzig who could arrange a meeting for me with Rek?"

"Do what I can," said Mauger. "Don't expect miracles. Telephone me the name of your hotel when you get fixed up. May take some time."

"In this particular case," said Mr. Calder, "time is not important."

It was in the evening, three days later, when Mr. Calder was debating whether he would dine out or sample the *table d'hôte* of the modest quayside hotel where he was lodging that the car drove up and a thickset man got out and said, "Herr Kaldor?"

"I expect that's me," said Mr. Calder. "Who are you?" His own Polish was elementary, and he normally spoke in German, which he found most Poles understood.

"From Tadeus," said the man.

"Splendid," said Mr. Calder. He was motioned into the front seat beside the driver. The thickset man climbed into the back beside a second man who was already sitting there. All three men wore dark, nondescript suits which might have indicated anything from a clerk to a workman in his best. All three, to Mr. Calder's practised eye, looked tough.

The car threaded its way through the tiny, cobbled streets around the waterfront, branching off finally into one so narrow that the overhanging roofs of the houses seemed to be propping each other up. The car stopped. The two men at the back got out, motioning sharply to Mr. Calder to follow. The driver, too, had climbed out and was close behind him. Mr. Calder had an uncomfortable feeling that he was a prisoner under escort.

Down a passage, through a side door, up a flight of steps and into a back room. The only window was shuttered. There was a table, with half a dozen chairs round it, but no other furniture. Behind the table sat a black-haired, hook-nose man in his middle forties. There were other men in the background, but he was the only one seated. He radiated the sort of authority which clothes a man who has fought a hard road to the top.

Mr. Calder stepped forward, held out his hand, and said, "Tadeus Rek?"

The hand was ignored. The man said, "That is my name. What is your name? Your real name, I mean of course. Perhaps you have several names, just as you seem to have several languages."

"My name is Calder."

Out of the corner of his eye he noted one of the men at the far end of the room stirring. Mr. Calder had an impression of snow-white hair, a brown face and a broken nose. A distant recollection. He turned his attention to Rek.

Rek said, "You must excuse my caution. The man who contacted me on your behalf is known to be a police spy."

"I'm sorry," said Mr. Calder. "He was the only contact available."

"I trust that your explanation for intruding on me will be satisfactory. The last man who forced his attentions on us, unhappily turned out also to be a police spy. What became of him in the end, Peter?"

The man who had brought Mr. Calder in the car said, speaking also in German, "He had an accident. He slipped and fell into the dock. Unhappily he broke both arms when falling. Not being able to swim, he drowned."

"I trust –" said Mr. Calder. But before he could say any more the white-haired man had come up to the table. He peered into Mr. Calder's face, then seized him and kissed him on both cheeks.

He said, "This is no Russian spy, Tadeus. It is a very old friend. An Englishman. A splendid person. He helped me to murder three Gestapo agents in Albania in 1943."

"One of the servants," said Mr. Behrens, "making a final round of the college, smelled gas coming from Pitt-Hammersley's sitting-room. He went in and managed to get a window open. The door to the adjoining bedroom was open. Pitt-Hammersley was in bed. They tried everything, but it was no good. So that, I'm afraid, is really the end of it."

"Why?" said Mr. Fortescue sharply.

"Because of what was found on his table."

"A confession?"

"No, no. Nothing like that. It was a paper he must have been working on for the last few months. His magnum opus, you might say. He'd just that moment finished it. Then, no doubt he pottered off to bed leaving the gas fire on, and it blew out. Air in the pipe. He told me that happened sometimes."

"But –" said Mr. Fortescue.

"It was the paper," said Mr. Behrens unhappily. "He has proved, using the most ultra-scientific modern computerised linguistic methods that Boswell didn't exist."

"If he didn't exist, who –?"

"Johnson *was* Boswell. He wrote his own biography."

"But that's mad," said Mr. Fortescue. "Quite apart from his life of Johnson, Boswell wrote other works. He was a known historical character. There are dozens of independent witnesses to his existence."

"Quite so."

"You mean that this paper proves that Pitt-Hammersley was mad?"

"Not exactly. But it does mean that if his version of linguistics is capable of producing a result like this, then one can surely place no reliance at all on his identification of Wycech with Thugutt."

"I see what you mean," said Mr. Fortescue. He was unaccountably angry. "It also means that his death may have been accidental."

"It never occurred to me that it could have been anything else," said Mr. Behrens. "I agree that it would have been an easy way of finishing off the old man. Anyone could have gone along when he was asleep and turned the gas on. Doors are rarely locked in a place like that."

"Exactly."

"Yes. But we're arguing in a circle. If Wykes really was a mole it would have made sense to remove *and* discredit the man who was threatening to expose him. But we've just concluded that he isn't."

The telephone on Mr. Fortescue's desk purred. He lifted the receiver, said, "No. I'm busy. Who? Oh, well perhaps you'd better put him through."

He listened in silence for some minutes while the voice at the other end spoke. Then he said, "All right, Ben. He's here with me. I'll tell him." And to Mr. Behrens, "That was Thom. He has now had a chance to analyse the paper which was found on Pitt-Hammersley's table, by the most modern ultra-scientific methods, and has concluded that Pitt-Hammersley didn't write it. I think you'd better get back to Cambridge."

"Maybe the same ultra-scientific methods will tell us who *did* write it," said Mr. Behrens hopefully.

"Certainly not," said Thom. "To do that I'd have to have lengthy samples of the output of everyone here. What I was able to do without difficulty was to spot that the Boswell paper was a clumsy fraud. Linguistics may not be an exact science, but it will show up a phoney right enough. Anyway, I think it's clear who wrote it. We've got a certain amount of dope back in Washington on this man Mitos. It was partly to keep an eye on him that I came over here."

"Then," said Mr. Behrens, who was slowly trying to absorb this new idea, "you think that there *is* something in Pitt-Hammersley's theory, and that Mitos was instructed to remove him and throw ridicule on it at the same time."

"There's no certainty about it, but that eminent functionary who watches over our incomings and outgoings –"

"The hall-porter."

"That's the joker. He sleeps over the gate. He tells me he heard Mitos' car driving off at about one in the morning. He thought it was unusual, because he's never known him stay so late."

"What the devil are we going to do about it?" said Mr. Behrens. He felt curiously helpless.

"I agree with your invocation of the devil," said Professor Thom, "because it's a diabolical situation. All that we have to go on so far is surmise and guess-work. But let's add two and two together for a moment and see where it gets us. Suppose Wykes is a plant. He'd be a very valuable plant. He'd need watering and tending. He'd also need a handy method of getting information back to base. Now Mitos has a bungalow on the river bank, three or four miles below Cambridge. He sits on his landing stage in the evening, fishing. Wykes is a punting and canoeing enthusiast. You follow what I'm thinking?"

"I follow you completely," said Mr. Behrens. "But if we're going to move against Mitos, on the sort of information we've got, we're going to need a clearance from higher-up."

"Right from the top," said Thom. "But if you figure on their reactions when they think that there's now a chance – an outside chance, I grant you – that the Russians have managed to get their hands on a big slice of the East-West Early Warning System, I would surmise that the gloves will be off and Queensberry Rules will be discarded."

"I must apologise," said Tadeus Rek, "for your somewhat dramatic reception, but we are well aware that the authorities are becoming frightened of our influence, and would give much to discredit us. In particular, by some purported involvement in espionage. Now that I understand what you want, I naturally acquit you of any such intentions. What you have told me is a curious story. It might be true."

"How well did you know Boris Wycech?"

"For two years, as boys, in Sweden. We had been very close. When we came back here, we both obtained places at the University at Cracow. Stefan Thugutt, fresh back from internment in Canada, was there too. Boris joined with enthusiasm in all the patriotic anti-Russian demonstrations. So did my brother. Me, I was not happy. I was younger then, and inexperienced, but not stupid. A riot was planned in favour of our war hero, General Anders. I saw trouble coming. I removed myself from the University, and took a job as a workman. The riot gave the Russians' puppet Radkiewiz and his political police, the chance they wanted. Thugutt acted as spy and *agent provocateur*. I learned of that later, after the riot had been stamped on, and the leaders shot, my brother among them. As you may imagine, when I learned of this, I took all possible steps to trace Thugutt. But he and Wycech had both disappeared. It was astonishing. It was as though they had never existed."

"One possible explanation would be, wouldn't it," said Mr. Calder slowly, "that Russian Intelligence saw an opportunity of carrying out one of their favourite substitution tricks? There was the superficial resemblance between the two young men, and the fact that their studies had been in the same field. Add to that the fact that all of Wycech's family were dead. His uncle's reputation would ensure his substitute a friendly reception in England. All that was necessary was to extract from Wycech every detail of his past, and to prime Thugutt with this background information. Wycech is obliterated. Thugutt comes to England, changes his name to Wykes, and lives quietly for at least fifteen years before he starts to move into a sensitive job. The chances of discovery would become smaller every year."

"As you say, it is possible. I suppose that I am the one person who could make the matter a certainty."

"Would you be willing to help? I could make all arrangements very quickly. And of course, at no expense to you."

"My dear Mr. Calder, if this man should turn out, in fact, to be

Stefan Thugutt, the pleasure of meeting him again would be an ample reward in itself."

The smile which accompanied these words was one of the coldest, thought Mr. Calder, that he had ever seen, on a human face.

"I had a message last night from my chief," said Mr. Behrens.

He and Ben Thom were sitting together, after breakfast, on a bench in the Warden's private garden. Bees hummed among the riot of July flowers in the deep borders. Pigeons cooed. The buttery cat strolled across the smooth shaven lawn, keeping one eye on the pigeons.

"Special Branch are picking up Mitos at his bungalow this morning and taking him to London. He has been told that some question has arisen over his papers. Since he is not operating under diplomatic cover, but is here as a private citizen, he was unable to object. The whole thing has been arranged to give me a chance to make a very careful search of the premises."

"You and me," said Thom.

"Really, Ben. There's no need –"

"You're not keeping me out of it. After all this cerebral work, a little activity will be a welcome change."

"All right," said Mr. Behrens. "If that's how you feel about it I'd be glad of your company. Can you pick a lock?"

"I majored in lock picking. We'll go in my car."

"No. We'll go by boat. Much the least conspicuous way. A two-oar skiff should get us there in an hour."

Mr. Behrens had over-estimated his skill as an oarsman but it was well before midday when he tied up the boat under a willow tree fifty yards short of the Mitos bungalow.

"On foot from here," said Mr. Behrens. "We can keep under cover until we get to the garden."

The bungalow was an isolated one, approached on the landward side by a long, dusty side road. The lawn sloped down to the river. On the other side the bank was wild and overgrown.

"A perfect pitch for a contact job," said Thom. They walked up the path together. They were twenty yards from the building when Mr. Behrens stopped.

"I'm not absolutely certain," said Mr. Behrens, "but I did think I saw the curtain in that window move a fraction."

"Then clearly the first thing to do," said Thom, "is to ring the bell. If there's someone there, they answer the door and we're two boat-trippers who forgot to bring any water for their kettle, and don't trust river water. OK?"

"That seems sound," said Mr. Behrens.

The back of the bungalow was a glassed-in verandah. There was no bell by the door but there was a knocker. Mr. Behrens executed a lengthy and lively tattoo on it. Nothing happened.

Professor Thom was already busy with a selection of thin steel spikes. Some had spatulate tips, some ended in hooks. He handled them with the familiarity and firmness of a surgeon. The lock was evidently more complicated than he had expected. "A curious lock to find on the back door of an innocent bungalow," he said to Mr. Behrens. In three minutes he had it opened and they stepped inside.

The verandah was full of stored heat and silence. A step led up to an inner door. This was unlocked. Mr. Behrens opened it, stepped inside and stopped.

"Something wrong?" said Professor Thom.

"Not really," said Mr. Behrens.

Mr. Calder was seated on the sofa with a stranger beside him.

"Allow me to introduce my friend," said Mr. Calder. "Tadeus Rek, of Danzig. Mr. Behrens. And –?"

"Professor Ebenezer Thom of Columbia University."

"I think," said Mr. Calder a little later, "that it's time we joined up the two sides of this affair. Tadeus has been very useful to us already. He identified Michael Mitos, from a photograph, as a minor functionary in Russian Intelligence. An unimportant intellectual who was probably blackmailed into coming to England. He is not a very brave man. His credentials are being examined. The supposition is that he was acting as link-man to someone much more important."

"That someone," said Mr. Behrens, "being Sir Boris Wykes."

"That we shall shortly find out. A message has been conveyed to a certain quarter – I said that Mitos was not very brave. If what we suspect is correct, it should result in someone attempting to contact Mitos."

"Coming here, you mean?" said Professor Thom. There was a look in his eye which seemed to suggest that further activity would not be displeasing to him.

"That is the supposition. The message stressed that a contact was urgent, but it might not be effective before tomorrow. Fortunately there is plenty of food in the house. However, I suggest" – he was looking at Mr. Behrens as he said this – "that a reception committee of four might be excessive."

"I think you're right," said Mr. Behrens slowly. "Besides, Ben, we must bear in mind we have hired our boat by the hour. A substantial monetary penalty will be exacted if we keep it out over night."

"Very well," said Professor Thom reluctantly. "If that's what you think would be best."

Rek said, with the justifiable pride of one employing a colloquialism in a foreign tongue, "That's the way the cookie crumbles, Professor."

Sir Boris Wykes, paddling his canoe expertly down the smooth reaches of the Cam, was not unduly alarmed. Mitos was inclined to panic. He had asked, more than once, for him to be replaced by a more reliable operator but it had been difficult to find anyone with the precise qualifications.

The message had reached him, through established channels, and verified by the current code-word, at five o'clock on the previous afternoon. He gathered that it was something to do with Mitos' papers. It had mentioned urgency. Wykes was too old a hand to be hurried.

Fortunately he had already mentioned to one or two friends that he was planning to take a boat out on the following afternoon and he had adhered to this timetable.

As he came round the bend he saw the familiar figure seated on the landing-stage, a fishing rod in his hand and the same floppy old sunhat on his head. So! The authorities had *not* detained Mitos. Another false alarm.

Three swift strokes with the paddle drove the canoe towards the stage. The fisherman looked up.

A moment of paralysed shock.

The man was a stranger. Or was he? He was certainly not Mitos.

"My name is Rek," said the fisherman. "Tadeus Rek." One brown and muscular hand had grasped the edge of the canoe. "We met once or twice, no more I think, in 1946 at Cracow. On the other hand, you knew my brother, Andreas, rather well. It was on account of your information that he was shot. That makes what we have to do much easier."

Wykes fended off wildly from the landing stage, hitting at Rek's hand with the paddle. It was an ineffective gesture. Mr. Calder had come up behind him, and was holding the other end of the canoe firmly.

"First Pitt-Hammersley," said the Warden. "Now Mitos. We are the playthings of fate." He was alone in his study with Mr. Behrens.

"I learn this morning that the authorities have not only detained Mitos, they have refused to allow him out of custody pending deportation. Is this a police state? Is there nothing we can do?"

"You could appeal to the Home Secretary," said Mr. Behrens, but he said it without much confidence.

The Warden's eye fell on the morning paper that Mr. Behrens had put down. "Boating Tragedy," said the headline, "Eminent Scientist Feared Drowned. A canoe, which had been hired on the previous afternoon by Sir Boris Wykes, the Government scientist in charge of the East Coast Early Warning System, was found this morning floating bottom up in the Cam five miles below Cambridge. The body of the canoeist has not been recovered. That stretch of the river is notorious for its underwater weed bed which is known to have trapped quite strong swimmers. The river above the point where the canoe was found is being dragged."

Mr. Behrens thought it very unlikely that the body would be recovered.

"I shall have to put up a notice," the Warden made a note on his pad, "urging students not to go boating single-handed. I've done so before, but young people take little notice of warnings." He reverted to his original grievance. "I suppose," he said to Mr. Behrens, "that you wouldn't care – just as a temporary measure – to take over Pitt-Hammersley's lectures? I understand you are something of an expert on the subjects that he covered."

"I'm afraid not, Warden," said Mr. Behrens. "I'd like to help, but I've come to the reluctant conclusion that the science of linguistics is too dangerous to be meddled with by amateurs."

10

The Killing of Michael Finnegan

"They burned him to death," said Elfe. He said it without any attempt to soften the meaning of what he was saying. "He was almost certainly alive when they dumped him in the car and set fire to it."

Deputy Assistant Commissioner Elfe had a long, sad face and grey hair. In the twenty years that he had been head of the Special Branch he had seen more brutality, more treachery, more fanaticism, more hatred than had any of his predecessors in war or in peace. Twice he had tried to retire, and twice had been persuaded to stay.

"He couldn't have put up much of a fight," said Mr. Calder, "only having one arm and one and a half legs."

They were talking about Michael Finnegan, whose charred carcass had been found in a burnt-out stolen car in one of the lonelier parts of Hampstead Heath. Finnegan had been a lieutenant in the Marines until he had blown off his right arm and parts of his right leg whilst defusing a new type of anti-personnel mine. During his long convalescence his wife Sheilagh had held the home together, supplementing Michael's disability pension by working as a secretary. Then Finnegan had taught himself to write left-handed, and had gained a reputation, and a reasonable amount of cash for his articles; first only in service journals, but later in the national press, where he had constituted himself a commentator on men and affairs.

"It's odd," as Mr. Behrens once observed, "you'd think that he'd be a militant chauvinist. Actually he seems to be a moderate and a pacifist. It was Finnegan who started arguing that we ought to withdraw our troops from Ireland. That was long before the IRA made it one of the main planks in their platform."

"You can never tell how a serious injury will affect a man," said

Mr. Calder. This was, of course, before he had become professionally involved with Michael Finnegan.

"For the last year you've been acting as his runner, haven't you?" said Elfe. "You must have got to know him well."

"Him and his wife," said Mr. Calder. "They were a great couple." He thought about the unremarkable house at Banstead with its tiny flower garden in front and its rather larger kitchen garden at the back, both of which Michael Finnegan tended one-armed, hobbling down between whiles for a pint at the local. A respected man with many friends, and acquaintances, none of whom knew that he was playing a lonely, patient, dangerous game. His articles in the papers, his casual contacts, letters to old friends in Ireland, conversations with new friends in the pub, all had been slanted towards a predetermined end.

The fact was that the shape of the IRA's activities in England was changing, a change which had been forced on them by the systematic penetration of their English groups. Now, when an act of terrorism was planned, the operators came from Ireland to carry it out, departing as soon as it was done. They travelled a roundabout route, via Morocco or Tunis, entering England from France or Belgium and returning by the same way. Explosives, detonators and other material for the job came separately, and in advance. Their one essential requirement was an operational base where materials could be stored and the operators could lodge for the few days needed for the job.

It was to hold out his house as such a safe base that every move in Michael Finnegan's life had been planned.

"We agreed," said Mr. Calder, "that as far as possible, Michael should have no direct contacts of any sort with the security forces. What the Department did was to lease a house which had a good view, from its front windows, of Michael's back gate. They installed one of their pensioners in it, old Mrs. Lovelock –"

"Minnie Lovelock?" said Elfe. "She used to type for me forty years ago. I was terrified of her, even then."

"All she had to do was to keep Michael's kitchen window sill under observation at certain hours. There was a simple code of signals. A flower pot meant the arrival of explosives or arms. One or more milk bottles signalled the arrival of that number of operators. And the house gave us one further advantage. Minnie put it about that she had sublet a room on the first floor to a commercial gentleman who kept his samples there, and occasionally put up there for the night. For the last year the commercial gent was me. I was able to slip out, after dark, up the garden path and in at the back door. I tried to go at least once a month. My ostensible job was to collect any information Michael might have for us. In fact, I believe my visits kept him sane. We used to talk for hours. He liked to hear the gossip, all about the inter-departmental feuds, and funny stories about the Minister."

"And about the head of the Special Branch?"

"Oh, certainly. He particularly enjoyed the story of how two of your men tried to arrest each other."

Elfe grunted and said, "Go on."

"And there was one further advantage. Michael had a key of this room. In a serious emergency he could deposit a message – after dark, of course – or even use it as an escape hatch for Sheilagh and himself."

"Did his wife know what he was up to?"

"She had to be told something, if only to explain my visits. Our cover story was that Michael was gathering information about subversion in the docks. This was plausible, as he'd done an Intelligence job in the Marines. She may have suspected that it was more than that. She never interfered. She's a grand girl."

Elfe said, "Yes." And after a pause, "Yes. That's really what I wanted to tell you. I've had a word with your chief. He agrees with me. This is a job we can't use you in."

"Oh," said Mr. Calder coldly. "Why not?"

"Because you'd feel yourself personally involved. You'd be unable to be sufficiently dispassionate about it. You knew Finnegan and his wife far too well."

Mr. Calder thought about that. If Fortescue had backed the prohibition it would be little use kicking. He said, "I suppose we *are* doing something about it."

"Of course. Superintendent Outram and Sergeant Fallows are handling it. They're both members of the AT squad, and very capable operators."

"I know Tom Outram," said Mr. Calder. "He's a sound man.

I'll promise not to get under his feet. But I'm already marginally involved. If he wants to question Sheilagh he'll have to do it at my cottage. I moved her straight down there as soon as I heard the news. Gave her a strong sleeping pill and put her to bed."

"They wondered where she'd disappeared to. I'll tell them she's living with you."

"If you put it quite like that," said Mr. Calder, "it might be misunderstood. She's being chaperoned, by Rasselas."

"I think," said Superintendent Outram, "that we'd better see Mrs. Finnegan alone. That is, if you don't mind."

He and Sergeant Fallows had driven out to Mr. Calder's cottage, which was built on a shoulder of the North Downs above Lamperdown in Kent.

"I don't mind," said Mr. Calder. "But you'll have to look out for Rasselas."

"Your dog?"

"Yes. Mrs. Finnegan's still in a state of shock, and Rasselas is very worried about it. The postman said something sharp to her – not meaning any harm at all – and he went for him. Luckily I was there and I was able to stop him."

"Couldn't we see her without Rasselas?"

"I wouldn't care to try and shift him."

Outram thought about it. Then he said, "Then I think you'd better sit in with us."

"I think that might be wise," said Mr. Calder gravely.

Sheilagh Finnegan had black hair and a white face out of which looked eyes of startling Irish blue. Her mouth was thin and tight and angry. It was clear that she was under stress. When Outram and Fallows came in she took one look at them and jerked as though an electric shock had gone through her.

Rasselas, who was stretched out on the floor beside her, raised his head and regarded the two men thoughtfully.

"Just like he was measuring us for a coffin," said Fallows afterwards.

Mr. Calder sat on the sofa, and put one hand on the dog's head.

It took Outram fifteen minutes of patient, low-keyed questioning to discover that Mrs. Finnegan could tell him very little. Her husband, she said, had suggested that she needed a break, and had arranged for her to spend a week in a small private hotel at Folkestone. She wasn't sorry to agree because she hadn't had a real holiday in the last three or four years.

Outram nodded sympathetically. Had the holiday been fixed suddenly? Out of the blue, like? Sheilagh gave more attention to this than she had to some of the earlier questions. She said, "We'd often talked about it before. Michael knew I had friends at Folkestone."

"But on this occasion it was your husband who suggested it? How long before you left?"

"Two or three days."

"Then it *was* fairly sudden."

"Fairly sudden, yes."

"Did he give any particular reason? Had he had an unexpected message? Something like that."

"He didn't say anything about a message. I wouldn't have known about it, anyway. I was out at work all day."

Outram said, "Yes, of course."

There was nothing much more she could tell them. A quarter of an hour later the two men drove off. As their car turned down the hill they passed Mr. Behrens, who was walking up from Lamperdown. Mr. Behrens waved to the superintendent.

"Looks a genial old cove," said Sergeant Fallows.

"That's what he looks like," agreed Outram.

When Mr. Behrens reached the cottage he found Mr. Calder and Sheilagh making coffee in the kitchen. They added a third cup to the tray and carried it back to the sitting room where Rasselas was apparently asleep. By contrast with what had gone before it was a relaxed and peaceful scene.

Mr. Calder tried the coffee, found it still too hot, put the cup carefully back on its saucer, and said, "Why were you holding out on the superintendent?"

"How did you know I was holding out?"

"Rasselas and I both knew it."

Hearing his name the great dog opened one brown eye, as though to confirm what Mr. Calder had said, and then shut it again.

"If I tell you about it," said Sheilagh, "you'll understand why I was holding out."

"Then tell us at once," said Mr. Behrens.

"Of course I knew something was in the wind. I didn't know exactly what Michael was up to. He was careful not to tell me any details. But whatever it was he was doing, I realised it was coming to a head. That was why he sent me away. He said it shouldn't be more than two or three days. He'd get word to me as soon as he could. That was on the Friday. I had a miserable weekend, you can imagine. Monday came, and Tuesday, and still no word. By Wednesday I couldn't take it any longer. What I did was wrong, I know, but I couldn't help myself."

"You went back," said Mr. Calder. He said it sympathetically.

"That's just what I did. I planned it carefully. I wasn't going to barge in and upset all Michael's plans. I just wanted to see he was all right and go away again. He'd given me a key of that room in Mrs. Lovelock's house. I got there after dark. There's a clear view from the window straight into our kitchen. The light was on and the curtains weren't drawn."

As she talked she was living the scene. Mr. Behrens pictured her, crouched in the dark, like an eager theatre-goer in the gallery staring down onto the lighted stage.

She said, "I could see Michael. He was boiling a kettle on the stove and moving about, setting out cups and plates. There were two other people in the room. I could see the legs of a man who was sitting at the kitchen table. Once, when he leant forward, I got a glimpse of him. All I could tell you was that he was young and had black hair. The other was a girl. I saw her quite plainly. She was dark, too. Medium height and rather thin. The sort of girl who could dress as a man and get away with it. I got the impression, somehow, that they'd just arrived, and Michael was bustling about making them at home. The girl still had her outdoor coat on. Maybe that's what gave me the idea. Just then I saw another man coming. He was walking along the road which runs behind our kitchen garden, and when he stopped, he was right under the window where I was sitting. When he opened the gate I could see that he was taking a lot of trouble not to make any noise.

He shut the gate very gently, and stood there for a moment, looking at the lighted kitchen window. Then he tip-toed up the garden path and stood, to one side of the kitchen window, looking in. That's when I saw his face clearly for the first time."

Sheilagh was speaking more slowly now. Mr. Calder was leaning forward with his hands on his knees. Rasselas was no longer pretending to be asleep. Mr. Behrens could feel the tension without understanding it.

"Then he seemed to make up his mind. He went across to the kitchen door, opened it, without knocking, and went in quickly, as though he was planning to surprise the people inside. Next moment, someone had dragged the curtains across. From the moment I first saw that man I knew that he meant harm to Michael. But once the curtains were shut I couldn't see what was happening."

"You couldn't see," said Mr. Calder. "But could you hear?"

"Nothing. On account of Mrs. Lovelock's television set in the room just above me. She's deaf and keeps it on full strength. All I could do was sit and wait. It must have been nearly an hour later when I saw the back door open. All the lights in the house had been turned out and it was difficult to see but Michael was between the two men. They seemed to be supporting him. The girl was walking behind. They came out and turned up the road. Then I noticed there was a car parked about twenty yards further up. They all got into it. And I went on sitting there. I couldn't think what to do."

There was a moment of silence. Neither of the men wanted to break it. Sheilagh said, "I do realise now that I should have done something. I should have run down, screamed, made a fuss. Anything to stop them taking Michael away like that. But I didn't know what was happening. Going with them might all have been part of his plan."

"It was an impossible situation," said Mr. Calder.

"When you thought about it afterwards," said Mr. Behrens, "am I right about this? You got the impression that things had been going smoothly until that other man arrived, and that he was the one who upset things."

"He was the one who gave Michael away," said Sheilagh. "I'm

sure of it." There was a different note in her voice now. Something hard and very cold.

"I agree with Calder," said Mr. Behrens. "You couldn't have done anything else at the time. But as soon as you knew that things had gone wrong for Michael why didn't you tell the police everything that you've just told us. Time was vital. You could give a good description of two of the people involved. Surely there wasn't a moment to lose."

Sheilagh said, "I didn't go to the police because I recognised the man, the one who arrived on foot. I'd seen his photograph. Michael had pointed it out to me in the paper. I only saw him clearly as he stood outside the lighted window, but I was fairly certain I was right." She paused, then added, "Now I'm quite certain."

Both men looked at her.

She said, "It was Sergeant Fallows."

The silence that followed was broken unexpectedly. Rasselas gave a growl at the back of his throat, got up, stalked to the door, pushed it open with his nose, and went out. They heard him settling down again outside.

"That's where he goes when he's on guard," said Mr. Calder.

There was another silence.

"I know what you're thinking," said Sheilagh. "You both think I'm crazy, but I'm not. It *was* Fallows."

"Not an easy face to forget," agreed Mr. Calder, "and it would explain something that had been puzzling me. We'd taken such tight precautions over Michael that I didn't see how they could suddenly have known that he was a plant. He might eventually have done something, or said something, which gave him away. They might have got suspicious. But not certain. Not straight away. It could only have happened like that if he was betrayed, and the only person who could have betrayed him was someone working in the Squad."

Mr. Behrens' mind had been moving on a different line. He said, "When they got into the car, and turned the lights on, you'd have been able to see the number plate at the back, I take it."

"That's right. I saw it, and wrote it down. I've put it here. LKK 910 P."

"Good girl. Now think back. When you were talking about the last man to arrive you called him 'the one who came on foot'. What made you say that?"

Sheilagh said, "I'm not sure. I suppose because he came from the opposite direction to where the car was parked. So I assumed –"

"I'm not disputing it. In fact, I'm sure you were right. Fallows wouldn't have driven up in a police car. He wouldn't even have risked taking his own car. He'd have gone by bus or train to the nearest point and walked the rest of the way."

Mr. Calder said, "Then the car belonged to the Irish couple. Of course, they might have stolen it, like the one they left on the Heath."

"They might. But why risk it? It would only draw attention to them, which was the last thing they wanted. My guess is that they hired it. Just for the time they were planning to be here."

"If you're right," said Mr. Calder, "there's a lot to do and not much time to do it. You'd better trace that car. And remember, we've been officially warned off, so you can't use the police computer."

"LKK's a Kent number. I've got a friend in County Hall who'll help."

"I'll look into the Fallows end of it. It'll mean leaving you alone here for a bit, Sheilagh, but if anyone should turn up and cause trouble Rasselas will attend to him."

"In case there might be two of them," said Mr. Behrens, "you'd better take this. It's loaded. That's the safety-catch. You push it down when you want to fire."

The girl examined the gun with interest. She said, "I've never used one, but I suppose, if I got quite close to the man, pointed it at his stomach, and pulled the trigger –"

"The results should be decisive," said Mr. Behrens.

Fallows was whistling softly to himself as he walked along the carpeted corridor to the door of his flat. It was on the top floor of a new block on the Regent's Park side of Albany Street and seemed an expensive pad for a detective sergeant. He opened the door, walked down the short hall into the living room, switched on the light and stopped.

A middle-aged man, with greying hair and steel-rimmed glasses was standing by the fireplace regarding him bene-volently. Fallows recognised him, but had no time to be sur-prised. As he stepped forward something soft but heavy hit him on the back of the neck.

When he came round, about five minutes later, he was seated in a heavy chair. His arms had been attached to the arms of the chair and his legs to its legs by yards of elastic bandage, wound round and round. Mr. Behrens was examining the contents of an attaché case which he had brought with him. Mr. Calder was watching him. Both men were in their shirt sleeves and were wearing surgical gloves.

"I think our patient is coming round," said Mr. Calder.

"What the bloody hell are you playing at?" said Fallows.

Mr. Behrens said, "First, I'm going to give you these pills. They're ordinary sleeping pills. I think four should be sufficient. We don't want him actually to go to sleep. Just to feel drowsy."

"Bloody hell you will."

"If you want me to wedge your mouth open, hold your nose and hit you on the throat each time until you swallow, I'm quite prepared to do it, but it'd be undignified and rather painful."

Fallow glared at him, but there was an implacable look behind the steel spectacles which silenced him. He swallowed the pills.

Mr. Behrens looked at his watch, and said, "We'll give them five minutes to start working. What we're trying" – he turned courteously back to Fallows – "is an experiment which has often been suggested but never, I think, actually performed. We're going to give you successive doses of scopalamine dextrin to inhale, whilst we ask you some questions. In the ordinary way I have no doubt you would be strong enough to resist the scopala-mine until you became unconscious. There are men who have sufficient resources of will power to do that. That's why we first weaken your resistance with a strong sedative. Provided we strike exactly the right balance, the results should be satis-factory. About ready now, I think."

He took a capsule from a box on the table and broke it under Fallows' nose.

"The snag about this method," he continued, in the same level tones of a professor addressing a class of students, "is that the interreaction of the sedative and the stimulant would be so sharp that it might, if persisted with, affect the subject's heart. You'll appreciate therefore – head up, Sergeant – that by prolonging our dialogue you may be risking your own life. Now then. Let's start with your visit to Banstead –"

This produced a single, sharp obscenity.

Fifty minutes later Mr. Behrens switched off his tape recorder. He said, "I think he's gone. I did warn him that it might happen if he fought too hard."

"And my God, did he fight," said Mr. Calder. He was sweating. "We'd better set the scene. I think he'd look more convincing if we put him on his bed."

He was unwinding the elastic bandages and was glad to see that, in spite of Fallows' struggles, they had left no mark. The nearly empty bottle of sleeping pills, a half empty bottle of whisky and a tumbler were arranged on the bedside table. Mr. Behrens closed Fallows' flaccid hand round the tumbler, and then knocked it onto the floor.

"Leave the bedside light on," said Mr. Calder. "No-one commits suicide in the dark."

"I've done a transcript of the tape for you," said Sheilagh. "I've cut out some of the swearing, but otherwise it's all there. There's no doubt, now, that he betrayed Michael, is there?"

"None at all," said Mr. Behrens. "That was something he seemed almost proud of. The trouble was that when we edged up to one of the things we really wanted to know, an automatic defence mechanism seemed to take over and when we fed him a little more scopalamine to break through it, he started to ramble."

"All the same," said Mr. Calder, "we know a good deal. We know what they're planning to do, and roughly when. But not how."

Mr. Behrens was studying the neatly typed paper. He said,

"J.J. That's clear enough. Jumping Judas. It's their name for Mr. Justice Jellicoe. That's their target all right. They've been gunning for him ever since he sent down the Manchester bombers. I've traced their car. It was hired in Dover last Friday, for ten days. The man they hired it from told them he had another customer who wanted it on the Monday afternoon. They said that suited them because they were planning to let him have it back by one o'clock that day. Which means that whatever they're going to do is timed to be done sometime on Monday morning, and they aim to be boarding a cross-Channel ferry by the time it happens."

"They might have been lying to the man," said Sheilagh.

"Yes. They might have been. But bear in mind that if they brought the car back on Saturday afternoon or Sunday the hire firm would be shut for the weekend and they'd have to leave the car standing about in the street, which would call attention to it. No. I think they've got a timetable, and they're sticking to it."

"Which gives us three days to find out what it is," said Mr. Calder. "If the pay-off is on Monday there are two main possibilities. Jellicoe spends his weekends at his country house at Witham, in Essex. He's pretty safe there. He's got a permanent police guard and three boxer dogs who are devoted to him. He comes up to court on Monday by car, with a police driver. All right. That's one chance. They could arrange some sort of ambush. Detonate one of their favourite long distance mines. Not easy, though, because there are three different routes the car can take. This isn't the Ulster border. They can't go round laying minefields all over Essex."

"The alternative," said Mr. Behrens, "is to try something in or around the Law Courts. We'll have to split this. You take the Witham end. Have a word with the bodyguard. They may not know that we've been warned off, so they'll probably co-operate. I'll tackle the London end."

"Isn't there something I could do?" said Sheilagh.

"Yes," said Mr. Calder. "There is. Play that tape over again and again. Twenty times. Until you know it by heart. There was something, inside Fallows' muddled brain, trying to get out. It may be a couple of words. Even a single word. If you can interpret it, it could be the key to the whole thing."

So Friday was spent by Mr. Calder at Witham, making friends with a police sergeant and a police constable; by Sheilagh Finnegan listening to the drug-induced ramblings of the man who had been responsible for her husband's death; and by Mr. Behrens investigating the possibility of blowing up a judge in court.

As a first step he introduced himself to Major Baines. The major, after service in the Royal Marines, had been given the job of looking after security at the Law Courts. He had known Michael Finnegan, and was more than willing to help.

He said, "It's a rambling great building. I think the chap who designed it had a Ruritanian palace in mind. Narrow windows, heavy doors, battlements and turrets, and iron gratings. The judges have a private entrance, which is inside the car park. Everyone else, barristers, solicitors, visitors, all have to use the front door in the Strand, or the back door in Carey Street. They're both guarded, of course. Teams of security officers, good men. Mostly ex-policemen."

"I was watching them for a time, first thing this morning," said Mr. Behrens. "Most people had to open their bags and cases, but there were people carrying sort of blue and red washing bags. They let them through uninspected."

"They'd be barristers, or barristers' clerks, and they'd let them through because they knew their faces. But I can assure you of one thing. When Mr. Justice Jellicoe is on the premises everyone opens everything."

"Which court will he be using?"

Major Baines consulted the printed list. "On Monday he's in Court Number Two. That's one of the courts at the back. I'll show you."

He led the way down the vast entrance hall. Mr. Behrens saw what he meant when he described it as a palace. Marble columns, spiral staircases, interior balconies and an elaborately tessellated floor.

"Up these stairs," said Baines. "That's Number Two Court. And there's the back door, straight ahead of you. It leads out into Carey Street."

"So that anyone making for Court Number Two would be likely to come this way."

"Not if they were coming from the Strand."

"True," said Mr. Behrens. "I think I'll hang around for a bit and watch the form."

He went back to the main hall and found himself a seat, which commanded the front entrance.

It was now ten o'clock and the flow of people coming in was continuous. They were channelled between desks placed lengthways, and three security guards were operating. They did their job thoroughly. Occasionally, when they recognised a face, a man was waved through. Otherwise everyone opened anything they were carrying and placed it on top of the desk. Suitcases, briefcases, even womens' handbags were carefully examined. The red and blue bags which, Mr. Behrens decided, must contain law books were sometimes looked into, sometimes not. They would all be looked into on Monday morning.

"It seemed pretty water-tight to me," said Mr. Behrens to Sheilagh and Mr. Calder, as they compared notes after supper. "Enough explosive to be effective would be bulky and an elaborate timing device would add to the weight and bulk. They might take a chance and put the whole thing in the bottom of one of those book bags and hope it wouldn't be looked at, but they don't seem to me to be people who take chances of that sort."

"Could the stuff have been brought in during the weekend and left somewhere in the court?"

"I put it to Baines. He said no. The building is shut on Friday evening and given a thorough going-over on Saturday."

"Sheilagh and I have worked one thing out," said Mr. Behrens. "There's a reference, towards the end, to 'fields'. In the transcript it's been reproduced as 'in the fields', and the assumption was that the attempt was going to be made in the country, when Jellicoe was driving up to London. But if you listen very carefully it isn't 'in the fields'. It's 'in fields' with the emphasis on the first word, and there's a sort of crackle in the tape before it which makes it difficult to be sure, but I think what he's saying is 'Lincoln's Inn Fields'."

They listened once more to the tape.

Mr. Calder said, "I think you're right."

"And it does explain one point," said Mr. Behrens. "When I explored the area this morning it struck me how difficult it was to park a car. But Lincoln's Inn Fields could be ideal – there are parking spaces all down the south and east sides, and the south-east corner is less than two hundred yards from the rear entrance to the courts."

"Likely enough," said Mr. Calder, "but it still doesn't explain how they're going to get the stuff in. Did you get anything else out of the tape, Sheilagh?"

"I made a list of the words and expressions he used most often. Some were just swearing, apart from that his mind seemed to be running on time. He said 'midday' and 'twelve o'clock' a dozen times at least. And he talks about a 'midday special'. That seemed to be some sort of joke. He doesn't actually use the word 'explosion', but he talks once or twice about a report, or reports."

"Report?" said Mr. Calder thoughtfully. "That sounds more like a shot from a gun than a bomb."

"It's usually in the plural. Reports."

"Several guns."

"Rather elaborate, surely. Hidden rifles, trained on the Bench, and timed to go off at midday?"

"And it still doesn't explain how he gets the stuff past the guards," said Mr. Behrens.

He took the problem down the hill with him to his house in Lamperdown village and carried it up to bed. He knew, from experience, that he would get little sleep until he had solved it. The irritating thing was that the answer was there. He was sure of it. He had only to remember what he had seen and connect it up with the words on the tape, and the solution would appear, as inevitably as the jackpot came out of the slot when you got three lemons in a row.

Visualise the people, pouring through the entrance into the building, carrying briefcases, book bags, handbags. One man had had a camera slung over his shoulder. The guard had called his attention to a notice prohibiting the taking of photographs in court. This little episode had held up the queue for a moment.

The young man behind, a barrister's clerk Mr. Behrens guessed, had been in a hurry, and had pushed past the camera-owner. He had not been searched, because he hadn't been carrying a case. But he had been carrying *something*. When Mr. Behrens reached this point he did, in fact, doze off, so that the solution must have reached him in his sleep.

Next morning, after breakfast, he telephoned his solicitor, catching him before he set out for the golf course. He said, "When you go into court, and have to tell the judge what another judge said in another case –"

"Quote a precedent, you mean."

"That's right. Well, do you take the book with you, or is it already in court?"

"Both. There's a complete set of Reports in court. Several sets, in fact. They're for the judges. And you bring your own with you."

"That might mean lugging in a lot of books."

"A trolleyful sometimes."

"Suppose you had, say, five or six sets of Reports to carry. How would you manage?"

"I'd get my clerk to carry them."

"All right," said Mr. Behrens patiently; "how would he manage?"

"If it was just half a dozen books, he's got a sort of strap affair, with a handle."

"That's what I thought I remembered seeing," said Mr. Behrens. "Thank you very much."

"I suppose you've got some reason for asking all these questions?"

"An excellent reason."

His solicitor, who knew Mr. Behrens, said no more.

"We'll get there early," said Mr. Calder, "and park as close as we can to the south-east corner. There's plenty of cover in the garden and we can watch both lines of cars. As soon as one of us spots LKK 910 P he tips off the others using one of these pocket radios. Quite easy, Sheilagh. Just press the button and talk. Then let it go, and listen."

"That doesn't sound too difficult," said Sheilagh, "what then?"

"Then Henry gets busy."

"Who's Henry?"

"An old friend of mine who'll be coming with us. His job is to unlock the boot of their car as soon as they're clear of it. By my reckoning he'll have ten minutes for the job, which will be nine and a half minutes more than he needs."

The man and girl walked up Searle Street, not hurrying, but not wasting time, crossed Carey Street, climbed the five shallow steps and pushed through the swing doors and into the court building.

Mr. Behrens had got there before them. He was standing on the far side of the barrier. A little queue had already formed and he had plenty of time to observe them.

They had dressed for the occasion with ritual care. The man in a dark suit, cream shirt and dark red tie. The girl in the uniform of a female barrister, black dress, black shoes and stockings, with a single touch of colour, the collar points of a yellow shirt showing at the throat.

As he watched them edge forward to the barrier Mr. Behrens felt a prickle of superstitious dread. They may have been nervous, but they showed no sign of it. They looked serious and composed, like the young crusaders who, for the more thorough purging of the holy places, mutilated the living bodies of their pagan prisoners; like the novices who watched impassively at the *auto-da-fé* where men and women were burned to the greater glory of God.

Now they were at the barrier. The girl was carrying a book bag and a satchel. She opened them both. The search was thorough and took time. The man showed very slight signs of impatience.

Mr. Behrens thought they've rehearsed this very carefully.

When it came to the man's turn he placed the six books, held together in a white strap, on the counter and opened the briefcase. The guard searched the briefcase, and nodded. The man picked up the books and the case and walked down the short length of corridor to where the girl was standing. He ignored her, turned the corner and made for Court Number Two. Although it was not yet ten o'clock there were already a number of people in the courtroom. Two elderly barristers were standing by the front bench discussing something. Behind them a girl was arranging a pile of books and papers. The young man placed his six books, still strapped together, on the far end of the back bench, and went out as quietly as he had come in. No-one took any notice of him.

A minute later Mr. Behrens appeared, picked up the books, and left. No-one took any notice of him either.

When the young man came out he had joined the girl and they moved off together. Having come in by the back entrance it was evidently their intention to leave by the front. They had gone about ten paces when a man stopped them. He said, "Excuse me, but have you got your cards?"

"Cards?" said the young man. He seemed unconcerned.

"We're issuing personal identity cards to all barristers using the court. Your clerk should have told you. If you'd come with me I'll give you yours."

The girl looked at the man, who nodded slightly, and they set off after their guide. He led the way down a long, empty passage towards the western annexe to the courts.

The young man closed up behind him. He put his hand into a side pocket, pulled out a leather cosh, moved a step closer, and hit the man on the head. Their guide went forward onto his knees and rolled over onto his face.

The young man and the girl had swung round and were moving back the way they had come.

"Walk, don't run," said the young man.

They turned a corner, and went down a spiral staircase which led to the main hall and the front entrance.

When they were outside, and circling the court building, the girl said, "That man. Did you notice?"

"Notice what?"

"When you hit him. He was expecting it."

"What do you mean?"

"He started to fall forward just before you hit him. It must have taken most of the force out of the blow."

Without checking his pace the young man said, "Do you think

he was a plant? Holding us up so they could get to the car ahead of us?"

"I thought it might be."

The young man put one hand on the shoulder-holster inside his coat, and said, "If that's right, you'll see some fireworks."

There was no-one waiting by the car. The nearest person to it was a small man, with a face like a friendly monkey, who was sitting on a bench inside the garden reading the *Daily Mirror*.

No-one tried to stop them as they drove out of Lincoln's Inn Fields and turned south towards the Embankment. "Twenty past ten," said the young man, "good timing." They were five miles short of Dover, on the bare escarpment above Bridge, before he spoke again. He said, "Twelve o'clock. Any time now."

Either his watch was fast or the timing mechanism was slow. It was fully five minutes later when their car went up in a searing sheet of white flame.

II

The Decline and Fall of Mr. Behrens

When Mr. Behrens had got into it, it had been an Underground train, and full of people. Now, emerging into the pale sunlight of a late January afternoon, shedding passengers at every stop, it was pottering unhurried and almost empty through the flat countryside of the Thames delta; past stations whose names ended romantically in Tree and Wood and Park, but which exhibited an unbroken vista of bricks and mortar; past back gardens, past allotments and small derelict factories; out to the furthest tip of the most recently constructed tentacle of the London Transport system, Wallingford Bridge, a brand new station built to accommodate the brand new University of Middlesex.

The overhead street lamps were glowing orange in the dusk, and there was a powdering of snow on the pavement as Mr. Behrens carried his battered suitcase out of the station, up the long slope which led to the High Street. As he reached it, he became conscious that something was happening.

A group of people was marching down the middle of the road. Most of them were singing or shouting. A lot of traffic had piled up behind them. As they approached, Mr. Behrens was able to make out some of the words. The battle cry was "Stoo-dent-Rep-res-en-TAY-shun". One group of hirsute singers was giving a rendering of "John Brown's body", with a chorus of "We won't shave until we get it." A second, rather larger group, was putting over "We'll hang Jack Harraway on a sour apple tree." The only people neither singing nor shouting were the policemen marching beside the leaders.

There were three people in the front rank, and Mr. Behrens was able to see them clearly as they walked past. In the middle strode a thickset, red-faced young bull. Sixteen stone of muscle and intolerance. On his right, a thin, coffee-coloured youth with black hair, a hairline black moustache and an appearance of serious gravity. On his left, and thus closest to where Mr. Behrens was standing, a girl with a white face and a head of copper curls. Even under the neon lighting, which was being unkind to her colour scheme, she made a striking figure.

Mr. Behrens stood watching, until the noise and shouting had faded into the distance, and the last frustrated motorist had ground past. Then he continued on his way. It had started to snow again.

Anyone, he thought, to whom the word University still conjured up visions of mellowed stone, creeper-covered walls and smooth lawns would have been in for a shock when confronted with the University of Middlesex. Particularly if the confrontation took place at dusk under a lowering sky. The buildings were not only raw, but seemed to have been designed on an over-ambitious plan, modified from motives of economy, and replanned in a hurry. The general effect was something between a council estate and an army cantonment.

He located the Rector's Lodge at the far end of this conglomeration and was welcomed by the Rector, Dr. Harraway, a plump, white-haired man with a professionally ready smile. He said, "Come in, come in. You look frozen. You had to walk? This shortage of taxis is a scandal. An absolute scandal. It's Behrens, isn't it? I'm so glad you've been able to join the faculty as a temporary member. At such short notice, too. You'll be covering Modern European Social and Economic History. When the Minister recommended you to us – a very warm, personal recommendation, incidentally – he mentioned that you were a linguist as well?"

Mr. Behrens said, "I have a smattering of most European languages."

"That should be very useful. Many of the leading authorities in your field are in German. As, of course, you will be aware. Is it too much to hope that you might be considering joining us permanently?"

"That will depend on how I get along with your students. I

passed a number of them when I was on my way here. An army with banners."

"They do demonstrate rather a lot," said Dr. Harraway. "What was it about this time?"

"The only slogan I could actually make out was 'Hang Jack Harraway.'"

The Rector laughed delightedly. "High spirits. They mean no harm. I must have been hanged in effigy a dozen times since I took over at the beginning of last year. It doesn't worry me a scrap."

"Just so long as they continue to do it in effigy, Rector," said Mr. Behrens, and took his leave.

It was two days later that he faced his first class. He was interested to find in it all three of the leaders of the demonstration. He had already discovered something about them. The girl was Alison Varney, daughter of Samuel Varney, the property millionaire. The big Irishman was Patrick Meaghan. His grandfather had helped to hold the Dublin Post-Office on Easter Day 1916 and had died in its ruins. The thin boy, as he already knew, was Ahmed bin Akbar bin Suleiman, heir apparent to the Ruler of Ras-al-Daar.

On the supposition that what interested him might also interest his students Mr. Behrens had chosen to discourse about conditions in Germany between the wars. He had dealt with Kurt Eisner and with the provisional government of Hoffman and was starting on Bela Kun's Communist regime when the flame-haired Alison interrupted him. She did it politely enough, holding up her hand, and saying, "Do you mind us interrupting you when we want to ask something?"

"Certainly not," said Mr. Behrens. "Why?"

"Oh, some of the lecturers get very shirty if we do."

"I can assure you," said Mr. Behrens smoothly, "that an amateur lecturer like myself, and one who is rather out of practice at that, positively welcomes interruptions. It not only gives him a breathing space but ensures that the notes he has prepared will last out the hour."

The laugh that greeted this sally was good-natured.

"It was just this," said Alison, "the period you've been describing. It must have been pretty ghastly. But we know what it was followed by, and that was Hitler. Do you think that Hitler's sort of rule was better, on balance, than what went before?"

"I think," said Mr. Behrens slowly, "that Hitler was an unqualified disaster. For Germany and for the whole Western world."

"Isn't that a judgment you're making from post-war books?" said Ahmed.

"If you mean, is it a judgment I'm making only from books, the answer is no. I can speak from personal experience also."

"You met him?"

"Twice."

"But those would be formal meetings. You could make no judgment from them."

"One was formal. One was informal," said Mr. Behrens, evasively. "I saw no occasion on either of them to question the verdict of history. Which brings us back to the point. Anarchy and political chaos are usually followed by dictatorship."

"Is that an invariable rule?" said Ahmed. He sounded interested.

"Not invariable. There are exceptions. In Ireland, for instance, political chaos is normally followed by political chaos."

This roused Patrick Meaghan, as, indeed, it had been intended to do. The rest of the hour passed pleasantly enough.

"Who is this man?" asked Meaghan, yawning prodigiously. The three of them were in Alison's cell-like room, Ahmed and Alison sitting on the bed and Pat Meaghan overflowing the only chair.

"He's taking Morovitz's lectures for the rest of this term," said Alison.

"That must be an improvement, however bad he is."

"I think he's rather sweet. And for God's sake stop yawning, Patrick."

"I feel sleepy."

"You can't feel sleepy at four o'clock in the afternoon. And we've got important matters on the agenda. Item one. Tomorrow's demonstration."

"You are determined it shall be violent?" said Ahmed.

"Yes. I am. Non-violence has failed. All we've done so far is to hold up the traffic. We've made no impression on the authorities at all." She gave Ahmed a look which was almost motherly and said, "There's no need for you to join in if you don't want."

"I shall join with the others."

"You don't sound convinced."

"I'm convinced of the rightness of what we are asking for. Not to be treated as children. To have a say in our own affairs. And I am not afraid of violence – I come from a violent country. Of its last six rulers, four have died by violence. But violence leads to a hardening of attitudes. At the moment, few of us feel any animosity towards the authorities. I feel none. To be violent without being provoked seems to me to be wanton."

Alison sighed. She said, "It's very difficult. We'll give Pat the casting vote." A strangled snore came from the chair. "For God's sake. He's asleep."

Alex Fraser was clearly a tycoon. His office, on the eighth floor of the building overlooking the Thames proclaimed as much. It had close carpeting, comfortable chairs, a desk the size of a tennis court, and, in one corner, a neat scale model of a drilling rig. Mr. Fraser's blonde secretary, herself a neat scale model, proclaimed it, too. The only unpretentious thing about the whole set-up was Alex Fraser himself. He was small, had a nut-brown face crowned by a mop of greying hair, and was wearing a suit which must have been ten years old at least, and far from well looked after. Mr. Calder took in these points at a glance. Being himself a man who disliked pretension, he was prepared, on balance, to disregard the tycoonery and approve of the person.

"It's a damned serious situation," said Mr. Fraser. "East Gulf Oil Company, which is one of our subsidiaries, has been working a number of concessions down near Muscat and Oman. They're very promising. And the most promising survey report I've ever read in my life is the one we've just completed in Ras-al-Daar."

"Congratulations."

"Congratulations would be premature. What we had was an exploration contract. Not a drilling contract. That has still to be signed."

Mr. Calder said "Ras-al-Dar? That's old Sheik Akbar. I used to know him quite well. He never struck me as being unduly greedy."

"He's not greedy. He's a desert Arab of the old stock. And he's got ideals. He's seen what money has done to other small Arab states."

"Instant Western civilisation. A package deal available overnight," said Mr. Calder with a shudder.

"It's not all bad. He realises that. The oil revenues will pay for hospitals and roads and education. It'll also bring in alcohol and traffic accidents and the quick-money boys. And jealousy from any neighbour who isn't lucky enough to possess oil. And unrest from his own subjects."

"Not a very attractive balance sheet?"

"Well, maybe I've falsified it a bit. Anyway, that's what the old man's thinking about. And to find out how Western civilisation is working out in practice, he's sent his son to an English University. The FO recommended Middlesex. Being new they thought it might be less troublesome."

"They may be new, but they're learning fast. Two days ago they heaved a couple of bricks through the Rector's window. I understand that the change in the Rector's outlook was positively startling. He stopped being a genial uncle or elder brother and became a roaring lion."

"It's wonderful what a well-placed brick will do," said Mr. Fraser. "I only hope the thrower wasn't Ahmed?"

"Ahmed was in the forefront of the battle. Mercifully he wasn't pulled in. The police had all their work cut out arresting a wild Irishman. But there's no saying he won't be in trouble next time. And if he spends one night inside an English gaol, I imagine your chances in the Eastern Gulf will look a bit sketchy."

Fraser got up, moved across to the corner of the room, and stared malevolently at the model oil rig. He said, "I don't suppose I need explain to you, Calder, just *how* valuable a good concession in that part of the world would be to us right now."

"You don't need to explain," said Mr. Calder. "We're taking it seriously all right. My chief, Mr. Fortescue, sent a colleague of mine, Mr. Behrens, down there at the beginning of term to keep an eye on things. Now he wants me to go down and lend a hand too. Normally Behrens would have been perfectly capable of dealing with a situation like this on his own. But there's a complication."

"What sort of complication?"

"This one's got auburn hair and her name is Alison Varney."

"Sam Varney's daughter?"

"That's right."

"It was bad enough without that," said Fraser, gloomily.

Mr. Behrens said, "There's the bell for lunch. Enough tuition for this morning. We'll knock off, shall we?"

Alison Varney shuffled her books and papers into a pile on Mr. Behrens' table, sighed, and said, "I'm not really hungry. How could anyone be, the food they serve up here."

Mr. Behrens was busy filling his pipe. He said, "Eating's a thing you either worry about a great deal, or not at all. I'm in the second category. When I'm at home, I'm cooked for by my aunt. She permutes on three dishes. Mince, chicken casserole and Irish stew." He had the pipe going nicely now. He added, between puffs, "I've got so little sense of taste that I find them indistinguishable."

Alison said, "Tell me something, Mr. Behrens. What are you doing here?"

"Endeavouring to lecture in Social and Economic History."

"Come off it. You're not a don."

"What makes you think that?"

"You don't look like one. Or talk like one. Or think like one."

"You've made a study of the species?"

"Indeed yes. This is the third University I've been to. I was sent down from the other two. For violent and subversive behaviour."

"Did they know that when they accepted you here?"

"Yes. But my father promised them a handsome grant to finish the library."

"I see."

"Do tell. You're some sort of official. An inspector?"

"Oh dear," said Mr. Behrens. "Am I such an obvious civil servant."

"Or are you something more exciting than that? I have it. You're a member of MI5. Come down to spy on us."

Mr. Behrens swallowed a mouthful of smoke and started to splutter. Alison patted him on the back, and said, "Own up."

"Since you have guessed half the truth," said Mr. Behrens, "I'll tell you the whole. I was planning to take you into my confidence anyway. I've been sent down here to keep an eye on Ahmed, and see he isn't led astray by wild companions."

"Meaning Patrick and me?"

"Yes."

"And how were you aiming to do it?"

"I've often found that in a tricky situation the best plan is to co-opt your opponents onto your own side."

"Cool. Tell me more."

"Ahmed's father is hereditary ruler of a patch of desert in the south-east corner of the Gulf. It's rather smaller than the Isle of Wight, has a population of nomad Arabs who live by date-growing and camel-farming with a side line in gold smuggling. Additionally, it looks like being the brightest prospect for oil that's been turned up for many a year. It would do us a power of good if we were allowed to develop it. Normally, we should be. We discovered it. And we're first in the field for a concession. But if Ahmed gets slung out of an English University or into an English gaol, our prospects will be dim."

"And you're suggesting that I should tell him to be a good boy so that an oil company can make some money?"

"Not an oil company," said Mr. Behrens. "England."

"Don't tell me you're going to start beating the patriotic drum? Rule, Britannia. The Army, the Navy and the Air Force."

"Yes, indeed. And since you mention it, the Air Force in

particular. It's amazing to think that thirty years ago there really *were* young men, who grew huge moustaches, and said things like 'Bang on' and 'Wizard prang' and fought their private battles five miles above the fields of Kent, and were burned to death, quite a lot of them, big moustaches and all. And when they knew they were dying, weren't entirely unhappy, because they were doing it for England. Does that make you laugh?"

In the silence that followed, Mr. Behrens could hear the distant trampling of feet down the corridors and the banging of doors.

Alison said, "I'm not sure. It's the sort of thing that either makes you laugh or cry. It depends how you look at it. But the point is that it's an anachronism."

"If you mean that we're never going to have another conventional war, I agree with you. More's the pity, I sometimes think."

"Do you mean you *want* another war?"

"It wouldn't affect me. I'm too old. It's the young people I'm thinking about. Fancy living your whole life without ever having a cause worth dying for. Maybe that's what makes them so discontented."

"We have got a cause."

"Breaking the Rector's windows?"

"You say that because you don't understand. He can mend his windows. He can't mend his public image."

"What's wrong with his public image?"

"It's a fraud. These places are selling second-class goods. Not even second-class. Shoddy third-class. But it's such a seller's market for Universities just now that they can get away with it. The teaching's a farce. Most of the students could get on faster if they sat at home and read the set books. The brighter ones do."

"You can't manufacture dons over night."

"Agreed. But what about the living conditions? One bathroom for forty students. When it works. Rabbit hutch cubicles with walls so thin you can hear people talking three rooms away. And the food! If you served up muck like that at Dartmoor you'd have a mutiny."

"And how would you improve it?"

"Simple. Hand over all administrative arrangements to a committee of students. Do you realise that we've got men here who'd be helping to run businesses if they weren't at University? Women who'd be married, keeping house, maybe looking after a couple of children. And they treat us as though we were children ourselves. That's what we're fighting against. And we're going to go on fighting. I don't suppose any of us will be killed. But we'll be uncomfortable, and some of us will be hurt."

"Suppose I were to agree," said Mr. Behrens, "that every word you've said is true? I think you've exaggerated it, but suppose it is true. Must Ahmed be one of the rebels?"

"He and Pat Meaghan are the leaders. Pat's in gaol. If Ahmed backed out, we'd have to start all over again."

"You underrate yourself. They're not the leaders. You are."

"Even if that was true," said Alison, seriously, "I'm not prepared to go on alone."

"You realise that if you go on at all, you're heading for real trouble. Few people fight dirtier than an aroused Establishment."

"If it's going to be a tough and dirty fight, we need a tough and dirty leader. Would you care to take on the job? I'm sure you'd be beautifully unscrupulous. What about it?"

Mr. Behrens sighed. He said, "I'm not involved in this fight."

"But you'd enjoy it, wouldn't you? Do you know *when* I spotted that you were different from the rest of the professors. It was when you were talking about Hitler. It's true, isn't it? You did meet him."

"Yes."

"When?"

"It was in Russia," said Mr. Behrens. "In 1943. He made me a personal presentation of the *Dresdner Kreuz* with crossed palm leaves. I don't think he'd have done it if he'd known that my reason for being there was to arrange for an explosive device to be placed in his private aeroplane."

"There you are," said Alison. "What did I say. You're just the man we need to run a student riot."

*

Mr. Calder sat in the saloon bar of the Duke of Pomfret public house in a back street of Wallingford. Thickset, middle-aged, nondescript in appearance and dress, he attracted no attention and desired to attract none.

The snow had changed to frozen rain. The bar was warm and crowded. Mr. Calder sipped his whisky and cast an occasional glance at the small serving hatch, through which he could see most of the public bar.

The stout man he was following was sitting in a corner by himself, spinning out half a pint of beer and occasionally glancing at his watch. It was getting on for nine o'clock before the second man joined him. This was a small, spruce character with the look of a prosperous jockey. He carried his drink over and the two men talked for a few minutes. When the packet was passed it was done so inconspicuously that if Mr. Calder had not been watching very closely he would have missed it.

Soon afterwards the stout man lumbered to his feet, wrapped a scarf round his neck, said a general goodnight to the bar, and made his way into the darkness of the street. With his head bent forward against the stinging rain he was unaware of anyone behind him until Mr. Calder put one hand on his shoulder. As he swung round Mr. Calder clipped him scientifically on the side of the throat, caught him as he fell, gasping for breath, and lowered him gently to the ground. He found the packet in a coat pocket and transferred it to his own. By the time he had done this the stout man was already recovering. Mr. Calder helped him up into a sitting position with his back against the railings and said, "If I were you, Mr. Ponting, I should go straight home now. You'll get a nasty cold if you sit about in this weather."

"Who exactly *is* Mr. Ponting?" said Mr. Behrens two days later.

"He keeps a small tobacconists and sweet shop," said Mr. Calder. "It's just behind the University and he has a lot of student customers. I'm afraid he sells them nastier things than cigarettes and sweets."

"Cannabis?"

"Yes."

"Hard stuff?"

"I don't think he's got round to it. At the moment, he's strictly on the amateur pot-line. It was because I recognised one of the carriers, a nasty little man called Jacko Sampson, that I was able to get onto him so quickly."

"Bad," said Mr. Behrens. "But not too bad yet. What are the authorities going to do about it?"

"It depends what line the Rector decides to take. Ponting, who has about as much courage as a small mouse, tried to buy himself out of the worst of the mess by identifying six students who had had stuff from him. My advice to the Rector was to let me throw a scare into Ponting which would shut him up for good, whilst he gives the students concerned the dressing down of their young lives."

"Will he do it?"

"The snag is that most of them have been in the forefront of the trouble. And one of them is Pat Meaghan."

"He's a vindictive beast," said Mr. Behrens. "He won't pass a chance like this."

"Yes, Miss Varney?" said the Rector, managing to combine in his tones hostility towards a known rebel and a degree of warmth appropriate to the daughter of a possible benefactor.

"It's about Pat Meaghan and the others."

"Which others?"

"The one's who've been buying cannabis, silly young asses."

"I should have used a stronger term myself," said the Rector. "What they have done happens to be a criminal offence."

"Only if you make it so," said Alison. "I gather the police will only push it if you make them."

"Might I ask exactly how you have – er – gathered any of this, Miss Varney? So far as I was aware the whole matter was, at the moment, entirely confidential between myself and the Home Office man who unearthed this scandalous state of affairs."

"These things get about," said Alison, evasively. "The point is, are you prepared to do a deal?"

"A deal?"

"If you'll persuade the police to back-pedal on these charges,

I'll guarantee you'll have no more trouble at the University. At least, as long as I'm here."

The Rector had gone very red. He said, "Do you imagine for a moment that I could contemplate an outrageous bargain of that sort?"

"I don't suppose you want a lot of trouble when the Minister comes down to open the Library wing next week, do you? He might get the idea that you weren't doing a very good job."

"I fear you misjudge me," said the Rector. His mouth was so tight that the words would hardly come out. "If I had been in any doubt before as to my proper course, this impudent attempt at blackmail and bribery would have made my mind up for me. Now, if you'll excuse me, I have a great many things to do."

"We're on collision course," said Mr. Behrens.

"She sounds a remarkable girl," said Mr. Calder.

They were taking tea in the Palm Court of the hotel where Mr. Calder was staying. A string quartet was playing selections from *The Arcadians*.

"Oh, she is. An arresting personality. Her father's a millionaire. She's a dedicated radical extremist. But with a lot more brains than that sort of person usually has. Make *her* Rector, and you'd have a University worth talking about."

"It sounds to me as if you've fallen for her."

"I have," said Mr. Behrens. "Hook, line and sinker. Incidentally, she placed me without any difficulty."

"The devil she did. What happened?"

"She offered to withdraw Ahmed from the leadership of the student protest group, on conditions."

"Which were?"

"That I took his place. Even to achieve our main objective I didn't feel able to agree to that."

The Arcadians was inducing a mood of nostalgia in Mr. Behrens. They were playing one of the catchy tunes from the second act. "*It's nice and fine. I think that we shall have a lovely day – Eighty in the shade they say – very, very warm for May.*" Mr. Behrens was humming the words to himself when he realised that Mr. Calder had said something.

"What's that about Ahmed?"

"I said, you won't have to bother about Ahmed. His father's ordered him to come home."

"Ordered him home?"

"Nothing to do with the University. The decision was taken on grounds of policy."

"When did you hear?"

"About an hour ago."

"Policy? What policy? Look here, something's up. Why wasn't I told?"

"I've been trying to make up my mind," said Mr. Calder, calmly, "whether I'd tell you at all. Since it's going to make you very angry, I thought I'd let you finish your tea before I did so."

"First we lose Pat, and most of the out-and-outers with him. *They* daren't move hand or foot until the court case is decided. And now Ahmed. Damn, damn, damn, damn, damn."

It was the first time that Mr. Behrens had seen Alison near to tears. He said, "I think it's time I gave you my well-known lecture on tactics. You made a mistake in offering the Rector terms. Never do that when your opponent thinks he's winning. The time for offering terms is when *you're* winning."

"I'm sorry. I don't see –"

"When you have suffered a series of set-backs, when your front is pushed in, your flanks are under fire and your rear is threatened, there's only one thing to do. You attack. The body of students are behind you. They all realise that the Rector is behaving vindictively. He's never been more unpopular than at this moment. The press will be here in force when the Minister comes down on Wednesday. You've got a golden opportunity to show the world what you think of him."

"It's all very well talking. Do you realise that almost every effective member of our organisation is out of action? You can't build a new committee in forty-eight hours."

Mr. Behrens seemed not to have heard her. He said, "The speeches will take place in the assembly hall. There is some sort of loft above the dais. The ceiling, I noticed, is wood or plaster board. A trap-door cut at the right point –"

"I could think up a lot of marvellous ideas," said Alison, "if we had the people and the equipment. For one thing, do you realise that the assembly hall is locked at night?"

"I have a friend who happens to be staying in Wallingford," said Mr. Behrens. "He has a way with locks. He could also get hold of any equipment, in reason, that you want."

"Why should he help? Why should you, come to that?"

"We're both *very* angry with the Rector," said Mr. Behrens, gently. "When we're angry, we like to do something about it."

Mr. Fortescue looked over the top of his steel-rimmed glasses and said, in tones of cold disapproval, "Do I gather, Behrens, that you had some hand in this disgraceful episode?"

"I organised it," said Mr. Behrens, "with a little help from Calder."

"Suppose you are implicated?"

"Not a chance."

"I'm glad you had that much sense." Mr. Fortescue resumed his study of the report. "I see that the newspapers speak of an avalanche of soot descending on the Rector *and* on the Minister."

"It was soot mixed with flour, actually. It gave them a very odd appearance."

"Like the black and white minstrels," said Mr. Calder.

"Suppose this girl – Alison Varney – is charged with complicity and gives you away?"

"Not a shred of evidence against her. She was seated in the third row of the audience, and could not possibly have had any hand in opening the trap."

"She didn't throw tomatoes either," said Mr. Calder.

"Tomatoes?" said Mr. Fortescue. "There is no mention in the paper of tomatoes."

"About twenty of the students threw them. Oddly enough, they were students who hadn't been particularly militant before."

Mr. Fortescue seemed to be visualising the scene. He said, "Soot, flour, *and* tomatoes. The Minister is a man who is rather conscious of his personal dignity. I can't think he was pleased."

"He was far from pleased," said Mr. Behrens, "and spent, I

233

believe, the best part of half an hour telling the Rector exactly what he thought of him, and his lack of control over his students. The betting is strongly in favour of a new Rector being appointed."

"I have noticed," said Mr. Fortescue, "that when you speak of the Rector, Behrens, you exhibit a most uncharacteristic spirit of personal vindictiveness."

"You know *how* he got rid of Ahmed?"

"I wasn't exactly clear about it," said Mr. Fortescue. "I was so relieved that he had left without embarrassment to ourselves that I didn't enquire too closely into the means."

"The Rector had a message conveyed to Ahmed's father," said Mr. Calder, "that his son was in danger of being debauched by a girl of Jewish parentage."

"My personal opinion," said Mr. Behrens, "is that he was lucky to get off with soot and tomatoes. He deserved boiling lead."

Mr. Fortescue rocked silently on his chair for some seconds. His eyes had a far away look. Then he said, "The experiment was tried, in the early twenties, in a Rectorial election at Aberdeen University. It was not an unqualified success."

12

The Last Reunion

A sharp, clear July morning had turned to a drizzle of rain, and
Mr. Calder and Mr. Behrens had retreated, with Rasselas, to the
sitting room of Mr. Calder's cottage. They had brought out the
chess-board, but so little was Mr. Calder's mind on the game
that, within ten minutes of the start, he had allowed Mr. Behrens
to manoeuvre himself into a position of impregnable advantage.

He said, "I am thinking of resigning."

"You can't think about resigning," said Mr. Behrens. "Either
you do resign, or you don't."

"I'm not talking about chess," said Mr. Calder crossly. "I'm
talking about our work."

"Why?"

It was fifteen years since both men had left the regular Intelligence Service, almost on the same day. Since then they had been
on a retainer. If a job seemed to be suitable for their particular
talents they had been assigned to it.

"Enough is enough," said Mr. Calder. "I'm getting old. My
reactions are slowing down. Rasselas is as bad as I am."

The great dog looked up.

"Yesterday, a rabbit ran rings round him."

Rasselas seemed to understand this. His expression indicated
that he thought the criticism unjust. Rabbits? Who cares about
rabbits. He could have caught it quite easily if he had wanted
to.

"It's odd you should mention it," said Mr. Behrens. "Because
the same thought had occurred to me. I fired a refresher course on
the Police range at Croydon last month, and barely qualified. If
you've made your mind up, we'd better get in touch with Fortescue."

As he said that, the telephone rang.

"And that," said Mr. Calder, "is probably more trouble."

His telephone number was not only ex-directory. It was changed every six months. He went out into the passage where the telephone lived. Rasselas followed him.

Mr. Behrens fiddled with the chess pieces, trying one or two moves to see whether the attack he had mounted could be circumvented. He had decided that the position was irreversible when Mr. Calder came back.

"Your instinct was correct," he said. "That was Fortescue."

"And he has a job for us?"

"Yes, and no. That wasn't the main point. He rang up to tell us that he was resigning his post at the Bank. Did you realise that he would be seventy next month?"

"I never thought about it. He could be any age."

"That being so, he has decided that it's time he gave up his other jobs too."

"He's the sort of man who'll live to ninety. What is he going to do for the next twenty years?"

"He plans to grow roses."

"He always was a stickler for tradition."

The two men sat for a minute, staring out at the rain, which was drifting across the top of the North Downs in a filmy curtain. What they had heard had underlined their own decision. They had enjoyed working for Mr. Fortescue, a man of intransigent realism who could be ruthless to his subordinates, but allowed no-one else, from the Prime Minister downwards, to interfere with them.

"I suppose it will be Rowlandson who takes over."

"I suppose so," said Mr. Calder. Since they were going themselves the matter was unimportant. "He's all right. A bit Royal Navy."

Mr. Behrens remembered something. "You said 'Yes *and* No.' Is there something in the offing?"

"There is a job. It sounds rather unusual. I said we'd go up tomorrow and discuss it."

"With liberty to say no if we didn't like the sound of it. I'd hate to get nailed at the fifty-ninth minute of the eleventh hour."

"It didn't sound like that sort of job," said Mr. Calder. "In fact, it doesn't sound like our normal sort of job at all."

"For the last forty-eight hours," said Mr. Fortescue, "the Department has had possession of Rudolf Sperrle's testament. Nearly five hundred pages of typescript. In that folder there."

He indicated a fat box-type folder on his desk.

Mr. Calder and Mr. Behrens looked at each other in astonishment.

"Rudolf Sperrle?" said Mr. Calder. "Hitler's personal aide-de-camp? I'd no idea he was still alive."

"He isn't," said Mr. Fortescue. "He's been living in retirement in Bonn for the last thirty years. After the decision was made not to prosecute him – and, indeed, there was nothing to prosecute him for – he slipped into obscurity. I've no doubt he was only too glad to forget his war-time experiences, and glad that other people should forget them, too. But there was a drawback. Obscurity declined into poverty, and poverty to near starvation. He was too well-known for any of the new industrialists to risk giving him a job. He had a minimum state pension and made a little money by doing other people's typing."

"There must have been times when he regretted the high old days at Berchtesgarten," said Mr. Behrens. "He was very close to the centre."

"He was at the centre. True, he took no part in decision making, but he heard the decisions being made. He accompanied Hitler everywhere. No-one was jealous of him, because he exercised no influence. An admirable position for a Boswell."

"And now he has written the *Life of Johnson*?"

"It is not exactly a biography of Hitler. Rather a commentary on his command methods. Why he took certain decisions, and how he achieved his ends. You might call it the sequel to *Mein Kampf*. It is a document which will be of incalculable value to historians. To psychologists, too, no doubt. When I had read it I came to two conclusions. The first was that it must be returned to the German Government. It belongs to them, not to us. The second was that I would have it photographed, which I have done. Both copies are in that file."

"How on earth did we get it?"

"For that we have to thank the foresight and patience of John Corrie, our representative at the Bonn embassy. After the near debacle over the Bartz affair, I persuaded them to create the office of Assistant Trade Secretary as cover for one of our men. Corrie was my nomination. He proved an excellent choice. One of the things he did was to keep in discreet touch with Sperrle. In spite of the ridiculous stringency of our Intelligence budget we were able to help him with money, from time to time. But it was more than money. It was sympathy. Corrie used to call on Sperrle in his tiny roof-top apartment up in the Leopoldstrasse and drink coffee with him, and gossip about old times. About a fortnight ago, when he called on him, he saw quite clearly that Sperrle was dying. That was when he handed over the typescript. According to Corrie, he said, very solemnly, 'I make this gift in the trust that no evil use will be made of it, and in the hope that our two great Anglo-Saxon nations will never again be in enmity.'"

"Not a bad epitaph," said Mr. Behrens.

Mr. Calder, more practically, said, "You mentioned a job."

"I want you, first of all, to read the last chapter. Sperrle, you will recall, was in the Bunker during the closing weeks of the war. Along with Goebbels and Martin Bormann, he was one of the witnesses at the macabre wedding of Hitler and Eva Braun. It was then that Hitler gave him this last assignment. Read it for yourselves. One of you can use the original, and one the photocopy."

For half an hour there was silence in Mr. Fortescue's dignified Victorian office where Millais' "The Angel Child", on one side of the chocolate-coloured porcelain overmantel smiled at Landseer's "Tug of War" on the other. At the end of it Mr. Calder said, "Jesus Christ," an expression of feeling which drew a frown from Mr. Fortescue. "I mean, what an extraordinary story."

Rudolf Sperrle, making his way through the sector of the ruined city which was still held by the Germans, had reached the appointed rendezvous where a battered staff car awaited him. He was carrying with him two sealed and padlocked canisters, a harness having been fixed to them so that he could carry one over each shoulder. They were very heavy. The staff car had taken him south, through the narrowing gap between the Allied advance on one side and the Russians on the other. Its objective had been the Austrian Alps, in the heart of which Hitler had planned his mountain fortress, a fortress which was half built and never manned. The unexpectedly fast progress of the Americans in the south had driven Sperrle eastward. Petrol and oil were difficult to get, and the car was on its last legs.

It had finally crawled into Straffelager Seven. It was clear that it could not go much further. There were reports that the Eighth Army, moving up from Italy, was already in Austria.

Straffelager Seven was a camp for British other ranks who had attempted to escape from the regular camps or had made nuisances of themselves to their captors in some way. It was the non-commissioned equivalent of Colditz; not a castle, but a quadrilateral of barbed wire at the foot of the Bohmerwald near the village of Abendreuth. To the commandant of the camp, but to no-one else, Sperrle had confided the details of his mission. He had been entrusted with a large collection of letters, records and memoranda in the Fuehrer's own hand, photographs, and personal mementoes, and a number of actual messages which had been recorded, on the somewhat primitive apparatus of the time, in the form of wire spools. "When the great German nation rises again, as it will," Hitler had said to Sperrle, "these relics will be the Ark of the Covenant. They must never, never, never come into the hands of our enemies."

(As Mr. Behrens read the words he could hear the Fuehrer's voice rising, as he had heard it once before, in a terrifying crescendo. "Never, never, never.")

Sperrle and the commandant had discussed the matter late into that night, and all through the next day, to the accompaniment, growing menacingly closer, of the Russian guns in the east. On the second night, taking only the camp adjutant into their confidence, they had buried the canisters in a bed of concrete under the floor of the commandant's own office.

"O.K.," said Mr. Calder. "So we go and dig it up?"

"With German co-operation. Yes."

"It doesn't seem a very difficult assignment."

"The difficulty," said Mr. Fortescue, "is that nobody now knows exactly where SL Seven was. Corrie will explain it all to you. I've arranged for you to meet him at Munich Central station at eleven o'clock, two days from now. You'll need a little time to get ready."

Mr. Calder and Mr. Behrens, who had grown used to being ordered to remote parts of the world at a moment's notice, looked at each other in some surprise.

"I should have explained," said Mr. Fortescue blandly, "that you will need to take camping equipment. Sleeping bags and – ah – groundsheets, and that sort of thing."

This he said with all the relish of a man who had a comfortable bed of his own to return to.

"It's like this," said John Corrie, as they drove north and east from Munich in Mr. Calder's roomy Ford Escort, packed with camping gear. "SL Seven was a temporary affair. It was run up, in a hurry, at the end of 1944 when the camps in Poland had to be evacuated. The usual prison camp style. A double barbed wire apron, a watch tower at each corner, wooden huts for the prisoners, and something a bit more permanent for the commandant and the guards, who were second line SS. It was a naughty boys camp, and the guards were fairly tough, but there don't seem to have been any particular atrocities."

"I expect it was too close to the end of the war," said Mr. Behrens. "Most Germans had their chins on their shoulders by the end of 1944."

"Could be," said Corrie. "Anyway, it was the Russians who got there first. The commandant and the adjutant stuck to their posts. Much good it did them. They were taken off to Russia, and I've no doubt were put straight underground. The SS boys scarpered. The prisoners marched out after them, in a rather more orderly fashion, made for the American lines and were repatriated. Sperrle got away into Austria. SL Seven ceased to exist."

"But, surely," said Mr. Calder, "*someone* must know where it was?"

"When we get there, you'll understand the difficulties better. The Russians drew back a little at this point, for some reason, and the Iron Curtain runs about three miles east of Abendreuth, which was deserted by its few aged inhabitants and is now a ghost village. All the useful roads in that area ran east-west, and since the Iron Curtain chopped them off, there was no point in keeping them up. The nearest place of any size is Plattling, thirty miles away on the Passau-Nurnberg road. It's got quite a decent *gasthaus*, incidentally. I've booked rooms for us there tonight and we're meeting our opposite numbers, Police Captain Bruckner and Lieutenant Brunz, there tomorrow morning."

Mr. Behrens had been considering the curious problem of the vanishing prison camp. He said, "What about farmers? Someone must use the land."

"It's open heath. There are two farms. One of them is about ten miles west of Abendreuth. The other twelve miles northwest. The owners share the grazing rights, such as they are. Their horses and bullocks have the run of the heath. They round them up twice a year, in spring and autumn. Like Dartmoor ponies. They're pretty wild specimens, I believe."

"Wasn't there some sort of road from the village to the camp?"

"I thought of that," said Corrie. "But a lot of marram grass and heather grows in nearly forty years. When I tried to trace it, I was reminded of that poem of Kipling's. Do you remember it? The one about the old lost road through the woods, '*It is underneath the coppice and heath and the thin anemones.*' Only in this case it isn't thin anemones. It's a particularly vicious sort of dwarf thorn bush. Discouraging to exploration on hands and knees."

Captain Bruckner and Lieutenant Brunz arrived at Plattling punctually at nine o'clock on the following morning, each in his own car, with a police driver. They set out in convoy, with Bruckner leading. The mist of early morning had cleared away, and there was promise of a fine day.

Ten miles out of Plattling the road they were on deteriorated into something not much better than a farm track. It crossed the open heath in a series of small dips and rises. Ahead of them the line of the Bohmerwald rose, blue and grey under the morning sun.

When they arrived at their destination Mr. Calder was surprised to see that a sizeable encampment was already springing up. There was a large transporter, from which its crew was unstripping two big Porta-cabins, ready-made wooden one-room buildings. The work was in charge of a police sergeant. Other men were setting up tents, and unloading posts and barbed wire. There were two caravans, and an old-fashioned field cooker. A modern gypsy encampment, thought Mr. Behrens.

The sergeant approached Captain Bruckner, saluted, and said, "Has any decision been made as to where the huts shall be placed?"

Bruckner said, "Find the best hard standing you can, and dump them there for the moment."

Mr. Calder had been making a calculation. The huts would each, he guessed, house at least ten men. The tents and caravans would take twice as many. Yet, counting the drivers of the vehicles and the unloading team, who were all policemen, he made the total no more than fifteen.

"We seem to be allowing ourselves plenty of elbow room," he said.

Captain Bruckner smiled at John Corrie, who pointed back the way they had come.

"Reinforcements," he said.

Two large army trucks were approaching them up the track from Plattling. They, also, had police drivers, beside each of which a civilian was sitting. As the trucks came to a halt the civilian jumped down, went round to the back, and said, "All out, chaps."

"Thank God for that," said a voice from the back. "It's nearly forty years since I've travelled in the back of one of these bastards, and I'd forgotten how bloody uncomfortable it was."

"Not like your air-conditioned Cadillac, Philip," said a second voice.

"You can keep your Cadillacs. Give me a good old English Humber every time."

In front of Mr. Calder's astonished eyes there emerged from the back of the lorries a dozen civilians, all of late middle-age, and all dressed in the sort of clothes that a business man likes to wear on holiday. One had evidently been a fisherman. There was an assortment of flies in his tweed hat. Another might have been a yachtsman. A third had simply put on the clothes he would have worn for a little light gardening.

Corrie evidently knew the fisherman.

He said, "Come along, Sam. Meet two friends of mine."

Introductions were effected all round. Mr. Behrens recognised the fisherman. He had been, until his retirement, the managing director of a company which ran a famous chain of food stores.

Corrie said, "We advertised for ex-inmates of SL Seven who had a little time on their hands and might enjoy an open-air holiday, at the joint expense of the German and British Governments. I thought we might have some difficulty in finding anyone. I was never more surprised in my life. Applications flowed in. We had to close the list."

"We're a picked bunch," said the man called Sam with a grin.

"You've got a lot of ground to cover," said Corrie. "You'd better spend the rest of the day getting organised. I've got to get back to Bonn." And to Mr. Calder, before he left, he said, "Don't forget. This is really a German show. We're helping them. Bruckner's in charge. He's a decent fellow. I'm sure you'll all get along splendidly. There'll be a daily shuttle to Plattling, so you can keep me in the picture."

For the next three days the weather remained fine, which was a blessing because they made no progress at all. One of the difficulties was that the prisoners had not been allowed into the village, which was out of sight of the camp, and their estimates of its distance and exact direction from the camp varied widely. It was agreed that it had been to the east, and more than a mile away, but that was all they could agree about. For long hours each day they prodded with poles in the thick heather and undergrowth and found nothing but a few nose-caps from Russian shells and an unexploded mortar bomb which they buried cautiously.

There were excitements of another kind. On the second day, a Russian helicopter had floated across and looked at them. A herd of wild-haired bullocks watched their efforts with equal, or even greater suspicion. Finally, deciding that the time had come to assert themselves, they had charged. One of the policemen drew his police carbine, and shot the leading animal dead at point blank range. The herd withdrew. That evening the diggers had enjoyed an excellent meal of steak and chips.

Not that they were short of food. The German commissariat had produced sound if unimaginative supplies. As soon as he had examined them Sam sent a message back, through Plattling, to the German associates of his old firm. They must have moved fast, because on the next afternoon a truck arrived loaded with delicacies. One of the policemen turned out to have been a cook before he joined the police force.

"I haven't eaten like this for years," said Lester.

"That's because you haven't taken so much exercise for years," said Sam.

Philip said, "He showed a nice turn of speed when that bullock came after him."

During those long days in the sun and cheerful evenings in Hut A (into which they had moved after their personal tent had been trampled on by a wild horse) Mr. Calder and Mr. Behrens came to know and appreciate the ex-inmates of Straffelager Seven. All of them were men who had made their very different ways in the world since 1945.

Chester was a Member of Parliament for a northern constituency. Albert, who had ended the war as one of the youngest sergeant-majors in the Brigade of Guards, had become a policeman in Kenya and then headed his own Security firm in London. Philip had worked his way up in a publishing firm from reader to managing director. Ronald had made a name for himself in horror films. He gave them a memorable impression one evening of Dracula at large in a nunnery.

It was on the fourth day that Alan, the yachtsman, made an observation.

He said, "We've been looking in the wrong place."

This had been said so often that nobody took much notice. But Alan seemed to have something definite in mind.

He said, "None of you chaps are sailors, so none of you notice the really important things, like the sun and the moon and the stars. Now I've remembered one thing quite clearly. In the last few weeks before the Russians came and let us out, I used to watch the sun going down *exactly* behind the top of the Grosse Arber."

He pointed to the jagged top of the peak, nearly five thousand feet up and the highest point in the Bohmerwald.

"I took a bearing at the time. You remember those little pocket button compasses we had in our escape kits. Ninety-three, twelve magnetic. I remember that because I had a great aunt of ninety-three and she had twelve Persian cats."

"All dead, I suppose, now," said Lester.

"Pipe down, Lester," said Sam. "I believe Alan's got something."

"I've had to make a few adjustments," said Alan ignoring the interruption, and producing a compass from his pocket. "Never travel without a compass by the way. We're nearly five weeks later now. And magnetic north doesn't stand still either. But I can give you a back-bearing from that peak – I took it at sundown last night when you chaps were soaking up the gin – and I'll guarantee it's correct to thirty minutes either way."

"So what do we do with it?" said Philip.

"We peg it out. You take one pole, Albert, and walk towards the peak. I'll give you 'move right' 'move left' signals. Then we do the same thing in the other direction. That gives us the line. Then we move along it, searching not more than twenty yards either side of it."

Under the sailor's directions, a line was laid out. It was nearly a quarter of a mile south of anything they had searched so far.

"I always told you we were looking in the wrong place," said Chester.

"What you actually told us was that we were too far *south*," said Philip.

"Have a heart," said Ronald. "He's a politician. You must allow him to change his mind once every twenty-four hours."

It was Ronald who struck pay dirt. He let out a scream which would have done credit to a maiden attacked by a werewolf. The others crowded round to see what he had found.

It was a slab of concrete, roughly eighteen inches square. When the moss had been scraped away they could see that there was a square hole in the centre of the slab, and a few rotting fragments of wood in the hole.

"There you are," said Alan complacently. "Trust the British

Navy. That was one of the four supports of a corner tower."

The others were already scraping in the earth.

In a few minutes they had located and cleared a neat square, composed of four concrete blocks. The excitement had attracted everyone to the spot.

"We can't tell which corner tower it was," said Alan. "But it won't take long to find out now."

By dusk that evening the perimeter of the camp had been established and staked out. Two lines of barbed wire had been run round, and the huts, tents and caravans all moved inside. This was a sensible precaution, as the bullocks were getting aggressive again.

"What I suggest we do," said Mr. Calder, "is reconstitute, as closely as we can, what the camp looked like. I'm told there were six huts for the prisoners. Right? So let's put our two huts down in the places occupied by two of them. If someone will be kind enough to indicate exactly where that was."

This led to a complicated argument, which was finally settled by Philip. He said, "I was in the hut nearest the wire, and I know *exactly* how far it was from the wire because two of us worked it out – by trigonometry, we daren't pace it – when we were planning a break. It was thirty-six feet six inches from the south-west corner of the hut."

"Which you remember," said Ronald, "because you had an aunt aged thirty-six who had six budgerigars."

One of the huts was transported by the carrier and positioned thirty-six feet six inches from the wire, with the other hut parallel to it, and fifteen feet closer to the entrance. The presumed position of the other four huts and of the administrative block and the commandant's office was then worked out with reasonable accuracy. The large double marquee was pitched over the latter. Smaller tents and caravans represented the guard huts and camp kitchens.

By the time this had been done it was dark, and they knocked off for supper. A crate of Bollinger was opened and they celebrated their progress.

Later that night, the inmates of Hut A discussed the excitements of the day.

"It's uncanny," said Chester. "As we were walking to the hut I looked round, and suddenly, I seemed to be back. The barbed wire, the guard tent, the huts, and then – that."

One of the policemen had brought a record player. On the other nights they had gone to sleep to the sound of mixed pop and classical music. Now he had produced – possibly saved up for the occasion – the record of German songs sung in the lovely husky contralto of Marlene Dietrich.

"Underneath the lamplight, on the barrack square –"

The words and the tune of "Lili Marlene" floated out into the night, carrying with it, to a handful of middle-aged and elderly gentlemen on the brink of sleep, a reminder of a time when they were young, and life was not a dusty path to look back on, but a long bright road stretching ahead of them.

"Do you wish you could put the clock back?" said Philip.

"Yes," said Sam and Alan simultaneously.

"Certainly not," said Albert.

"Not on your life," said Ronald.

"That gives me a casting vote," said Chester, sleepily. "But I can't tell you, because I'm damned if I know."

Back in their own tent Mr. Calder and Mr. Behrens were thinking about the present, not the past.

"I don't want to alarm our nostalgic friends," said Mr. Behrens, "but I fancy we've reached a point where we may have to take a few sensible precautions."

"Were you thinking of the Russians?"

"You mean that helicopter? No, I wasn't particularly worried about the Russians. I've no doubt that everything we've been doing has been photographed by them and examined and debated, but I don't see that they have any reason to interfere."

"So?"

"So I've remembered something which I find a little alarming. That manuscript that Fortescue gave us to read. You wouldn't have noticed it, of course, because you only had a photocopy. I had the so-called original. Only it wasn't the original. It was a carbon copy."

Mr. Calder thought about this for a minute in silence. Then he said, "And you think that the top copy might have got into other hands."

"I can think of one set of people," said Mr. Behrens, "who'd give their front teeth or their back teeth – and since a lot of them are getting on in years – their false teeth, too – to get their hands on what's in those canisters."

Mr. Calder thought about it. He said, "Did you bring a gun with you?"

"I didn't, because it didn't seem to be that sort of party."

"Nor did I," said Mr. Calder sadly.

Next morning they found that the search was by no means over. Rudolf Sperrle's story had been specific, up to a point. With the whole night to work in the three men had dug a hole in the earth under the commandant's private room, had put the canisters into it, and covered them with liquid cement. Then they had piled back the earth on top, and restored the surface.

"It would have been more helpful," said Captain Bruckner, "if he had told us the depth of the hole."

"And even more helpful," said Lester, "if we hadn't all been such good boys. I mean, if old Barney was here he'd have given us the lay-out of the block. He spent more time in cells than out of them. I don't think any of us ever set foot inside the place."

The possible area was not enormous, but when the only method of search was to drive a series of spikes into the packed earth, going at least five foot down on each occasion, it was bound to be laborious.

At the end of a hard day's work, as they were sitting down, a bit dispirited, to their evening meal, Sam suddenly said, "What you're all forgetting is that you're looking for the commandant's office."

When the insults which this remark provoked had died down, Sam went on. "I was a sort of commandant myself. When we moved the organisation out of London, and opened a new complex at Slough, I was consulted about where my own office was to be. I said, put it as far away from other people as possible, and give it as much sun as you can. OK? Apply that here. He'd want to be at the far side of the block, which also happens to be the south side. Maximum peace. Maximum light. So I say, stop messing about here. Start on the south, and work inwards."

Captain Bruckner had listened seriously to the argument. He said, "I agree, that would be logical. The first rooms inside the entrance would be the offices. Then the stores and the armoury, and the cells for offenders. The commandant's private quarters would be at the far end. We will start there tomorrow."

"Why not this evening?" said Philip. "I wouldn't mind putting in a little overtime to find out whether Sam's talking nonsense or not."

This seemed to meet with general approval.

"We'll make it a mass assault," said Lester. "Let's all line up along the southern edge, and work our way inwards."

The tables were cleared, everyone was armed with some sort of implement, and they set to work. Even the policemen, who seemed infected by the prevailing excitement, joined in.

Half an hour later, just at the moment when enthusiasm was beginning to flag, Philip said, "Hold it chaps, I think this miner-forty-niner has struck pay dirt."

He was prodding with the iron bar which he held. He said, "It feels quite different. Not nearly so packed. Quite loose."

He drove the point in again.

"And there is something there. I just hit it. See that? Fetch a spade."

The others crowded round him, and the earth flew out. Soon they could hear the edge of the spade scraping a rough surface.

At this exciting moment Mr. Calder happened to be outside. He had walked across to look for extra spades in the guard tent. The moon was full and was bathing the camp and the heath in a theatrical wash of yellow limelight. As he strolled towards the entrance, he met Hans, one of the youngest and solidest of the policemen, coming back.

Hans said, "I did not know, Herr Calder, that we were expecting visitors."

Mr. Calder said, "What visitors?"

"In cars. I heard them just now. They stopped a little distance away down the track. I wondered –"

He had no time to say any more. Mr. Calder had grabbed him

by the arm, jerked him to one side, and pulled him down onto his face in the shadow of the guard tent.

Men were advancing, spread out in line, across the open space between the entrance of the camp and the marquee. Mr. Calder counted fifteen of them as they went past, the nearest almost treading on his fingers. He could see that they were all carrying automatic weapons.

As soon as they were past, Mr. Calder started to wriggle backwards, keeping in the shadows, and as flat as possible on the ground. Hans came with him. When they were behind the tent Mr. Calder said, his mouth close to Hans' ear, "Get into the tent. Squeeze in under the canvas. See if you can find me one of those field telephones."

Hans nodded, and wormed his way into the tent. Five minutes passed before he reappeared, pushing the instrument in front of him. Meanwhile Mr. Calder had been making a reconnaissance. The ground was uneven and he led the way, still keeping flat, down a shallow depression, under the wire and out of the camp. After this they continued their advance on hands and knees until a clump of bushes hid them. By this time they were nearly a hundred yards from the camp. Mr. Calder noted that Hans had not opened his mouth. It confirmed his good opinion of the boy.

He said, "Now we must find the telephone line. I think it was laid on the left-hand side of the track."

They found it without difficulty. He said, "You know how to use this thing?"

Hans nodded. He was already baring the insulation with his jack-knife, and twisting in the wires from the terminals. Then he put on the headset, and spoke softly into it. Softly, but to no purpose. He said, "The line is dead."

"I was afraid of that," said Mr. Calder. "But we had to try it first. They will have cut out a section of the wire. It might take all night to find it. We'll have to go for the cars. You heard them arrive. How far down the track?"

"Two hundred metres I would judge."

There were three bulky Steyr touring cars and a smaller Volkswagen, parked in a line. As they came up they could see the man who had been left to guard them. He was sitting in the front seat of the leading car, and he was smoking.

"No time for finesse," said Mr. Calder. He stalked up to the car and shouted, in German, "That's no way to stand guard, you lazy lout."

As the man scrambled out Mr. Calder hit him scientifically and he went down flat on his face.

"Take his boots off," he said. "We'll use the laces to tie him up. And gag him with his scarf."

"Then we take the little car, yes?"

"Yes," said Mr. Calder. "But we don't start it up here. It's much too close to the camp. We'll have to push it."

They turned the light Volkswagen without much difficulty, pushed it up the track for ten yards, and then had the benefit of a short downhill run. Ahead of them the track rose steadily for about a hundred yards to a crest. After that, as he knew, they would have a free run down for about the same distance.

Mr. Calder thought about it. They were now about three hundred yards from the camp. The night was very still. With any luck they would not have been missed. What they needed to do was to complete their getaway as inconspicuously as possible.

"We shall have to push the car over that next crest," he said. "We'll set the wheels as straight as we can, and both get behind her. And we won't try to do it all at once. I'm not as young as I was."

Mr. Calder soon realised one thing. Hans was the right man for this job. Mr. Calder himself had surprising reserves of strength in his barrel chest and thick arms, but Hans was twice as strong as he was.

It would have been easier if the surface of the track had been harder and smoother. After forty yards Mr. Calder demanded a breather. The sweat was pouring down his body inside his shirt.

He said, "Did you ever play rugby football?"

"Rugby football," said Hans. "I have watched it. It seemed a very rough game."

"You'd be an asset to any team in the second row of the scrum."

"Those are the ones who put their heads between the bottoms of the other ones and push?"

"That's right."

The thought seemed to amuse Hans. He said, "Perhaps I will try it."

Then they resumed their labour. Mr. Calder thought with sympathy of Sisyphus. By the time they reached the second halt, some twenty yards from the crest, something seemed to be troubling Hans. He said, "Have you considered, Herr Calder, that the keys of the car are missing. How shall we start it?"

"You don't need keys to start a car. Just a small piece of wire."

"Is that so? That would be the way in which a car thief would operate?"

"Certainly. I've stolen a lot of cars in my time."

"Indeed?" said Hans. Clearly his opinion of Mr. Calder was now very high.

At the top of the rise the passage of vehicles in either direction had thrown up a low ridge of packed earth.

"We'll have to move that," said Mr. Calder. "There should be a kit of sorts in the back."

Armed with a jack handle and a large spanner they started to dig out the obstruction.

The men in the tent were taken totally by surprise. The first sign was the irruption of fifteen armed men into the marquee. A hard voice said, in German, "You are advised to make no stupid moves," and repeated this in English.

Everyone swung round.

Captain Bruckner said, "Who are you? You have no right here. Lay down those arms at once."

When the newcomers made no move to obey him, Lieutenant Brunz, who was the only man who was armed at that moment, put his hand onto the gun in his hip holster. The man who had spoken raised his own machine pistol, and shot the lieutenant through the shoulder.

"You see," he said, "we mean business. We do not shoot to kill, unless we have to. But a bullet in the shoulder or the knee can be painful. It can also cripple you. If anyone wishes to try whether I mean what I say, he is at liberty to make the experiment."

His men had spread themselves along the far side of the tent, and were covering every angle of it.

Mr. Behrens stepped forward slowly. He said, "You will all do exactly what this man tells you. There is a first-aid box in the corner. Albert, would you get it, and see what you can do for the lieutenant." Brunz was sitting on one of the chairs by the table. His left hand was clasping his right shoulder and his face was contorted.

The leader of the newcomers had been looking curiously at Mr. Behrens. He said, "I think I know you. But I have forgotten your name."

"I have not forgotten yours," said Mr. Behrens. "You are – or you were – *Obersturmfuehrer* Otto Lessner. You were, for a time, in charge of the guard at Ravensbruck camp. I did my best to get you hanged. I am only sorry that I was unsuccessful."

Lessner came forward and peered into Mr. Behrens' face. He was smiling. It was not an agreeable smile, more a lifting of the lips.

"Behrens, of course," he said. "This is indeed a reunion. Where is your inseparable friend Calder?"

"He died two years ago, otherwise I'm sure he would have been happy to be here. It would have given him great pleasure to see you in such an uncomfortable position."

"Uncomfortable, Herr Behrens?"

"Certainly. You have shot and wounded a police officer in the presence of a number of witnesses. Forty years ago you might have got away with it. Not now, my friend. Not now."

Lessner had taken off his left-hand gauntlet, and was holding it loosely in his right hand. Now he swung it, hitting Mr. Behrens in the face.

"Running true to form," said Mr. Behrens. "A bully and a coward." He was speaking in German, loud enough for the newcomers to hear. They were a curious mixture, some of them hardly more than boys, others as old as Lessner, or even older. Mr. Behrens ran a sardonic eye over the representatives of the resurgent Nazi movement. "This is a curious platoon you've brought along, *Obersturmfuehrer*. Half from the kindergarten and half from the old folks' home."

Lessner's face was dark red and his hand was sliding towards the butt of his machine pistol when he stopped.

He said, "I know you, Herr Behrens. I know your ways. You are an old fox. Why do you seek to provoke me? I answer my own question. You are playing for time. You expect assistance. It will not come. We have taken all necessary steps to ensure that. Nevertheless, we will waste no time exchanging compliments with you. Maybe when we have finished our work we will have a little sport."

He signalled to two of the young men, who laid down their weapons and stepped forward smartly. Mr. Behrens saw that one of them was carrying a length of wire rope fitted with a shackle. Evidently Lessner had studied Rudolf Sperrle's manuscript and had come prepared.

The rope was passed under the exposed block of cement and fastened. The two men pulled. The block lifted a little, and fell back.

"Two more," said Lessner. The remaining gunmen spread themselves out to maintain their arc of fire. Four men pulling together lifted the block clear of the hole and swung it onto the floor of the tent. Two of them unloosed the rope. The other two went outside and returned with a sledge hammer and a heavy steel chisel.

"Well rehearsed," thought Mr. Behrens. He looked down quickly at his watch. Thirty minutes had passed. It might take them another thirty to crack the cement. Not quite long enough.

The men were using the hammer and chisel cautiously. It was more than half an hour before the metal canisters had been broken free of their concrete shell and were standing on the ground.

Mr. Behrens said, "Would it not be of interest to all of us, to ascertain at least that the recordings of the Fuehrer's voice have survived."

He noted the stir of interest which this produced from the listening gunmen.

"No doubt it would be interesting," said Lessner, "but unfortunately we have not brought the necessary apparatus with us."

"I have," said Mr. Behrens. He went to the back of the tent, opened a suitcase, and brought out an old-fashioned dictaphone. "The description of the wire spools was detailed enough for me to be able to procure a machine which should enable us to play them. Would you care to try?"

There was no doubt about the sentiments of the audience, German and British alike.

"Ninety-nine per cent in favour," thought Mr. Behrens.

Lessner hesitated. Then he said, "We have the night in front of us. I see no reason not to humour you in this matter."

The canisters were fastened with stout padlocks which had rusted solid and which, as Mr. Behrens had hoped, took a lot of removing. In the end, the shanks had to be sawn through. The first cylinder contained bundles of papers, tightly packed, each wrapped in oil skin.

"It would seem that what we are looking for must be in the other one," said Mr. Behrens smoothly.

Lessner hesitated again, and glanced down at his watch. He did not overlook the possibility that someone might have escaped and gone for help. But the nearest effective help was nearly fifty kilometres away, and all the camp vehicles had been immobilised.

He smiled thinly, and said, "Very well."

This time they knew what they were about, and less time was wasted. There were packets of papers in the second canister. Under them was a wooden box, the size of a larger cigar box.

"Allow me," said Mr. Behrens. He had set up his machine on the table, and now took one of the spools from the box and fitted it into the machine. He tried not to appear hurried, but he was wasting no time, because he had already heard the noise he was hoping for. It was faint as yet. Probably he only picked it up because he was listening for it. The attention of every other person in the tent was on the apparatus on the table.

A voice filled the tent. Harsh, staccato, unmistakable.

"To the people of the great German Reich, your Fuehrer speaks."

Mr. Behrens looked round. The youngsters, newcomers and police were attentive. The older men were much more than attentive, they were rapt, spell-bound. He noted, with sardonic amusement, that Captain Bruckner was holding himself rigidly to attention.

"We stand at one of the turning points of history. The storm clouds are rolling up, from the East and from the West. At this moment the sky overhead looks black."

For God's sake, thought Mr. Behrens, they *must* hear it soon. The three giant Hercules transporters had cut their engines as they came in at two thousand feet.

"But do not fear. Be of good courage. The sun will break through."

At the last moment Lessner realised what was happening. He switched off the recorder, and raced to the entrance of the tent. Fifty parachutists were already on the ground. Another hundred were floating gently to earth under the full moon.

"I confess I was surprised that he dared to shoot that policeman," said Mr. Behrens. "He couldn't hope to get away with it. Unless he killed us all and buried us. Which seemed improbable."

"If he had secured the contents of those canisters," said Mr. Fortescue, "he'd have had every chance of getting away with it. I understand, unofficially, that there was enough material there to embarrass two of their High Court judges, a police chief, and a number of very successful industrialists. With material like that he could have bought his way out of trouble easily enough."

"Do you think the authorities will use it?" said Mr. Behrens.

Mr. Calder said, "You remember what Sperrle said? 'Put it to no evil use.' Forty years is a long time. Let the dead bury the dead."

Mr. Fortescue said, "It is a decision for them, not for us. But I hope that you are right."